MW01140402

THE BRIDGE OVER
CEDAR CREEK

MICHAEL W. PAUL

ISBN: 1481826964
ISBN 13: 9781481826969

DEDICATION

This account of human decency and true celebrity is dedicated to all of the children in dysfunctional families who long for a loving parent and the knowledge they are worthy. The love and affection I will always shelter in my heart for the kindness of Frank and Lillie Kunce can never be measured.

My sincere thanks go out to the Captain and his Lady on the "Flying Pig", living their dream. Further thanks to Diane Swofford and other friends who have heard the story, for their insistence that I put it on paper.

I am most thankful for the love, encouragement, respect and honesty I have enjoyed for forty six years married to my help mate Dianne. Frank would be proud that I took his advice and married a "hasher". She is one "hell of a Jane".

Also, a thank you to my children enduring the "Frankisms". I will carry to my grave the most annoying, "Action, not words".

This book is based on true events. The characters may be authentic, composites or fictitious.

PRELUDE

The phone rang at that time of night when no one expects good news. The voice on the other end of the line had the timbre of an older man and cracked with the greeting. I recognized it instantly.

I had only met the man on a few occasions but when I answered, I could see him on the other end of the line half a continent away. "Hello, this is..., in Colorado. Is this...?" There was static on the line that sounded like light rain on a spring morning.

"It is," I said.

The caller launched immediately into the reason for his call without preamble but I had known what was coming before he uttered the first syllable. My chest tightened and my throat closed. I had been expecting the call for months, if anyone can truly expect and accept life's inevitabilities. I dreaded it and felt the emotion well up as soon as I heard the disembodied voice over the telephone line.

"I just wanted you to know," the voice said, "that he passed today, after dinner. He quietly slipped away with no pain while resting in the afternoon. When the nursing home staff found him, they thought he was sleeping. He was fully dressed in Payday overalls with his hat resting on his stomach and a hint of a smile on his face. The services will be Sunday at White's Funeral parlor."

I could not speak. Seconds passed in silence while I breathed heavily and tried to regain my composure. All I could say was, "Thanks, I will be there."

When my family and I arrived at the funeral home at the center of the now growing community, I was acknowledged, and we were ushered to a seat in the family section by the man who had been at the other end of the phone just a day and a half earlier. I recognized few of the mourners but was surprised not to see a friend Frank had made who worked for the National Park Service and had taken him on his last Elk hunt following his ninetieth birthday. I remembered the last time I saw him living in the nursing home and how he had pleaded with me to "Get the truck, and get me the hell out of here." I had always wished that I had.

The service was solemn, and it was clear the speaker had no idea who the man was. He uttered some of the usual platitudes, referenced passages from the Bible and seemed to be figuratively wringing his hands. I was sure that the frail little man in the flower-covered casket would have had some earthy response, like "just start dividing."

We all drove to the cemetery for a final few words by the minister. The excavation where he was to be interred was bordered by a mound of dirt covered with artificial turf and next to the grave of his wife of sixty-five years and the brothers he had loved. A very simple bronze plaque denoting the name, date of birth, and date of death marked the graves.

Once the churchman finished speaking and the crowd turned to walk away, I looked over my shoulder with tears streaming down my cheeks and saw a US Forest Service truck parked on the dirt lane in the distance. A man was approaching in the uniform of the Park Service with his hat pulled down over his eyes wearing dark glasses. When he reached the grave site, he stood quietly for a moment in contemplation and then placed a pine bough on the casket. He saluted, turned, and walked away.

Years later, one beautiful Bahamian evening, the sun was settling into the ocean. The sky was a deep scarlet, striated with hues of coral and magenta. High cirrus clouds and mares tails swept across the horizon, accenting it. I was waiting to catch a glimpse of the green flash that I had been told could be seen at the instant the sun disappeared beneath the sea. To see the green flash is said to be good luck.

What a blessed life I have lived, I thought, yet it certainly had not been luck. My wife and I had worked hard, educated ourselves, raised our children, and saved our money. I had only dreamed of such a life. I could not imagine how my life could be much more enriched even if I had set my goals higher. I remember thinking as a child, if I could just live in a neighborhood where cars were not parked on the street at night, where dinner was served when the street lights came on, and no one drank too much, I would have it all. My goal was to live on Hunting Lodge Drive—an area of middle-class homes that were set back off the street with long drives and expansive lawns. It was where the "swells" lived.

My wife and I had just flown our own airplane to the Exuma Islands to spend a week on a private yacht with some new friends. She had gone below to get our cabin ready for the night. We had risen at dawn every day since our arrival in Georgetown, Exuma and been in our bunks just after sunset. The yacht owners had already adjourned to their quarters, and their eighty-five-year-old mother had closed the bulkhead door to the forward cabin. This was our last night, and I wanted to sit quietly for a moment on the swim platform, contemplate the week, dangle my feet in the crystalline water, and enjoy the nightfall and one more spectacular sunset.

There were towering anvil shaped clouds in the distance lighted occasionally with Mother Nature's strobe-lightning. The storms were no threat.

The heavy yacht swung gently at its anchorage fifty feet from one of the most beautiful beaches I could remember seeing. Lights in the homes and shops of Georgetown were just starting to come on, and a gentle breeze ruffled the American flag that hung from its staff on the stern of the yacht. The halyard rattled against the mast, and I could see movement in the cabin of a trawler anchored off our port bow. A small fish had just broken the surface of the water with a splash sending ripples in every direction. The beach, with variegated vegetation and beautiful white sand, rose over one hundred feet to a summit topped by a decaying concrete monument, which was highlighted by the occasional lightning flash...what a stunning night! What a week! We were leaving in the morning.

I met the yacht owners serendipitously but not by coincidence. I do not think there are any coincidences in life. Several years previous I had negotiated a loan in connection with a piece of property in the North Georgia Mountains. The garrulous woman on the other end of the phone seemed almost a lifelong friend, yet we had never met. While we discussed the property, the annual percentage rate of the loan, the closing costs, the term of the loan, and the attorney who would handle the closing, we primarily talked about ourselves: where we had grown up—she in England, me in Florida, New York, Texas, Georgia, and Colorado—our families, our recreation. She saw that I had listed a small sloop on my financial statement. I had just arranged for the financing of a beautiful mountainside cabin that my wife and I hoped to enjoy in our retirement, while she, on the other hand, had just sold everything and told me this would be her last loan. She and her new husband had purchased a forty-six-foot, ocean-going sailing yacht and planned to travel the world. The boat needed some refitting, so she would join her husband in Florida to help finish the job. Surprisingly, she told me that neither of them had any "real" sailing experience and had never owned a sailboat. "Now this is going to be interesting," I thought. I had a small plaque over my office fireplace that was engraved, "Oh Lord, thy sea is so large, and my boat so small...HOPE." I hoped for them. I have always enjoyed knowing people with the kind of strength and courage it took to do the extraordinary, to change course and never look back.

The woman's husband had already moved to a marina in Florida and had been working on the yacht for more than a year. She said, "It's time to go." She had been living in a friend's guesthouse, her children were settled, and virtually everything she had accumulated during her life had been sold or given away. She had experienced all the small town gossip and corporate politics she could stand, she said. They were going to live the rest of their life "off the grid". "We were settling in, and she and her husband were striking out.

Toward the end of our conversation, she said, "You sound like someone I would like to know. May I put you on our list of people to receive our travel log? What do you think?" I thought to myself, *Hell, why not, what do I have to lose. I will never hear from her again, but if I do, it will be interesting to see how their new life unfolds. Always being practical*, I thought. *I will be able to cancel my subscription to Cruising Magazine.*

Our telephone conversation had taken place more than three years previously. We had kept in touch by email. I had followed my new friends' refitting of the boat, the "shake down" cruise, and the first attempt to set off on their sailing adventure.

On a dark night, not long after they departed the boatyard, after several years of preparation and spending thousands of dollars of their seed money, the boat struck a reef just before arriving in Marathon, Florida, in the middle of the Florida Keys. Their email to those of us following the first voyage seemed final.

The Coast Guard had rescued them, and they thought the yacht was lost. It was stuck on a reef offshore and thought to be "holed." "What were they to do now?" the email read. Miraculously, the boat was saved; people reached out to them, and before long, they were back on their way to the yard for repair and a fresh start.

Sitting quietly on the swim platform of the "Flying Pig" that beautiful Bahamian night, I looked back over my life and tried to put our new friends' adventure in perspective. What had made the difference? The answer seemed: to keep moving no matter how difficult life's shoals and reefs seem and to keep sailing on no matter how much shallow water passes under the transom.

Although I believe in divine presence and know in my heart that the unfolding of a new flower in the spring or the birth of a child is not an accident, I do not understand it all. Many have told me over the years, including our new friends on the yacht, that I should write about one special person and special time in my life. I loved to read but never seemed to find time to put my thoughts on paper. It was time.

The following pages are an effort to put on paper the thoughts about what has made the difference in my life. I write it because someone might have a passing interest in the journey of a young man alone. I also write it to try and understand the journey and perhaps convey to my wife and family who I am, why I think the way I do, and hope that my words will create a little more understanding. We are all complex people affected as much by our genetics as our experience.

While there have been many people who have come and gone in my life, who have passed on or passed through, and who have had an effect on me and will always be in my heart, some stand above the others. Some were difficult, troubled people with their own agenda; some were kind, gracious, fair minded, and loving. Some just passed through, and I never even knew their names, but all of these people delivered painful or painless lessons that I will never forget. There has not been one thing and certainly no one person of prominence, but the person I write about who entered my life that summer over fifty years ago stands out as one of the great influences in my life and one of the finest men I have ever known.

CHAPTER ONE

The bus was empty except for a woman and her infant, both sleeping on the bench seat at the far end of the aisle. Her luggage was piled around her, and it looked as if she must be traveling with everything she owned. The bus had the dank, humid, penetrating smell of burned diesel fuel, stale cigarettes, cheap whiskey, and the fetid Louisiana night.

Most Greyhounds were air conditioned by the late fifties; many were "Scenic Cruisers" with an opaque, sun-blocking window in the ceiling at the second level just above the restroom. They were luxurious as defined by this belching, old leviathan with its wool and leather seats and small open windows. The tired old bus had all the allure of a sweaty sock discarded in a high school locker room. The driver stopped every few minutes to pick up passengers. Every time it stopped, its air brakes hissed and gave off a guttural groan as if it were in pain. Some passengers waited along the roadside and called the driver by his first name when they boarded. "Hey Al, you're late this morning. Did you have another fight with the ole woman?" said one late middle-aged white man with slicked down hair, wearing a grey soiled uniform with "Edgar" stenciled over his right breast pocket. My ticket was for an express bus to Dallas, but the bus had been oversold. I found myself on an antique "local," which should have been taken out of service years ago.

The child had been crying softly until just a few minutes before our station stop. The mother, a pretty teenaged Negro girl, not much older than myself had placed a towel over her shoulder and put the baby to her breast. The driver addressed the passengers loudly as if the bus were full. "Fifteen-minute rest stop, don't be late, we gotta be in Shreveport by five o'clock." I had been able to nap for only moments at a time all night. The incessant stopping, the heat, and uncomfortable gait of the old bus just wouldn't let me sleep. I thought I would stay aboard and catch a few winks before we started again. It had been an awful night.

The driver had stopped and put two drunken sailors off the bus at a wide spot in the road. I watched the disbelief in their faces as the bus pulled away and one of the two slumped on his sea bag and became enveloped in the darkness, while the other stumbled into the guardrail on the other side of the road. The driver had warned them. They had been drinking since New Orleans, and their banter had become louder and louder. When they had propositioned a young woman passenger and reached for her breast, it was the last straw. Either they get off the bus, the driver said, or he would stop at the police station in the next town and that would solve the problem.

I had just nodded off when the entire seat settled to the floor. The seat groaned, and the new occupant uttered a deep harrumph. A large, heavy-breasted Negro woman had sat down next to me. She cradled a huge mixing bowl of ice in her ample lap and said in a husky, deeply accented Cajun voice, "Mine ifin I sit here?"

The bus was still only half full, and although rows of seats were unfilled in front of and behind me, she had chosen to sit with me.

She was traveling with her daughter who took the aisle seat next to her. Her daughter, like the young mother in the back of the bus, was a teenager who looked away shyly when her mother tried to introduce her. "Dora and I are a goin' to Shreveport to visit our cousin for the weekend," she said in a breathless, long, unpunctuated exultation.

CHAPTER TWO

Lighting in the old bus was almost nonexistent. A small, steady beam of light illuminated the three steps leading onto the bus and shined down the aisle at floor level. The muted instrument panel lighting projected dapples onto the ceiling. The engine idled and emitted a cacophonous rattle in the humid night air.

I could see the driver standing in the café doorway. His hat was cocked at an angle and perched on the back of his head. Sweat stained his underarms as he gestured to the remaining passengers to return to the bus. He was holding the door for an elderly, colored man who carried a tattered suitcase bound four ways and wearing a far too large checkered suit coat, baggy pants, and an old straw hat. The man limped, shuffled really, toward the bus. The driver apparently knew him as I could hear him expressing sympathy for the recent loss of his wife.

In the light of the café I could see a soldier in dress uniform with his elbows resting on the lunch counter, carrying on an animated conversation with the waitress. A desultory ceiling fan barely turned while the light in the café was sharp and bright. There were dozens of drinking straw wrappers stuck to the ceiling as if someone had held target practice with the turning fan.

It was early June, yet the heat of the night was oppressive. A slight breeze pushed through the open windows. As the bus rumbled out of the parking lot, wheels crunching on the gravel apron, the neon sign over the café door was being devoured by fluttering moths. Tiny crusted insect husks littered the ground and wall.

The woman in the seat next to me crunched down on a piece of ice and said, "Where you goin chile?"

It was 1958. I had never had a conversation with an unknown colored person. My mother called them "colored" or "negras." An aunt and uncle, whom I lived with most summers, had a colored maid named Sara, and to my knowledge, she was the only colored person I had ever spoken to.

This woman seemed truly interested in me, in whom I was and why I was on a bus in the middle of Louisiana at four o'clock on a June night.

I said, "I am going to Colorado."

"Lordy," she said, "I heard of it, but I don't know where it is. Dora and me never been any farther than Shreveport. You just a chile. I'll bet you no older than my Dora. Are you alone?"

I said, "Yes, I was. I had started the trip in Miami, Florida and had been on the bus for a day and a half."

"Lord, Lord, Lord a mercy, I sure woulda no let my Dora go no such a trip." She had a big friendly face with a bead of perspiration across her top lip. She crunched down on another piece of ice and said, almost under her breath, "How old could that boy be, Lordy mercy, Colorado!"

We talked about her cousin in Shreveport, her daughter growing up, and the loss of her husband in the Korean War. The few minutes we rode together were a pleasant respite from the stops and starts, the noise of the sailors, the grunts and groans of the old bus, and the dreadful heat and humidity of the night. When she and Dora got off the bus in Shreveport, I waved good-bye and felt I had spent time with an old family friend. I did not know her name.

"Coloreds and whites are different" is all my mother would say when I had wondered about the separate water fountains, restrooms, and beaches. The answer was always the same. We lived in a small Miami suburb where coloreds were not allowed at night. There wasn't any real antipathy, just separation. Occasionally, we would drive through Liberty City, and I would wonder why so many colored lived in crumbling row houses and shacks and yet they had shiny new Buicks and Cadillacs in the driveway or parked in the street.

While coming home from school on a city bus one afternoon, I found myself the only white person on a bus full of coloreds. They were seated in the back, two and three to a seat, and standing in the aisle behind a white line painted on the floor just beyond the rear entry door. There was not room for another person to either sit or stand, yet the entire front of the bus was empty except for the driver and me. The bus stopped, and an elderly Negro woman carrying two heavy shopping bags and an umbrella appeared in the doorway. Her hair was flecked with white and stuck to her forehead with perspiration. Her toes protruded from shoes that were old and misshapen. She placed one old shopping bag on the bus and then the other, dropped the umbrella, and nearly stumbled while climbing the short flight of steps into the bus. She was barely up the stairs, the door not yet closed, when the driver released the brake and started the bus with a jerk. I jumped up to prevent her from falling. She reached for the grab bar connected to the ceiling and swung heavily into a seat just before the white line. The driver accelerated, and then with a hissing of the airbrakes and squealing of tires, brought the bus to a sudden stop.

Passengers in the rear of the bus were thrown against one another, and several people were catapulted down the aisle. I had grabbed the bar on the top of the seat in front of me to protect myself. The driver shouted, "Nigger, get behind that white line, or this bus ain't moving."

I had never thought about segregation, "whites only," "colored not allowed," or the white line on a bus. It had just been an abstraction. Sara, my aunt's maid, would never have been treated this way. All I knew was, "coloreds and whites don't mingle. Don't ask why, that is just how it is."

Watching Dora and her mother round the corner on that sultry, early June, Louisiana morning was the beginning of my epiphany.

CHAPTER THREE

The Shreveport bus station was small and dingy. The neon Greyhound sign flickered in the steamy night. Cooking smells assaulted me from all directions. Harsh body odors mingled with the sharp sweet smell of disinfectant that stalked the waiting room. The Dallas bus had not arrived, and the New Orleans bus was just departing. Moments before the overhead speaker announced in a male's clipped, nasal tone, "All aboard, Na Awlins, gate three." I had a quick breakfast and walked outside to stretch. It was still dark, and the neighborhood was a little down on its luck.

Goose bumps arose on the back of my neck, and my hair stood on end. I felt a subtle shiver roll down my spine. I quickly went back into the building. I was afraid of the dark. It shamed me, but I was terrified. I was the proverbial whistler in the graveyard. *Fourteen*, I thought, *and still afraid of the dark.* I didn't want anyone to know.

The early morning air was heavy, and there was still a shadow on the horizon. People hustled in and out of the building, and every time the door opened, a new sound rushed in: a police siren, a loud laugh or guffaw, bus and car noises, and the click of high heels. I heard the hushed tones of a train whistle and remembered my childhood train trips between Miami and Jacksonville. Coffee cups clinked, and subtle conversations hummed inside the building. A radio played country music, while an old man, unshaven, mumbled to himself indistinctly. I shivered again and thought, *I'd better find out when the bus is arriving and how soon I can board.* I felt safe and protected while on the bus. Most people appeared to be travelers, but a few were just hangers on, and a couple of men had the dark countenance and piercing looks of predators.

My mother advised me when I boarded in Miami: "Keep your eyes open; look around; the world is full of bad people. Be careful." I was reminded of the story she told of an encounter she had with a disreputable-looking man in the darkened parking lot of a bank. The large man approached all five foot two of her and asked, "Lady, did you vote today?"

She assessed the situation and announced in husky voice, "Mister, I can't vote; I killed a man." The stranger turned on his heel and made a hasty retreat. I hoped that I would be able to think that quickly if threatened. My mother had a quick mind when she was sober.

I sat next to a middle-aged man. He was hidden behind a newspaper but peering occasionally over the top nervously. He would glance at his watch and look toward the door. Suddenly, a woman burst through the door carrying a baby with a small child in tow. "Sorry, I'm late," she said as she crossed the lobby. "The car wouldn't start. Janice drove me. She is waiting in the car. Do you have your bag? How was your trip?" she said. The man and woman headed toward the door while the child looked back at me and stuck out her tongue.

The dispatcher picked up his microphone and said, "Dallas bus, gate two, boarding, fifteen minutes." I approached him and said I was ticketed to Dallas. He said, "Son, better get in that there line early if you want a good seat. There are lots of college students going back to school for final exams. The driver will take your ticket. The bus is completely sold out."

I mounted the steps and climbed aboard. I wanted a seat just behind the topside bulkhead beneath the skylight. The behemoth trembled as it idled and I could hear the driver addressing each passenger while he slid luggage into its bowels. "Bags need to be first in, last out." "Where are you going?" he asked each passenger. I slid into the seat and slouched against the window. Air conditioning filtered through the vent under the window, and the humidity started to die. It was a new Scenic Cruiser. The seats were leather and spotless. The aisles were not crowded. There was a crisp smell of leather, wool, and cleaning solvent.

The bus lurched forward, and I settled back in the seat. Once leaving the city limits, the landscape flattened, and the horizon stretched on forever. The bus gained speed and rocked gently from side to side, much like a boat on a gentle sea. Fence posts and telephone poles came and went. There were very few sounds other than the noise made by the tires on the pavement and the creaking of people settling into their seats. A child whispered to his seatmate and rose to go to the restroom. The morning sun shimmered on the concrete roadway, cattle grazed in green pastures, and pine trees lined the highway. The endless landscape, the whirring of telephone poles and fence posts coupled with the intensity of the sun was hypnotic. I settled into my seat and braced myself with the footrest and stared out of the window at the solemnity of the morning.

CHAPTER FOUR

Buster referred to his houseguest as his "fat Uncle Frank." The man was neither fat nor his uncle. He was a family friend, who with his wife, wintered in Florida. He was not a tall man, perhaps five feet, six inches, but he seemed a big man to me. When we first met, I had just turned fourteen. I had seen him come and go on many occasions. He always wore a straw hat with a multicolored band, and colorful suspenders held up his trousers. He had large ears and the normal protruding abdomen of many older men, but he moved with confidence and had a way of looking at people thoughtfully. We had never spoken. His eyes were deep set and penetrating, though he was not intimidating or unkind. He had the look of a man who was in control and had confidence but in no way haughty or arrogant. When he removed his hat or slid it back on his head, he had a noticeable tan line crossing the center of his forehead. It was obvious he spent a lot of time in the sun, seldom bareheaded. When hatless his hair was combed straight back, and while it was thinning, he could not be considered bald. I never recall seeing him wear eyeglasses, but I learned later he would put on a pair of reading glasses when he became serious about a project. He appeared to be in his sixties, but it was difficult for me to judge the age of older adults.

Buster explained that Frank was retired and spent the winter in a small one-room apartment at the rear of a friend's home in Hialeah. Buster thought him cheap, because his Christmas gift was always "only" a basket of apples. His Hialeah friend owned an old established filling station on Fourth Avenue. Frank had owned an automobile business in Colorado prior to retiring, so the association was mutual—a busman's holiday. He moved as if he was a much younger man with a quick stride. Frank's friendship with Buster's aunt and uncle extended back to their youth in Colorado. He and his wife of many years visited Miami to enjoy the warm weather and attend both the dog and horse races—"the dogs and ponies," he said.

A city bus passed noisily in front of the house. An elderly couple walking their dog and talking to each other distracted me for a moment. I did not hear or feel the presence of someone approaching me from the rear. There was a small low-growing ornamental pine hedge separating my neighbors' apartments from our house. That mid-January morning I had been in the side yard on our side of the hedge, which served as a boundary between my mother's house and the Ramsay's house. It was a grassy space between our two houses where we ran the wire for our "walkie-talkies." I had mounted a wire-bound fruit basket on a small tree as a basketball hoop. The grass was worn thin at the base of the tree from the many sneaker-clad feet that had tried to lay up basketballs in the crude hoop. Raymond—that was Buster's given name—and I would call each other on the walkie-talkies at night after both houses were asleep and talk about girls and the many plans and dreams we had for the future. Buster was only a few months younger than me, yet he was a year behind me in school. I had started first grade at age five while living in New York, and he had begun at six. We did not share any classes or teachers, but we shared the same anxieties of all adolescents. We had just come to realize that girls were no longer things to be avoided, and at the same time, we found out they were avoiding us. Teachers never understood our need to talk among ourselves in class, and there was always someone's honor to defend on the playground or an insult to be avenged when not picked early for a team.

Although it was early morning, the sun was intense, yet the grass was still wet from the heavy South Florida morning dew. I had been trying to "kick start" an old Cushman three-wheeled truckster. It had spent most of its life as a baggage cart for Eastern Airlines terminal and was still painted in the company's blue and white corporate colors. I had painted the fenders red and added a red stripe to the body in an effort to disguise its origin.

The small hedge was no barrier between the houses, and the Chinese cherry tree where the basket was mounted added little shade. I was soaking wet with perspiration. I had tried everything. I had been struggling to start the old baggage scooter for what seemed like hours. If the truth were known, it probably had not been more than a few minutes, but with the intensity of the heat, the oppressive humidity, and the absence of a breeze, it seemed much longer. I was exhausted from the up-and-down motion of raising the kick starter and jumping down upon it with my full weight, only to have the engine grunt. A few times the starter pedal would catch upright, and my foot would slam against the metal floor sending a sharp, painful sensation throughout my entire leg. Nothing, not even a subtle cough came from the scooter's mechanical throat. "What the hell is wrong with this thing?" I muttered. I started swearing, adolescent profanity but swearing nevertheless. "Damn, damn, damn it to hell, son of a bitch," I said louder than I realized. It just would not start. It almost seemed to defy me in its inanimate, merciless way.

I had purchased the scooter from the airline with money I had saved from my paper route—forty dollars. Actually, it was not a route but rather a patch of pavement. I sold the evening edition of the *Miami Daily News* on the corner of Thirty-Sixth Street and LeJune Road. After school I would ride my bike several miles to my station, meet the *Miami Daily News* distributor, and stand in the middle of four lanes of traffic and yell until my voice faded. "Blue Streak, Blue Streak, Blue Streak, read all about it!" ("Blue Streak" meant the evening edition of the paper.) I would add the most titillating news of the day, or yell out the headline in an effort to capture the attention of the afternoon commuters. The paper sold for five cents a copy, but occasionally some generous commuter would give me a dime and say "keep the change, kid." I would start at the light when it changed to red and walk back through the line of traffic and the rising heat and exhaust fumes until the light changed to green. If I was lucky, there would be no cars at the end of the line. When I had to make change, I often would get stuck in the middle of the line of traffic and not be able to get back to the safety of the curb. I would have to remain in the middle of the street and skip between the on-coming cars to avoid being hit while waiting for the light to change. My hands would be black from handling the coins and the newspapers. I always had dark, dirty chevrons on my sleeves resulting from rubbing my nose and mouth across my shirt at the shoulder.

The truckster was going to allow me to move up in the news-paper world, and now it would not start. "All that money wasted," I thought. "A fool and his money are soon parted," my mother often said. The truckster had a small stake body that was attached to a frame propelled by a Cushman step-through scooter. It was steered by a steering wheel much like that found in an automobile and had two small tires on the front with one in the back. The three-wheel vehicle was propelled by an eight-horsepower, four-cycle, air-cooled engine. The newspaper distributor promised me a home delivery route once I purchased the scooter. Now that I had the scooter, I could not make it start.

The old man asked, "Do you really think all of that bad language will help start that 'machine'?"

I noticed that he referred to my scooter as a machine. I had never thought of it that way. A machine. I guess it was mechanical after all, but at the moment, it was merely an inconvenience preventing me from roaring down the street, wind in my face, tossing newspapers to my promised customers. I really did not know what to say. I was a little embarrassed that someone had overheard my language, so I mumbled an apology and tried to explain my frustration.

He said with a smile, "I understand. The machine is not the problem. It's just a mechanical thing. It conforms to mechanical rules. If you break one of the rules, it will not do what it is expected to do. All of the foul language and all of your effort to jump up and down on the kick starter in this heat will be a waste of time. It won't change a thing," he said. "I think it's flooded. There's not enough spark to ignite the gas in the combustion chamber, and I'd guess the spark plug is soaked in gas. If there is no spark to ignite the gas to begin the combustion process, nothing will happen, nothing except perhaps foul language. Do you understand how it all works?"

"No, I don't. I really don't," I answered. "I just know I paid forty dollars for the thing, all the money I had, and it won't run. If I can't make it run, I lose my paper route, and all I have is a scooter that won't run, have no money, and I'll be forced back to LeJune Road and Thirty-Sixth Street on hot afternoons."

He must have been watching my struggle at a distance for some time. I suspect Mrs. Ramsay, Buster's aunt had told him about my mother's drinking and the hurt and embarrassment it caused me. She had seen me sleeping many times in the front seat of the car after being locked out of the house.

My mother was an honest, decent person when she was sober. She was attractive, smart, and caring, but unfortunately she drank too much. One drink and she changed from a Doctor Jekyll to a Mr. Hyde. She had grown up on a middle Georgia farm with five sisters and brothers during the early part of the twentieth century. It was a family farm, but her father was a tenant, and times were tough for everyone. The farm failed during the Depression, about 1930, and the one hundred acres were sold at a sheriff's sale for $125. She and her older sisters had escaped to the city, while her younger brothers and baby sister and mother struggled to subsist in a small South Georgia town doing whatever was necessary to generate enough money to feed themselves. Her father was a whiskey-making drunk. During her sober moments, she swore she would never be like him.

I don't know what caused Frank to enter my life that day. Looking back I can only sense that there must be a Divine Plan. Life is unfolding as it should. At the time I could not be so philosophical. I only wanted the "machine" to start and get on with my paper route.

Frank said, "Would you mind if I give it a try?"

OK, why not give it a try, I thought. I said, "Thanks." I was ready, so any help would be welcome. "I can't make it do a thing."

He reached down, made a minor adjustment to the carburetor needle valve and mused half under his breath, "It is flooded! See all of that gasoline dripping from the carburetor, don't ya smell her?" he said. "Let her set a spell. I have some tools in my car." Almost to himself he said, "Let's take a look at the spark plug; maybe we should clean it while we wait for the gas to dry. I'll be right back." He turned toward the hedge and disappeared into Mrs. Ramsay's apartment.

When he returned he had removed his hat and rolled up his shirt sleeves. He had a pair of glasses on his nose and was carrying a small canvas bag. It looked like a woman's purse. I remember it had a flowered design, an opening across the top but was held closed with a small clasp. It was entirely full of tools: wrenches, screwdrivers, sockets, pliers...*everything,* I thought, *anyone would need to fix anything.* My tool supply consisted of a rusty set of pliers, a flat-bladed screwdriver, and a claw hammer. He removed a large socket from the bag and handed it to me.

"Remove that spark plug; let's have a look. No, no, no, turn the thing counter clockwise, lefty loosey, rightie tightee, that is how to get her out," he said. Once I had removed the spark plug, he harrumphed and held it up to his nose. He sniffed it as if it were an overripe tomato; his forehead wrinkled as he squinted. He removed a tool from his bag and said, "I'll adjust the gap. The gaps gotta be just right or the plug wouldn't give enough fire to ignite the gas. Screw her back in, not too tight," he cautioned, "and remember to turn the hickey to the right." I put the plug back in and tightened it. I later learned he called lots of things "hickeys."

"Ok, let's give her a try," he said. He adjusted the needle valve once more and raised the kick starter. "Jump down on her!" I did, but nothing, not a murmur. "Try her again." He reached down and adjusted the needle valve again. "One and a half turns oughten to do her," he said to himself. The flywheel whirled, and the engine sputtered, but it still did not start. "Try her again, but this time put all you have in her." He said, almost to himself again, "Let's try her at two and a half." He adjusted the needle valve one more turn. He said, "Have patience, believe, it will start—ya gotta believe."

I raised the kick starter in what I thought would be another futile attempt. *After all,* I thought, *what does this old man know about Cushmans?* I put one hand on the steering wheel, raised the kick starter to its full height, and jumped down with my right foot with all my weight. "Cough, sputter, cough, sputter, clunk, clunk." It started. The little engine was running!

"Yep, she was a flooded," the old man said. I looked at him with incredulity. With the twist of a needle valve and the sputter of an old worn-out engine, something happened that day that would change the entire course of my life.

CHAPTER FIVE

My thoughts went to meeting Frank for the first time. By the time he walked into my life, I had found refuge with virtually all of my aunts and uncles, my mother's friends, and a private school in upstate New York. Following my birth in North Carolina, and as soon as I was able to travel, I lived with my mother's sister and her husband, Inez and Barney. Barney worked for a trucking company, and Aunt Inez had just lost a baby. I became the surrogate she needed to get through the long days and nights that followed while Barney was on the road. The trucking business kept them on the move.

We lived in Miami, Fort Lauderdale, West Palm Beach, and Atlanta before moving to Jacksonville. I left my aunt and uncle's care once my aunt learned she was pregnant again, and I was taken to live with my mother, her sister, and their several housemates in Coral Gables. I became the community child.

After a year or so of community living, I moved on to the home of my mother's new husband. My stepfather was quite a bit older than my mother. While I was much too young to really come to know him before he died, I was told that he was a professional gambler (who would bet on the sunrise), a World War I fighter pilot and a World War II ferry pilot. My mother said he flew the Burma hump. To a child, he seemed quite a romantic figure.

He was a pilot of considerable skill and was well known in the aviation community. I learned that he started and managed the Miami Seaplane Base on Miami Beach causeway. He owned and flew all sorts of aircraft. I never knew his real origins or lifestyle, but it was later hinted that he was not a terribly scrupulous individual and that guns were kept throughout the house in easy reach to protect him from adversaries. I have never known the truth about who he was. He was larger than life and always good to me. I remember dining in a large dining room most evenings. My stepfather would summon the maid by stepping on a buzzer under the carpet at the head of the table. I was only allowed in his bedroom—where he kept most of his guns—if he or another adult were present. He and my mother did not sleep in the same room.

One convivial afternoon my mother, Cap, short for "Captain" as he was known to his friends, and my aunt and uncle were having cocktails in the living room in the front of the house. Returning from the bathroom, my uncle Charley absentmindedly picked up a weapon ensconced in an umbrella stand by the front door. Thinking it was a relic or at the very least unloaded, he pointed it at the ceiling and pulled the trigger. The room came alive with bullets. Bullets struck the living room wall within inches of my mother's and aunt's heads. My mother's marriage to Cap lasted a little more than a year. Soon after the divorce, Cap died.

I spent a year living both in the Martinique Hotel near Broadway in New York City and the school year at Mac Fadden School in Tarrytown. My mother would put me on the subway near the Empire State Building with a note pinned to my shirt advising the conductor to make sure I got off the train when it arrived at the Tarrytown station. During school holidays I spent my days in the barbershop in the basement of the Empire State Building. I would ride the elevator up and down all day. I became friends with many of the building's occupants and referred to the elevator operator by name. My mother had moved to New York to locate my father and convince the court he should pay child support. He had been medically discharged from the Navy and was living in Brooklyn with another woman. He had left before I was born. He just walked away, no word and no destination. It had taken her several years to locate him. He had served as a communications officer in the Navy, assigned at the time of my mother's pregnancy to an obscure naval station in Louisiana. Just prior to my birth, he told my mother that he had orders to New York where he was to "ship out" with the Atlantic Fleet. The truth was he had learned that the Navy was going to discharge him for medical reasons, and he did not want the responsibility of a child. He had left his first family, and now he was leaving another. My aunt invited my mother to come to Charlotte, North Carolina for the delivery, but upon arrival, the only hospital willing to offer medical care to military dependants was in Asheville. She arrived in Asheville by train with a suitcase, heavy with child, just weeks before my birth. She moved into a boardinghouse just blocks from the hospital.

By the time I settled into the seat on that Greyhound bus late afternoon in June 1958, I'd had fifteen addresses, attended eight schools, and lived with at least as many families. My best friend's mother was a stripper. My other closest friend, Buster, lived next door with his aunt and uncle. He had also been abandoned by his natural father. Although I never knew for certain, it was said that his mother died in a house fire, and his father just could not bear the responsibility of raising a small boy alone. Two other close friends either lived with single parents or dealt with alcoholism and emotional abuse.

My two closest personal friends were Buster and Jimmy. We were thrown together more by circumstance than choice. My best friend was a clear choice. I first met him one late afternoon, when my mother pulled a box out from under a bed in a stranger's house somewhere in the city of Miami. A close friend of my mother's, whom I lovingly referred to as "Aunt Lyda," though not related to me, thought that a small boy with no siblings must at the very least have a dog. When I first looked into the darkened and not-very-good-smelling box, I saw five or six tiny rodent-like animals squirming around in a mass of dampened cut newspaper and soggy cardboard, squeaking like mice. Several, I was told were taken, but there were a few remaining to claim. I'd had a dog briefly while living with my stepfather, but without permission while he was working in the backyard on a gate, I took my new friend for a walk without a leash and soon ran home to inform my mother and her several party guests that he had been "run over" by a speeding car. The last I saw of him was his tiny little blond corpse in a trash can by the street.

Of the three remaining, two lay quietly together while the third, which I was told was the runt of the litter, attacked me with his tiny pink-and-purple tongue, as if radar homing in on a target. He shook all over, and his little rat-like tail vibrated with the frequency of a radio signal. He seemed to wink at me and say, "I'm your guy! Chose me, and I'll never let you down." The choice was clear, although he was half the size of the others and looked like a dirty mop and smelled worse. His nose was black; his eyes, although barely open, were the deepest liquid brown I had ever seen, almost as deep as my own. His coloring was black, interspersed with dark brown fading to a rust color, and his tail, though almost bare, curled over his tiny back. He was truly a mongrel; my mother referred to him as a Heinz—fifty-seven varieties. As I gently picked him up, my mother said, "No, not that one son. I don't think he will even survive. He is the runt. You will be disappointed if you choose him," she said. "What about this little girl curled up here, or maybe her sister? They are precious."

It was settled. I knew instantly which pup I wanted. I was just six, but if you wanted to know my opinion, all you had to do was ask. The runt would be coming home with me; no other would do. All I needed was a name. *What will I name this potential champion?* I thought. As I looked over and saw my aunt Lyda's huge smile, I knew I had selected the right one. My mother commented, "Don't worry about a name yet, Son, because he cannot come home today. He is too young to leave his mother, because he has not been weaned." That was the first time I had ever heard that word, and it became a word I forever associated with disappointment. The tiny, almost helpless little critter was warm and soft in my hands. He wet all over my hand and wiggled like a newly dug night crawler. He was the puppy I wanted, and nothing would do but that I have him. I don't think I had ever wanted something so badly. I put him back in the box gently as the breeder slid it back under the bed. I could see him clearly in my mind and knew we would be friends forever and ever and ever.

Weeks passed and I asked every day, "Is this the day? Is this the day? Can we go get him? Can we?" I wrote my father and asked his thoughts on an appropriate name. When the day finally arrived, my mother was sure I would be disappointed in the name I had chosen, because she was certain that one of the remaining females would be the only live puppy, and the name I had chosen certainly didn't sound very feminine. The breeder had promised her she would save a puppy for me. When the woman pulled the box out from under the bed, there was only one pup remaining. Rowser was four times his original size, had a bushy tail and a long nose, and looked every bit the part of the Shepherd-Chow mix that he was. He had to be the most beautiful dog I had ever seen. Sergeant Preston's dog, King, paled in comparison.

We took him home, and over the years, he became the neighborhood dog and love of the entire community. If anyone wanted to find me, they only had to find my "shadow." He followed me to school and slept under the portable classroom all day for years until some "do-gooder" threatened to call the dog pound. Rowser slept outside of the Circle Theater every Saturday morning and often had to endure a double feature. He would raise his head off his paws every time a child opened the door, and the ticket taker always had a large bowl of water for him. One time he was left in the front of a drug store while I thoughtlessly exited the back door, not thinking of him until well after dark. When my mother and I drove up, we watched briefly from a distance as he raised and lowered his head every time the door opened in the dark. Since my mother was working from home at the time, he was banished from the schoolyard, much to the chagrin of many of the teachers and my classmates; she was able to restrain him until after I left for school. She would keep him locked on the back porch. Somehow he had the good sense to wait until three o'clock, but when his internal clock told him to go fetch me and "carry me home," off he went. He would meet me at the school gate, his bushy tail going a mile a minute. His entire body would shake and then he would roll over to have his tummy scratched. When we slept together in a tent, appropriately called a "pup tent," I would come home smelling like the underside of a car and wet dog. He would allow me to use him as a pillow until he sensed that I was asleep and breathing deeply. He would follow me the fifteen miles I rode my bicycle to reach my horse, Smokey, until his paws were bloody and raw. He would dive in the many borrow ditches along the roadside and keep coming with his pink-and-purple tongue waving like a tattered red-and-blue Confederate battle flag in the wind. He would slide down the school slide and swim with me at Bare Ass Beach. He had his picture published in the local newspaper riding in the front of my truckster scooter with his ears blown straight back and pinned against his head. He was hit by two cars, a school bus, and a pick-up truck but was never seriously injured. Once he was smacked so hard that an intestinal sac broke somewhere in his bowels, causing him to smell like flatulence for days, but he didn't even whimper. He finally learned to cross at the crossing lights and would always look both ways before he scampered across a street. There were no leash laws in the fifties, so he ran free all of the time except when sleeping on the screen porch, where he created a long black line six inches off the floor from wall to wall from his seldom-washed body. On hot afternoons Mrs. Ramsay chased him lovingly out of her cool, wet flower beds hundreds of times, only to have him return and start digging before she closed the back door. The headmaster of the Catholic Church school across the street allowed his two Doberman pinschers to attack him and soon learned that the vocabulary of a preteen boy could be quite colorful and that the Doberman was not nearly the dog a determined runt chow was in a honest fight—one ran, and the other whimpered and jumped back into the car.

Rowser was my dearest friend, my closest confidant, and the most loyal and devoted little brother a small boy could ever have had. I knew he would always be waiting for me. He would always be waiting by the back door with his head resting on his paws, looking forward to the next adventure.

CHAPTER SIX

The bus slowed suddenly and then swerved off the road. I had been alone with my thoughts when the bus suddenly fishtailed; it lurched to the right and then left, while the wheels clawed at the pavement and gravel shoulder. A 1957 Chevy darted between the bus and an oncoming truck. "Whew, that was close," I said out loud. The bus driver sounded his air horn and jockeyed the behemoth back onto the pavement while swearing quietly under his breath. I was suddenly awake. A car full of teenagers, not much older than me, were laughing and carelessly weaving in and out of traffic on a very narrow state highway. They had darted in front of the bus. *This was surely an accident waiting to happen*, I thought. I knew the make of virtually every car made beginning with the '38 Ford through the '58 Impala. Cars and motors were a fascination to me.

Perhaps that is what attracted Frank to me. He loved machines and told me once after I got to know him that he had only attended school through the third grade. He just couldn't concentrate on schoolwork; his mind was always jumping around to mechanical things. He doodled pictures of bicycles, motors, and machinery while daydreaming about working in his father's bicycle shop. "Bicycles were a big deal," he said, "at the turn of the twentieth century."

The woman seated next to me was reading a *Modern Screen* magazine. The cover displayed a picture of Debbie Reynolds and Eddie Fisher with the caption, "Why Eddie Walked Out on Debbie."

Debbie Reynolds was one of my favorite movie stars. She and Doris Day epitomized the woman I wanted to have in my life someday. They had cute button noses and the fresh looks of the girl next door. Not that a girl actually lived next door, but if one ever did, I thought she should look like Debbie Reynolds or Doris Day.

What did Eddie Fisher see in Elizabeth Taylor? I thought. *Sure, she was pretty; yeah, she had big boobs, but she didn't hold a candle to Debbie Reynolds.* I had always had the "white picket fence" syndrome. As the car of teenagers sped away, I returned to my thoughts. I wanted my life to be perfect; my future home to sit back off the street in a quiet neighborhood, and my wife to look like Debbie Reynolds.

CHAPTER SEVEN

It was a state highway with narrow pavement and shoulders. The roadbed fell off quickly into a grass-covered ditch full of water. The bus slowed as we passed a sign announcing Tyler, Texas. As we passed the city limits sign, "Welcome to Tyler," I saw a police car, fire truck, and several bystanders peering into a drainage canal. The rear section of a '57 Chevy was pointed up the hill, and the door to the driver's side was open. A fireman was bending over the driver and appeared to be comforting a young woman on the passenger side who had blood on her forehead. The car was partially submerged in the ditch. A second car was stopped on the opposite side of the road but did not have any damage. Apparently, the teenagers who had passed us earlier had passed one too many cars. No one seemed to be seriously injured, but the car was twisted, and the back window of the Chevy was lying on the shoulder of the road.

The Dallas bus station was in a rundown section of town. Buses were parked parallel under a canopy, and people were scurrying everywhere. I had to change buses one more time. This was my sixth change since Miami—Miami, Jacksonville, Pensacola, New Orleans, Shreveport, and now Dallas. What an experience. *Would I ever get there?* I wondered. I spoke to the dispatcher, and he said the express to Denver would be leaving at 4:00 p.m. It was routed over Raton Pass and into Colorado from the southern end of the state. I hoped that I would get a glimpse of the Rocky Mountains before dark.

Unfortunately, when we finally reached Raton Pass, it was dark and snowing. Snowing in June. I couldn't believe what I was seeing. The driver had the windshield wipers on, and snow was piling up on the edges of the windshield. Forward visibility was virtually zero. We had slowed to a crawl, and the windows were foggy and ice rimmed. It had been eighty-five degrees in the shade at four o'clock in the afternoon when I departed Miami. The sky was blue with cotton-ball clouds and a slight breeze off Biscayne Bay. I was wearing Levi's and a pull-over shirt. Arriving in Colorado approximately forty-five hours later, the temperature was freezing, and snow was falling in big flakes, covering the windshield and roadbed. Every so often the rear wheels of the bus would hit a patch of ice and would fishtail slightly.

This had certainly been an experience. I was still wearing the same Levi's and pull-over shirt. It was time for a blanket. I never thought that I would experience snow in June. I should be in Denver in about three or four hours, my seatmate said. Wow. Snow in June.

Jimmy was one of my two closest friends. Buster was the other. Jimmy's mother was Cuban and danced with an exotic cat in the local "cabaret." My mother said it was a "strip joint." I loved visiting Jimmy's house, because his mother had pictures of herself in some state of undress on every wall. I think it embarrassed Jimmy, but he never really said anything. We had become friends when we both learned that we were free to do just about anything we wanted to do. Our time was our own. Often he would stay at my house, or I would stay at his for days without either of our mothers asking about or being aware of our absence. His mother worked in the clubs at night, and my mother often passed out by eight o'clock. Jimmy's mother owned three small apartments and worked every night until daylight. She slept during the day, so when we were not in school, we would spend our days roaming the streets, hanging out at my house, or working at Jim's Delicatessen. It was the perfect arrangement. Jimmy had plenty of "uncles" that would give us a ride in their Ford convertibles and Chevrolet Bel Airs. I saw my first Corvette in 1953. Another of Jimmy's "uncles'" cars. Many men came and went in Jimmy's house, but John was the most interesting. He was a local motorcycle cop by occupation who drove a pink-and-black 1955 Ford Sunliner convertible. He and Jimmy's mom were an item or had at least been together for a few months.

The Sunday morning before I left Miami, Jimmy and I were working for the local grocer. The store was actually a small delicatessen. The owner's name was Jim; we called him "Big Jim." He sold groceries and had a small meat counter in the back of the store. He liked us and would often let us operate the cash register, stock shelves, or just hang around and keep him company. His family was still in New Jersey, and he worked all the time. The store was open seven days a week, fifteen hours a day. Big Jim was legally blind but had enough vision to determine the denomination of currency if he held it close to his nose, squinting through his thick lenses. My mother had rented a spare room to him and his business partner when they first arrived from New Jersey. He and his partner, also named Jim, "Little Jim," bought the store from an elderly couple and worked together for the first few months. It was soon apparent that Little Jim's family was not going to leave New Jersey, so he sold his interest to Big Jim, and I never saw him again. He went home to save his marriage, while Big Jim stayed and operated the store. The store was open from seven o'clock in the morning until ten o'clock at night. Big Jim was there every minute. He sold sandwiches and beer and wine along with a few basic groceries. He could not wait for Jimmy and me to meet his beautiful daughter.

One Sunday morning, soon after the store opened, Jimmy was in the back sweeping up, and I was stocking shelves. A man had approached the cash register the night before and had collapsed of a heart attack. He died on the spot. Jimmy and I still had not gotten over that experience when we suddenly heard a loud crash, and the glass storefront exploded inward. The front half of a pink-and-black '55 Ford convertible was resting on the stem wall that had supported window. The back of the car was on the sidewalk; the car was half in the store and half out.

"What the hell!" Big Jim yelled. Jimmy ran from the rear of the store, and I peered around the shelves. It was Jimmy's mother. She opened the driver's side door and stepped into the store as if nothing had happened. She was wearing a white, terry cloth bikini and high-heeled shoes. When Big Jim finally regained his composure, he said without enthusiasm, "Good morning, Delores; out kinda early, aren't you?" Jimmy's mother then slumped to the floor with one foot beneath her ample rear end and the other leg stretched out in front of her. One of her high heels had slid across the floor. With one hand on the floor and one on her brow, she said, "Mornin Jim. I came to get some coffee." She was obviously very intoxicated. When she tried to stand, she fell backward, legs akimbo in a rather unladylike posture. Big Jim bent over slightly, reached down, and took her hand and helped her up. While doing so he called to Jimmy. He said, "Jimmy, your mother's here. Could I ask you to take her home?"

She did not appear to be hurt. The car was not severely damaged with only a few scratches and one broken headlight. We put our backs to the front of the car. Big Jim lifted the front bumper, and we pushed it back off of the wall. "Delores, better get on home before the cops come," he said. "It's early, but never can tell, they could drive by. Get her on home, son." Jimmy helped his mother into the passenger side of the car, slid into the driver's seat, backed out of the parking lot, and disappeared around the corner of the building.

A few minutes later, I heard Big Jim talking to the police on the phone. He said, "Got to the store this morning, and the front window was smashed. Looks like a car musta rolled into it during the night. Nothin seems to be missin, just kind of a mess, glass everywhere! If ya want to send a car around, okay. I'll probably have to get it boarded up until I can replace the glass." Jimmy walked back into the store about half an hour later. He went into the back, picked up his broom, and continued sweeping. He and I were used to it. I do not remember Big Jim ever saying another word to Jimmy about that morning. Jimmy and I never discussed the incident. When I spoke to his mother a few days later, not a word was said. I was curious, however, what John the cop thought about the damage to the headlight on his pink-and-black convertible. *It was probably worth it,* I thought. Jimmy's mom was one sexy, good-looking woman!

CHAPTER EIGHT

Once the old engine started, it became immediately obvious to Frank that it was in serious need of attention. Heavy black smoke poured out of the exhaust pipe. The little engine skipped and coughed but ran, haltingly. It would accelerate and then slow down. It made wheezing and sucking sounds, faltering and skipping to a strange beat. "Valves, I think. Rings bad too, maybe. Oughten to fix that machine," he said. "Needs to go into the shop. It'll never make it the way it is. Do you know where to take it to have it fixed?" he asked. "I think the engine needs overhauled."

"Overhaul," I said. "I don't have any money. It took everything I saved just to buy it," I said, tears welling in my eyes.

He hesitated a moment, as if contemplating what to say next, then he said almost to himself, "We can fix it, ain't much trouble. Would you like for me to help you fix it, overhaul it I mean?"

"Would I, would you, could you help me, I mean. Would you really help me fix it? Boy, that would be great! I would love it," I said. I did not know what to say or how to express myself. I stood there for a full minute on one foot and then the other, before I said, "Are you serious, would you help me, seriously?" That is how it all began.

The weeks went quickly. Frank, Buster, and I would meet about three times a week to work on the scooter. We disassembled the engine. I scraped and scrounged to raise the extra money I needed to purchase the parts I needed. I would help fold and substitute for other boys who could not, for some reason, deliver their papers.

I still had my bike. Big Jim would allow me to stock shelves and sweep floors at the delicatessen for a few extra bucks. I scoured the roadside and drainage ditches within a few miles of my house for returnable soda bottles. I retrieved golf balls for golfers from the lakes and canals at the local country club.

We replaced the piston rings and connecting rod bearings, ground the valves by hand, and reassembled the engine with new gaskets and seals. Throughout the process Frank explained the function of each part, its relationship to the combustion process, and why and how it all interrelated. We talked about a lot of things. Frank never spoke to me as a child; he had a way of speaking that I could understand. If I did not understand, he would take the time to repeat himself, and on some occasions, he would make a drawing on a scrap of paper or cardboard.

Frank had always loved machinery. He told me that he had raced motorcycles on dirt and board tracks in Colorado during the early part of the century. He frequently took Buster and me to Royal Castle for lunch and would tell us about early attempts to deliver the mail by motorcycle. He described it as a motorized pony express. "The roads were all dirt and sometimes almost impassable after a rain or snowstorm," he said. "Riders would motor along hours at a time without seein a house or town. We would ride them machines in relays with our saddle bags full of mail," he said. "At times we would be so covered with mud that the only skin visible would be around our eyes after removin our goggles! The rain, the cold, and snow was brutal, but we loved it. For many of the riders, it was a dream come true. We were ridin motorcycles, and we were gettin paid for it. What a life," he would say. "We would have done it for nothin." He described his service in the motorcycles corps in the Army in World War I and told of his friendship with Mr. Harley and Mr. Davidson.

His father had owned a small bicycle shop in Colorado. He described the shop with loving detail and recalled so much about the time. He said that in the early 1900s, bicycles were the principle mode of transportation. He told us how some of the first motorized bicycles were developed in Europe.

Many of the early roads were dirt or gravel, he said with the cities often having brick pavers or hard-packed rock-and-gravel roadbeds. Bicycles became the fashion and then the motorized bicycle became a common means of transportation. Frank's father, soon after the turn of the twentieth century, learned of Messieurs Harley and Davidson's development of a motorized bicycle. After contacting them arrangements were made to purchase one of their earliest machines, allowing Frank's father to open one of the first Harley Davidson shops on the eastern slope, while he continued to repair bicycles and build motorized bicycles of his own creation.

The first motorcycles were little more than a heavy duty bicycle with a one-cylinder engine mounted between the front and rear wheels inside of the frame. They were started by placing the machine on a rear–fender, mounted kickstand and pedaling until the engine started. Once it started the "velocipede," as Frank referred to early motorcycles, was pushed off its kickstand and mounted like an ordinary bicycle. Many of the first motor bicycles were advertised to cover a mile in two minutes. Frank said, "Ya better be headin down a hill to go that fast." He said there was an Indian, Clement, Mitchell Mile a Minute, Excelsior, and a Minerva Speed King, among the many.

Motorcycle clubs began to spring up all over the country, and both men and women were drawn to riding. Before too long it became obvious to Frank's father that the Harley Davidson was the best of the best. While Frank knew of other machines that would compare, "There was nothing like a Harley," he said. By the time his father began selling Harley Davidsons, Sarah Bernhardt

was a leading lady, Mary Pickford was America's sweetheart, and
Will Rogers was a famous satirist. Woodrow Wilson was president. Frank could tell you about them all. He thought Woodrow
Wilson was one of the worst presidents in American history, second to FDR. He thought Sarah Bernhardt was an interesting
"Jane." He referred to most women as "Janes." Will Rogers, in his
opinion, was one of the funniest men alive.

He said when sidecars became popular with the "Janes," he became even more interested in motorcycles. His father built a way-
side motorcycle barn just beyond the canyon as a midpoint for his
customers to stop for the afternoon, picnic on the river, and ride
on to the national park. That barn, I learned later, was to become
his home and my refuge during that summer. It was located in
Cedar Cove at the end of a winding dirt road just above the river
and Cedar Creek.

Frank told Buster about his father and about how he and his
brother spent a winter in a small frame house adjacent to the river
across from his house. He said it was one of the coldest winters ever
recorded. The house had little insulation other than cardboard and
was heated by a potbellied stove. He had known Buster's mother
and told him a little of his father's marriage and early life.

The most fascinating stories were about motorcycle racing.
He rarely spoke of his own record-setting accomplishments. He
spoke of the evolution of racing. He described the dirt and board
tracks and personalities of the riders. He and his future brother-
in-law had raced throughout the west up Pikes Peak and rallied
across the country. He told of racing up hills and mountainsides
on "machines" with no brakes and the throttle "wide open." He
related stories in a matter-of-fact way, without braggadocio, and
often spent more time recounting the deeds of others than accomplishments of his own.

I did not learn until years later that he had personally set speed records on "singles" and "twins" (with sidecars) that had never been broken. I learned that he was quite well known in racing circles, as a celebrity, but he concentrated entirely upon the feats of others.

He spoke fondly of Floyd Clymer, who was not only a competitor but a close personal friend. "Floyd," he said, "set a record on a Henderson K model between Chicago and Denver, but it wasn't long before those big Harleys beat Floyd's record like an ugly stepchild. Them Harleys were quite a machine. Ole Clymer learned early on that the Harley was the machine to beat. Unfortunately for Clymer, Hap Scherer beat his record on the Henderson in just a few weeks. Hap averaged over twenty-five miles an hour on a Harley sport model and while that don't seem fast," he said, "ya gotta remember them roads were gumbo when it rained and were dry, dusty, and full a holes and ruts when it didn't. Making any kinda time would jar your bones and beat a rider's body silly. Twenty-five miles an hour was quite an improvement over the wagon and the horse and buggy. There were few cars in them days, but they would take a beatin on them roads and none would average twenty-five miles per hour." He spoke of many other personalities: Cannonball Baker, Red Parkhurst, Otto Walker, and of course his future brother-in-law, Lester Foote. Lester became Frank's brother-in-law, his lifelong friend, and sidecar partner throughout the 1920s. Later, I learned that he and Lester, riding together, set speed records that were some of the highest attained at that time anywhere in the world.

CHAPTER NINE

The sun had just started to rise when the bus pulled into the Colorado Springs station. The eastern sky was lavender, streaked with salmon-colored, pewter-tipped clouds. The sky was kaleidoscopic. Colorful hues of silver splashed across the horizon. The windows on the left side of the bus were still dark, but I could see the dark silhouettes of mountains and fresh snow glistening in the early morning shadows.

My seatmate was an army private on his first assignment out of boot camp. He and I marveled at the beauty. We had been seatmates since Amarillo. He had spent several months at Fort Benning, Georgia, and later at Fort Stewart learning the mechanized skills of the Army Tank Corp. His childhood experience was entirely antithetical to mine. He had grown up on a ranch and had never left the county prior to basic training in Georgia. He had not experienced the heavy morning dew and languid afternoons of the south. "It was overwhelming," he said. "I don't think I had a dry uniform the entire time I spent in Georgia. How do you stand that humidity?" he asked. "I could not live there," he said with emphasis. "The bugs are everywhere, and the heat is oppressive." He asked if Florida was the same or worse, and I quizzed him about ranch life.

Although a good five years older than me, he seemed impressed with my story. I told him how I had met Frank and been invited to Colorado to work on his friend's ranch. I told him about the long bus ride and some of the people I had met along the way.

He knew very little about the racial segregation of the south and said that there were very few coloreds in West Texas. He said Mexicans worked the fields alongside him, but his first experience with the races came after joining the army. He was surprised how this man, a stranger, certainly no family connection, had invited me to Colorado to work on the ranch of his childhood friend. I had no idea what to expect, I told him. "What was it like to grow up on a ranch?" I asked.

"It was hard, dusty, tiring work," he said. He had risen at 4:00 a.m. as long as he could remember. He and his father and a few hired hands had worked together often from sunrise to sunset six days a week. Sundays were devoted to church and rest, but the cows still had to be milked. It was rare to have a day off.

"Haying was a brutal task," he said. His father would operate the mowing machine, and he would ride behind the baler. He called it a "sled." When the bales of new hay emerged from the machine, it was his job to load them on the sled and stack them in the field; he called it "bucking bales." Each bale weighed about eighty pounds, and the stalks would penetrate his clothing and scratch his arms bloody. He said he looked like he had been in a fight with a polecat when he finished, and the cat had won.

He could drive a truck and operate every kind of tractor. He said the soil was so hard that they had to use a bulldozer for some of the work and kept it around to enlarge and clean the ponds on the place.

He loved horses and had several he entered in rodeo events when he had time. Calf roping was his specialty. He and his dad would team rope. He said he thought his interest in operating machinery was what drew him to the Army's mechanized division.

Amarillo was brutally cold in the winter, and the wind blew all of the time. There was no place to hide as the land was virtually barren. The summers were dusty, hot and dry. His family lived forty miles from the city, and there were only rare occasions when he could go to town. The family ranch consisted of over a thousand acres, and it took five acres to support one cow. Girls, he said were hard to find, and if you found one, the days were so long and the distance so great, it was hard to have any kind of relationship. Many of the girls left for the city right after high school. High school had given him the most pleasure, he said, but he did not want to go to college, since he knew his father would expect him, as the oldest, to manage the ranch sometime in the future. He wanted to see the world before he settled in.

"I put in for Europe," he said. "I had hoped to be stationed in Germany, but you know the Army; tell them where you want to go, and they will send you to the opposite end of the earth. Had I been smart, and knew what I know now, I would have asked to go to Colorado. I would have been shipped to Germany for certain. Take my advice: if you ever join the Army, don't forget, and if you want to go one place, ask to be sent in the other direction. You will then likely go exactly where you want to go!"

I could tell that he loved and admired his father. He had been one of the first to invade Omaha Beach in France and had been shot through the shoulder. He said his father had been evacuated to England and had spent the remainder of the war recuperating from his wound and preparing to return to Texas to manage his ailing father's ranch and reunite with his wife and young family. He had been there ever since, first living in a small trailer on the ranch and moving into the family home. His father's father had cared for his grandmother until she died. His grandfather died soon after of a broken heart, he said. "Ranch life is difficult and tends to wear people out," he also said. His father never left Texas after the war and seldom went to town. It was almost as if his war experience had "hollowed him out" and left him but a shell. His father rarely spoke of his experience, and when he did, it was only to praise his buddies and remember those who had died. The battlefield on that long ago French beach and the hospital in England seemed almost a Texas mirage, the soldier said. "I know he is proud of me, but the ranch takes so much care that during my absence, it is going to be a real hardship." He knew as soon as his tour was over, he would be expected to return to West Texas and continue the tradition of a Texas land owner. Leaving didn't seem an option.

In the predawn, as the darkness softened, I thought of my own father. He had left my mother before I was born. He had been a warrant officer in the Navy, stationed on some obscure naval base in Louisiana. My mother and father had been married for about three years when they left Miami for San Diego and then Louisiana. It was my mother's first and my father's second or third marriage as far as anyone knew. My father was somewhat of a mystery man. There were twenty years in his life that no one could account for. He was forty, and she was thirty. He was on the rebound from a long-term relationship, and my mother was at a point chronologically where a woman thinks the clock has been ticking long enough—marriage or spinsterhood. She chose marriage. I do not know whether it was a marriage of convenience or how it might be described, but it was doomed from the very beginning. There were no two more unlikely people. She was red-headed with a temperament to match, and he was tall, handsome, and black Irish.

My mother learned, after they were married, that he had a grown daughter. He had abandoned his first wife and child much like he would later abandon my mother and me. It was 1943, and the war in Europe was raging. He convinced her that he had to meet the fleet in New York and "ship out" to Europe. My mother was very pregnant and unable to work. She believed his story and made ready to hunker down in Louisiana for the duration.

Whatever their relationship she never expected him to just disappear. He did. Unfortunately, my father had been free of responsibility too long; he was "reckless with the truth" (an expression I later learned from Frank) and just hit the road. It would be several years before my mother found him in New York City, and she was able to convince a judge to grant her a divorce.

My seatmate gathered up his few belongings, and we said our good-byes and good lucks. While several new passengers boarded and settled in their seats, I stretched out and mused, *what a total alien life.* There could be no greater difference in the way the two of us grew up. I could almost not contemplate living in one house, in one town, or in one state for that matter, for a lifetime. It had seemed a lifetime to me already. I had attended six or seven schools, had recorded more than fifteen addresses, and had slept on beds, couches, car seats, and porches of nearly every relative and friend the family knew. I had never felt a grown man's beard, no less knew a father. I did not have the discipline to rise early and work hard. I had little discipline at all. I came and went as I pleased and often would be gone for days with nothing more than a note or an occasional phone call to alert my mother of my whereabouts. "Gone to Jimmy's" I'd scribble. Although I am sure she worried, she had her own demons, and I was but one of them. I had become a not-so-happy reminder of a handsome man and a relationship gone sour.

What exactly will it be like to live in a male-dominated household, I wondered. I had lived with several relatives but found the households to be primarily matriarchal. Either the husbands were gone often or were sleeping during the day. I wondered if I would be able to conform. *Will I be able to take direction,* I thought as the bus pushed through the cold morning air. I recalled that an uncle had once threatened to beat me with his belt for some supposed infraction, and I had run and was gone two days—I was eleven. I wouldn't return until he agreed to an armistice. *What would Frank expect of me?* I did not know him well. *Can I make the transition from total freedom and staying up all night swimming in the Green Mansion's apartment pool at three o'clock in the morning with my few friends and running from the police when the apartment dwellers could no longer stand the noise? This is going to be interesting,* I thought. The morning sun was bright and penetrated every crevice of the big bus. Motes of dust danced in the streams of light. *What a beautiful part of the world,* I thought. The mountains on the left side of the bus were spectacular with their dark shadows and blanketed with snow. Pikes Peak was the most prominent and loomed in the window of the bus. Colorado Springs was beginning to awaken, and the morning was fresh.

CHAPTER TEN

Denver was not unlike the many large cities I had traveled through since the start of my odyssey. The bus ride had almost come to an end, but my travels that summer were just beginning. The city was spread out for miles. The mountains looming in the western sky offered a pleasant, new perspective that was absent in Dallas, New Orleans, or the several other cities I had passed through. They offered what metaphorically seemed to be the end of the journey, yet this was just the beginning. It took the bus about thirty minutes to weave through the suburban neighborhoods and the sprawling communities of the outlying area to finally enter downtown where the bus station was located. Downtown was much like the many I had already visited; I could no longer see the mountains for the building obstructions.

The station was well lit and crisscrossed with bench seats accommodating people sleeping or sitting distractedly waiting for their bus. Bags were piled everywhere, and the noise of children and adults competed for attention. Some were reading while others seemed to be merely staring at the ceiling. I saw two sharply dressed military policemen speaking animatedly to a young soldier in uniform whose countenance was filled with expectation. Much like the many cities I had passed through, the station was located in an area that was run down at its heels and wore the clothing of an earlier day.

There was a street person sleeping in an alleyway leading to the terminal and a large yellow-colored cat with his backside protruding from a trash can searching for his breakfast. The bus garage was cavernous and smelled strongly of diesel fuel and the waiting area was packed with expectant travelers. One more change of buses and a short sixty miles and I would meet Frank.

What if he isn't there, what will I do then? I thought. I had an aunt in Denver that I had met the year before. I felt some safety in that knowledge. She was my father's sister, and I had not known she existed until I received a surprise card on my thirteenth birthday. I knew almost nothing about my father or his family, and now I knew he has a sister. I was more familiar with neighbors and my few friends' families than I was my own. My mother did not speak of my father except in derision, and none of the rest of my family had met him.

I had a few hours to kill until my local bus departed. I was hungry and tired of the greasy bus station fare. I thought I would walk a few blocks from the terminal and see if I could find a restaurant open for breakfast. Although I had been careful on the trip, I had very little money left to spend. I hoped I could find someplace that served eggs, grits, and bacon with a biscuit and gravy on the side and perhaps a few pancakes. I was not sure what I would find, but I knew I didn't want another greasy hamburger, French fries, and Coke for breakfast. It seemed that was about all that was edible at bus terminal lunch counters.

I had rarely eaten breakfast while living with my mother; she was often too hungover to tolerate the smells of food cooking, and she slept in on the weekends. While living with my aunt and uncle in Jacksonville during the summer months, I always experienced an unending supply of pancakes, eggs, and bacon on Sunday morning. My uncle traveled during the week and worked long hours. He spent his evenings studying the *Wall Street Journal* and the stock market, but on Sunday morning, he loved to cook. My cousin and I would awake to the commingled aromas of coffee and bacon and the hushed sounds of Sunday morning preachers on the radio. It was Sunday morning!

I had walked several blocks when I noticed a small coffee shop in the lobby of an old hotel. There was a waitress in a blue uniform with a cap pinned to the side of her head, hurrying between the few tables and lunch counter. A man behind the counter in checkered pants and a tall starched chef's cap was facing the cooking surface.

This will do, I thought. The cooking surface steamed with activity. I sat at the counter and enjoyed the first good meal of the trip. Several people came and went, and the waitress bustled around the room. I finished my breakfast, paid the tab with what little cash I had left, and discovered I had only eleven dollars left to finish out the summer.

I walked through the hotel lobby and into the fresh morning, Colorado air. It was cool and a slight breeze, strengthened by the effect of the tall buildings and narrow streets, picked up the local section of the *Denver Post* and scattered it down the street. I was a little confused when I left the restaurant and not quite certain which direction to head in order to return to the bus station. Since I did not own a watch, I was concerned about the time. I had not seen a clock in the hotel lobby or in the coffee shop.

Everything looked the same until I spied a western storefront on my left that I remembered passing. I remembered that the store would be on my right on my return to the Greyhound depot. I stood on the curb for a moment waiting for the light to change and thought I had better head east. "Head east," I muttered half aloud to myself and stepped off the curb. *I had better hurry,* I thought, *if Frank is waiting for me, I did not want to miss him.* I realized I did not have his telephone number.

Earlier, I had exited the bus station, crossed the street in the middle of the block, and walked several city blocks before discovering the old hotel lunch counter. I had done a little window shopping

along the way and had admired the western clothes on the manne-
quins in one of the store windows. I was truly in the West. I couldn't
believe it. Just as I stepped off the curb and was in the middle of
the street in the crosswalk, I heard a masculine voice behind me say,
"Are you lost, lad?" By the time I reached the curb on the opposite
side of the street, the man was at my elbow. He was a big man with
a long face, who appeared to be in his late twenties or early thirties.
He had long sideburns cut at an angle, a western string tie, and
a huge silver belt buckle. He did not appear threatening, but my
mind was already racing. *Who is this guy,* I thought.

"You look as if you are lost," he said. "Are you new to Denver?"
he asked. "What are you looking for? Can I help you? Are you
meeting someone?" he asked in an uninterrupted string of ques-
tions. "I was in the restaurant having breakfast when I saw you
come in," he said. "It seemed so unusual for a young man to be up
so early on a Sunday morning in this part of town."

Is he just making conversation, I thought, *or does he have other
intentions? Who is this guy, and why is he on my heels?* My mind
started to race again.

I thought of my mother's response to the man at the night de-
pository. She told me that the man had hastily departed when she
told him she could not vote because she had killed a man.

*What should I say, what should I do? He does not seem threatening,
but there are very few people around, and he is a big guy,* I thought. I
wondered if my mother's comments would work for me. *How was
I going to work the idea into a conversation? Oh, what a nice morning,
sir, by the way I killed a man. Nope that wouldn't do!*

When I originally stepped on to the bus, my mother, almost as
an afterthought, had admonished me, "Be careful, there are a lot
of predators out there. Don't put yourself into a situation that does
not give you an exit. Keep your eyes and ears open, and be aware of

your surroundings. Always look for an escape, and be alert," she had warned. *Was this one of those times,* I thought, *is this guy a predator?*

The trip so far had been uneventful, but I admitted to myself I had always stayed close to the bus station and was quick to reenter if I felt ill at ease. I remembered an afternoon while hitchhiking home from a movie. I was only about a mile from my house, but I was accustomed to hitchhiking. It seemed a challenge. On one occasion a Cadillac with New York license plates stopped and asked for directions. It was clear the occupants were not going to give me a ride, so I sent them in the opposite direction. Hitchhiking was my most frequent mode of transportation. I thought I was just too old to ride a bicycle—that was for kids. A man stopped near the Texaco station on the traffic circle and offered me a ride. Once I entered the car, he almost immediately made an excuse for turning down the next street and headed away from my destination. Not listening to my immediate protest, he told me he had to stop by his sister's house for a minute and asked would I mind riding along. He never gave me time to answer. He just kept driving. He soon began making sexual comments and innuendo and turned down several more streets and crossed several intersections without stopping. We were getting farther and farther away from my home, and although it was mid-afternoon my senses were in overdrive. It had become very clear to me that this ride was not one I should have taken. This was not the first bad decision I had made hitchhiking, but it was the most immediate, and I had to figure out how to get away from the man. He slowed the car and seemed to be looking for an address before suddenly turning into a driveway. I heard him say "nope, this isn't it" as I yanked the door open and leaped from the car almost before it stopped. The house appeared to be vacant, and there were several newspapers on the sidewalk. I stumbled but recovered while he was racing in reverse down the street in the opposite direction and reaching to close the passenger door. I do not know who was more frightened, him or me. I walked the rest of the way home admonishing myself for hitchhiking and telling myself how stupid my decision was. I was going to take the jitney or bus next time and no more soliciting rides. It wasn't a week before I had my thumb in the air again. So much for commitment...

I began to feel the same sensation at the back of my neck as I did on my ride with the stranger. The hackles I had seen rise on my dog's neck when an adversary approached him. *This is not a good situation, and it seems to be deteriorating,* I thought. As the man and I continued to walk in the direction of the bus station, I realized I had walked farther than I had originally thought.

While hurrying beside me, the man reached into his pocket, removed an object, and extended his hand in front of me as we walked. He shoved it in my face. "Have you ever seen a silver dollar?" he asked. "Take it, take it, look it over," he said. "Have you ever heard of Silver Dollar Tabor? Silver Dollar was famous for them, silver dollars I mean!" He kept holding the silver dollar in front of me. "Silver Dollar Tabor was a nineteenth-century prospector who had discovered one of the richest silver mines in Colorado. It was said that he purchased the Brown Derby Hotel and fired the manager who had not allowed him to register with the woman accompanying him. Her name was Baby Doe. Tabors were quite a story," he said. "The hotel is right up the street. I heard it told that Baby Doe would stand in a corner balcony and toss a handful of silver dollars to passersby."

The light changed, and we started across the street together. He seemed more insistent that I accept the silver dollar. "Take the silver dollar, it is free," he said. "Take it! Come on take it; it is just a gift, no strings attached." *Right! No strings*, I thought. I was starting to get a little frantic. *Be calm, the bus station is here somewhere, relax!*

The street was desolate, and the man continued at my elbow. As I picked up my pace, he picked up his. At times he walked backward facing me. He began telling me about a younger brother who was sleeping back at the hotel. He told me he thought I would like him, because he was about my age. "We should go back to the hotel and wake him up," he said. He was becoming insistent that I accompany him and did not want to take no for an answer. I must accompany him to the hotel, he insisted, and meet his brother. He had business to attend to that day, and I could spend the day with his brother. He would pay me, he said. Couldn't I use some money?

I heard a noise that I recognized approaching behind me. The noise was moving closer and growing louder. I knew the sound. I saw a sign on a pole about a half block ahead that I recognized. I looked over my left shoulder to confirm what I knew. The man did not appear to be aware of the noise. He kept up the banter about his brother, and there was a higher pitch to his voice. "Won't you help me with my brother?" he asked. "Why are you in such a hurry, kid?" he asked oblivious to the noise. "Don't you want to make some money? Wouldn't you like to meet my brother? We can all have some fun together. I know you will like him; he is just about your age! I have money."

I raised my left arm and looked over my shoulder at the Denver City bus displaying Larimer Street as its destination and then looked back at the "Bus Stop" sign. It was pulling up to the curb. I stopped, the driver opened the door, and I quickly stepped in. As I mounted the two steps and reached into my pocket for the fare, looking over my shoulder I said to the man, "Nice meeting you, sir; this is my bus!" The driver closed the door, released the hissing air brakes, and we pulled away from the curb. I watched the man getting smaller and smaller in the side-view mirror and shuddered. The Greyhound depot was two stops away.

CHAPTER ELEVEN

It was noon when we passed the bus station. A clock on a stand advertising Bettes' Jewelry was pointing to twelve. The sun was directly overhead, and the sky was the bluest blue I had ever seen. The few passengers on the bus were moving around in their seats, and one woman was standing in the aisle reaching for her luggage in the overhead rack. We had passed the Cosmopolitan Hotel which served as the bus stop in the small town, and I saw Frank leaning against the hotel façade talking to another man. The bus circled the block in order to stop at the curb in front of the bus stop. It was a curbside stop. I saw several people sitting on stools at the lunch counter in the hotel as Frank and the other man approached the bus. The man Frank was speaking with was tall and thin and towered over him.

As I stepped off the bus, Frank's face showed recognition, and he looked back and summoned his friend. As they approached both were wearing overalls and long-sleeved shirts. Frank wore a summer hat with a band dark with sweat stains. The other man was hatless and seemed to try and disguise his height by stooping at the shoulders. His eyes were rheumy and moist, and he had long creases that fit his long face.

When Frank reached his hand out to me, the other man's face lightened, and he flashed a toothy grin. "This here is the boy I told you about, Clay," he said. "He is from Florida but was born in North Carolina. I think you North Carolinians would call him a 'Tar Heel.' Boy, this here is Clay Wells. I been knowin him for fifty years. He was born in North Carolina but got here as soon as he could," he said with a twinkle in his eye. "Clay has been in a thousand fights but never won a one."

The man stuck out his big gnarled hand and said "howdy" with a southern drawl and asked about my trip. He said he had hitched to Colorado years ago. He had originally planned to wind up in California but never made it. He had never been to Florida, but he had heard it was "real purdy." He winked at Frank and said there was a woman involved, but he didn't want to go into that.

Frank did not introduce me by name, he just said, "this here boy." The driver had opened the baggage compartment and was setting several bags on the curb. My old Samsonite suitcase was easily recognizable. After some more pleasantries and a little laughter, Frank picked up my bag and said his goodbyes to Clay. We walked through an alley adjoined by an old gas station, and he put my bag in the bed of a red Dodge pickup truck that had a worn-out broom sticking out of one of the corner posts. "That there is the shop I told you of. It is on the site of my dad's original bicycle shop. I worked there for fifty years. I bought one of them surplus Army Quonset huts in '46, I think it had been an airplane hangar, and erected it. I had a showroom big enough for two cars," he said. "Army surplus was cheap. A fella could buy an old Steerman airplane or a jeep for a couple hundred dollars after World War II. Typical of our government to just throw money away," he said. "When you get inside, you can still see the rounded steel roof."

Frank started the truck, and we turned out of the gravel parking lot onto Cleveland Avenue and then onto First Street. After we had driven about a block to the south, Frank pointed out a small bridge culvert. He slowed the truck crossing some railroad tracks and said, "One cold night about forty years ago the sheriff was killed right there on that bridge. He was a bully," he said, "and someone just shot him dead. I don't know if he deserved killin, but a real good beatin with a croaker sack over his head would have served the purpose. He abused his authority and was a sneaky sort of fellow. I know they found him with another man's wife, and all the while, he sat in the first pew at the local Methodist church. Don't know who ever did it as never was anyone to step up or any clues, so the killin was never solved. Don't think he was missed much, but then that is a story in itself. Sometimes the only way to have fairness in this life is to take matters into your own hands. Don't be thinkin life is fair; fairness is sometimes getting even. Someone truly believed that notion and shot the bastard twice in the head! As in the case of old Clay Wells, there was a woman involved, but I don't know the whole story. I wouldn't have put it past old Clay as he was a tough hombre in them days. That shootin was one of the biggest things to happen in this town in the past fifty years. That don't mean to say we don't have our troubles, but I can't even remember another murder. The long and the short of the story is there weren't much time spent on the investigation, and his successor turned out to be an honest man with a level hand."

We turned west and passed the local high school with its green athletic field and wooden bleachers and continued down First Street. We crossed a second small bridge and Frank turned into an area adjoining the river, fenced up to the road. There was a small white, sun-bleached house badly in need of paint just inside of the fence with several burros nearby, their muzzles buried in the dust.

"Remember I told you about Chili; well, that's where I found him, over there in that hay loft and that's where he lived, in the white house, I mean. I used to feed hogs right here in this feedlot. It would stink to high heaven and them town folks would have a time of it. One day I backed my truck up to the shed where I stored hay and grain for the horses and started loadin up the truck. I threw a few bales on the truck when I come upon this place hollered out in the middle of the stack. There was some cardboard threw in there and a couple of old mule shoes. It was kinda like a coyote's den. Out crawled this little Mexican kid. He was scared to death and looked at me as if he thought I were gonna eat him on the spot. He couldn't have been over seven or eight year old and looked like he hadn't had a bath in his lifetime. I had seen him hangin around a few times before but didn't know he was livin in my hay loft. I have no idea what he had been doin for food. Turns out his old man had helped me around the place, and best I can figure had so damn many young un's that they just forgot him when they went to find other work. Hard to understand, but when I did run up on them, they said I could keep him if I wanted. He stayed with me and then lived in the white house until he joined the Navy. I took him in and never met a harder worker. We called it the 'dog house.'" He pointed to the weathered shack. "He slopped the hogs, swept up the garage, and helped me around the farms. He would drive a beet truck by sitting on a pillow when he was about eight years old. The kid would work all day and cat around all night. Never seemed to complain. Damnest thing I ever seen.

"He married some Jane when he got back from the Navy, but that didn't work out too good. He didn't care much for school but could ride a bull better than most and build an engine almost with his eyes closed. Him and 'Old Spot' got the shop now.

"Maybe tomorrow we can stop, and you can meet them both." He seemed proud of the man I had never met and would learn later that he considered him the son he never had.

We continued west on First Street and passed several small farms and ranches. The foothills grew larger. I was overwhelmed by the expanse of the horizon—the blue, blue sky that seemed to reach forever and the dappled green beauty of the mountains. They were capped with snow, and one long lens shaped cloud stretched for miles above their peaks. The foothills grew larger in the windshield, and the roadway became gravel.

Frank pointed to a small rise on the left side of the truck just above a lake at the water's edge and said that the clearing on the top was once the site of a dance hall. "A lot of drinkin, cuttin and fightin went on out there. It was told that the sheriff I spoke of that was killed was a silent owner. They say lots of money changed hands before the place mysteriously burned down. Just beyond that small rock-strewn hillside on your side of the truck was the summer campground of the Ute Indians. There are very few descendants around here these days," he said, "but they brought a lot of color to the community. They would get a little firewater in them, and there would be hell to pay. It is called Marianna Butte, and for years local children would find arrowheads and pottery shards.

"I used to run cattle up in the canyon with old Willie PaPa. I will show you where his cabin was once we get to the house. There is nothin left but a few large stones and a cold well in the river where he kept milk and butter."

We passed the old homeplace of Freddie Grimes and his family whom I would meet that summer and passed under a concrete water slew that crossed the road on pillars. "Water has always been a problem in the valley before the Reclamation Department built the big diversion at the base of the canyon. Water had been transported from the snow melt above Estes Park by way of a wooden flume and later a concrete flume that passed this way. Water, or the absence of it, created quite a stir early on," he said. "A man that controlled the water around here was mighty powerful and generally accumulated the most wealth."

We turned north toward the main highway, and he stopped the truck to point out his brother-in-law's family ranch and homestead. "My brother-in-law's father owned all of the land as far as you can

see. All the way to the flat irons," he said. Flat Irons were foot hills
shaped much like an old-fashioned iron used to press clothes.

He said, "Lester Foote married my sister Fonte. Ole Les came
to be my best friend in the world. His father lost everythin in
'29. In addition to the ranch, he owned the feed store and was the
president of the local bank. The bank is what did him in. He tried
to protect his customers and his friends by not foreclosin on them.
He protected his depositors as long as he could and lasted a few
years, but the bank just didn't have the reserves to stand up to it.
Folks wanted their deposits, so he had no choice but to pay all he
could and shut her down.

"The old man died shortly after the bank failed, and Les and
Fonte moved to Wyoming and bought a small place. They had to
start over. They scraped up enough money to buy a small parcel of
land and kept addin to it until they had over one hundred thousand acres. He and his boy are workin it now. The land is pretty
sorry," he said. "It takes about five to ten acres to feed one damn
cow, but it is beautiful. It ain't nothin like this grass valley here,
but they have enjoyed it, worked hard, and created somethin out
of nothin. It has been a hard scrabble life, but that is what the
country is all about."

We entered a canyon with rock walls ascending hundreds of
feet straight up. The canyon walls were solid rock, and a beautiful
white water river ran swiftly at their base. "That there is the 'Pillar
of Hercules,'" he said. "If you look close, you can see where the
old timers drilled through the mountain and built them wooden
flumes to carry water to the valley."

The road followed the river and seemed to have been carved
out of the rock. The deeper we drove into the canyon, the longer
the shadows became muting the reflected light of the river and
darkening the canyon walls. We rounded a curve in the road, and
Frank pointed out a small group of bighorn sheep several hundred

feet up the mountain looking down at us and grazing the grasses that grew out of the rock. One was a magnificent ram and his flock of four or five ewes.

"They come down from the high country in the spring with the sweet grasses and keep migrating down as they look for more food," he said. You can see em up to huntin' season, but as soon as the first deer tag is sold, those critters cannot be found. It's almost as if a bell rang, and they went to their corners. Most deer and elk hunters apply for a sheep tag. Some are for female, and some are for male. They ain't many issued, so if a fella gets one, he is excited. The excitement don't help none. The first time you hunt one of them fellas it is for the challenge; the next time it is for revenge. Some folks hunt for a lifetime and never even see one. Them fellas are elusive," he said. "They are skittish now, but they are smart enough to know that no one can get at them."

We left the canyon and slowed so Frank could point out his older brother's house. "That's Cliff and Emma's place," Frank said. "They been livin there since he retired. Ain't more than a shack, but that is what they want. Cliff don't put on no airs. He is as plain spoken as any man I know, but there is no better, more generous man in the county. He is eight years older then me and was a hell raiser as a young man. Surprised ole Emma put up with him. He would take a drink and couldn't get that gamblin out of his system. He smoked them cigarettes most of his life and can't breathe easy because of it."

We turned down a small dirt road, crossed a steel truss bridge, and forded a rocky creek before snaking around a mountain for a few hundred yards. We entered a wooden gate and passed a small white cinder-block house adjacent to the river. "That's Fred's place," he said. "He and Anna live there. Fred is the brother between me and Cliff."

Frank's home was at the end of the lane. It was clapboard sided, painted white, and carved into the mountainside. It was two levels with a half basement and five large picture windows overlooking the river. The first sound I heard when he stopped the truck was an ear-piercing scream that sounded as if someone sitting in the tree above the truck was screaming for help. It was one of Frank's many peacocks.

Frank told me that he had received a call from the Railway Express agent in town some time back. The agent told him he had a shipment from Florida, and he needed to pick it up immediately. A former guest and friend from Florida, who followed the horse races, had sent him two mature peacocks unexpectedly, a male and female. The birds were unsolicited and quite a surprise. Since he thought them to be tropical birds, he had no idea they would survive the harsh Colorado winters or even stay on the place. He said, "I didn't think the damn things would stay in the county, no less on the property. They have powerful wings and can fly off any time they want. It has been the damndest thing I ever seen; they took to us. They even get in there with them bantys and scramble for their feed. There are seven of them now."

He pointed to one of the largest males and said, "That there is old Tony; he is the grandfather of them all. Watch how them males preen for the ladies." Just as he said it, as if on cue, one of the larger males opened his beautiful fan and began shaking it. Several others were wandering the road, perched in the tall pine trees or strutting across the roof gable.

"Get your bag boy," he said, "you are goin to be stayin here with us this summer. Freddie's been sick since spring, and Francis thought he shouldn't take on no kid. Good thing really, I can use some help around the place anyway. I'll take you to Grimes's as soon as we get settled good."

My bedroom was in the basement. Entry was through an out-side door just below ground level. There was no access to the house. A bed and two sets of chests of drawers lined the far wall. The room was cooler than the outside temperature and had a slightly musty but not unpleasant odor. Another door allowed access to an open room under the center of the house that had mid-level concrete walls, a concrete floor, and dirt at the level of the crawl space. The room was cooler than the bedroom. I had never been in a basement before; Florida's water table was about six feet be-low ground level. The basement had the musty pungent smell of soil, leather, and sweat. There were three western saddles, a pack saddle, and several assorted, colorful horse blankets mounted on wooden trees at the back of the room. Several sets of harness and horse collars hung from the floor joist. A large piece of dried elk meat hung from a nail in the floor joist in the middle of the room. The walls surrounding the entire room were lined with a series of old refrigerators containing an assortment of tools and other para-phernalia. I had never seen so many tools and odd pieces of small equipment and appliances.

There was a small kick starter-activated engine mounted on a wooden platform with an automobile generator connected directly to a pulley on a flywheel. Frank said he was designing a way to generate power to charge batteries that would light the cow camp at Freddie Grimes's place. There was an assortment of bicycles hanging from the ceiling and lined up neatly in the corner of the room. He appeared to own just about any kind of tool necessary to build, fix, or repair anything mechanical.

As we left the room, he reached up and broke off a piece of the meat hanging from the ceiling. He broke it in half, offered a small piece to me, and took a bite. "Ever have a piece of jerky?" he asked. "This here is salt-cured elk meat. Give her a try; you may like it." It tasted a little like salt lick and saddle leather at first, but I finished it, smiled and said, "That's good." He laughed when he saw the difficulty I was having chewing the stuff and said, "It is more to suck on than chew on. A fella could break a tooth if he weren't careful." I did not know at the time that I would develop a taste for jerky and just about finish off the entire slab by the end of the summer. It was almost like eating potato chips; I couldn't eat just one. "You gotta tender it up a little before you swallow," he said. "Eating jerky is much like life; when a fella looks back, it seems all worth it, but it sure does take a while to tender it up."

We had not yet been in several of the other garages on the place. Two were at the end of the lane built against the mountainside. They held a couple of automobiles of varying vintage; several motorcycles were hanging from the ceiling, and a Cushman motor scooter was parked at an angle between a 1923 Harley Davidson motorcycle and a drill press.

I did not need to unpack. The few articles of clothing I brought could easily be contained in my suitcase, and there wasn't room in the chest of drawers. There were several drawers full of tanned deer and elk hide and bed clothing. It would be easy for me to live out of my suitcase. Everything I owned was packed in the old laminated tourister that I had borrowed from my mother. It was much older than I was and showed a lot of wear. Printed on a tag on the front of the bag was my mother's full name.

"Once you get situated," Frank said, "come on up to the house. I want you to meet some old friends." Once he left the room, I could hear the subtle sound of the river outside and the sound of the peacocks as they flew from one pine tree to another.

CHAPTER TWELVE

I entered the kitchen/dining area through a screen door that I quickly learned to close quietly. Frank said, "Don't let that damn door slam." There was a green, yellow, and red parrot in a cage just inside the door that screeched, "Hello, hello, hello." "That's Pinky's parrot," he said. "She and Tennis brought it from California. It goes everywhere with them, just like a dog, only it talks to you. It is the damnest thing to talk you ever seen. Tennis and Pinky are leaving in the mornin."

Frank introduced me as the kid from Florida he had told them about and said that I was supposed to spend the summer on Freddie's ranch. Tennis was Freddie's brother. I could not help but stare. Tennis was one of the smallest full-grown men I had ever seen. I had seen Eddie Arcaro at a distance when my friend Buster and I had worked on the Hialeah race track, but the distance did not put his size in perspective. Both Tennis and his wife Pinky were the smallest two adults I had ever encountered. They were literally Tom Thumb and his bride. It turned out that Tennis had been a jockey and a horse trainer in California. He rode and trained horses for many of the celebrities of the thirties and forties but was now retired. He and Frank had grown up together. After some pleasantries Frank offered to show me around the property.

"You don't need to go into the house to get a drink," he said. "I have fixed a cup on a hook just inside that wooden access door on the side of the house. There is a key inside there in case you ever get locked out and we ain't around." He pointed up the hill to an outhouse and said, "You can use that too; just remember to keep lime in the thing. It'll get to stinkin if you don't. I don't need for Lillie to be cleanin up after you all the time." He pointed to a hose hung carefully on the side of the house and said, "The water is from a deep well and cold. Make sure you leave the hose just the way you found it. You take it down, you put it back."

He ran the water and filled a small tin cup that was hanging on a nail just inside the access door. The water was cold enough to condense on the side of the cup and had a slight metallic taste. *Wow, I thought, ice water without having to keep a bottle in the refrigerator.* Frank said that the well was over three hundred feet deep.

We walked toward the garage and turned down a gently sloping path at the river's edge. We followed the path and pushed through some overgrowth until we reached a small footbridge. "This here is Grandma's Island," he said. "My mother had an apple orchard on the island years ago, and there are still several of the old trees bearin fruit. They are some of the best eatin you can find anywhere. You'll see. It is a great place to fish and just daydream. Over there is Grandma's hole where some of the biggest rainbow ever caught in these parts have lived. I'll teach you how to fly fish, and you can come down here in the evenin when the bugs are hoppin'. Best time to catch em is in the late afternoon when the bugs start hittin the water. A fella cannot help but catch a mess of trout down here if he just has a little patience. Patience is what it is all about. Patience is a virtue, they say."

We walked back up the path to the first garage, and he pointed to the old red Cushman motor scooter. "You can ride her when all the chores are done," he said. "But don't raise too much dust, or Fred will have a cow. May even let you ride the old Harley if you mind your manners."

The antique Harley Davidsons hanging from the ceiling fascinated me. They had white tires and were covered with dust. It was obvious they had been hanging from the rafters for many years. Both had indentations in the gas tank from holding on tight, and the handlebar grips were worn where a thumb holding a tight grip had eroded the rubber. We closed the garage doors and walked through a flock of banty chickens when I heard "hello, hello, I love Pinky" coming from the house.

We all ate supper around five o'clock. When we finished, I took a walk down the dirt lane leading from the house. I passed Frank's brother's house and several small cottages outside of the gate. The road crossed a small stream that held about six inches of water and immediately came upon a metal truss bridge. There was a fisherman standing in the middle of the river with water swirling around him. There were few sounds other than the whisper of the river passing over the rocks and boulders in the riverbed. The fisherman seemed almost a sentinel waiting to challenge the darkness.

When I crossed through the gate back onto Frank's property, a large iron-grey draft horse and a palomino were drinking from the edge of the river as a fish broke the surface. I took off my shoes to wade in the river, but it was so cold my feet and ankles soon ached. I was accustomed to swimming and wading in the warm Florida canals and beaches of Crandon Park. The coldness of the water was a shock.

I scouted the area for an hour or so and slowly drifted back toward the house. Night had come silently to the mountains. As the shadows lengthened and the sounds of the night quickened, I walked past Fred's small cottage. It was constructed of cinder block much like the homes in South Florida. A sprinkler was painting a half-round pattern on the whitewashed sides of the house, and there was a faint yellow light coming from a lamp in the living room. Fred had been sitting on a metal chair in front of the house, when Frank and I passed earlier, balancing a small rifle in his lap.

He was a bony, wizened man who had darkly tanned skin that seemed almost leather like and a long thin face. His deeply tanned face housed penetrating eyes and the bushiest eyebrows I had ever seen. Frank had introduced me earlier as the boy from Florida. "Looks like he is going to help around the place," he said. Fred nodded, leaned his rifle up against the wall, and stuck out his hand. He grunted a "how do you do." His facial expression did not change. I muttered a "nice to meet you sir," and we continued down the lane. As we pulled away, Frank said, "A goddamn cat took up in the shed and had a mess of kittens. They been killin the bantys, so Fred's been a killin them. They usually don't come out till it's dark, but he got one just sitting quietly. There is a couple of them kittens left, but the momma is pretty cagy. We tried to catch them, but she wasn't havin it. We had to go about shootin them. Them bantys laid a lot of eggs before them cats showed up but have been barren since. We will look in the mornin after we feed and see if we can find them eggs."

As I passed Fred's house the second time I saw the short, cropped grey hair of a woman sitting with her back to the window. She appeared to be occupied with something in her lap. It was Fred's wife. I learned later that she often read late into the night.

The last of the peacocks had flown into the several pine trees, and the noise of the river had increased to a quiet crescendo. The twilight was shades of grey with patches of blue, and the night was still except for the sudden shudder of jake brakes on a truck descending the highway somewhere up the mountain. *Now that is more like home*, I thought at the noise of the brakes. My bedroom was right under the final approach path of runway eighteen at Miami Airport. It was seldom used, but when it was, the television screen rolled, and the dishes would rattle in the kitchen cabinets. I was accustomed to the sound of aircraft engines being run up in the Eastern Airline maintenance hangars at all times of the day and night and the cacophonous noise of diesel busses and traffic on the street in front of my house. There were the occasional wail of sirens, the muted hum of the first air conditioners, and people talking as they walked along the sidewalk. I could often hear the sound of neighbors' televisions, and occasionally, the raised voices of an argument in an adjacent apartment.

I was not accustomed to this kind of quiet. Approaching the house from Fred's, I saw Frank and Lillie and the Grimes backlit by a floor lamp sitting quietly looking out at the river. No one appeared to be talking, just looking quietly out into the lengthening shadows of the night and listening to the steady flow of the river.

I was still wearing a short-sleeved shirt and dungarees, and the night air was cold. I had chill bumps on my arms and neck. The iron grey horse on the other side of the river now rested his big head on the shoulder of the palomino. It had been a long day.

Twenty-four hours ago, I had been sitting in the Amarillo bus station watching an assortment of people arrive and depart from all over the country. The air had been heavy with diesel fuel, cooking odors, and stale cigarettes and unwashed bodies. Tonight the night air had a fresh clean fragrance of pine and freshly mown grass; it was an ethereal scent that touched gently on everything. I had no idea what to expect when I stepped off the bus that day. My thoughts and emotions had run rampant when I first spied Frank and Clay Wells leaning against the hotel façade.

The surrounding beauty of the mountains and the river was overwhelming, the openness and friendliness with which Frank and his wife and friends welcomed me was comforting, and the anticipation of the remainder of the summer was incomprehensible.

CHAPTER THIRTEEN

I was terrified of the dark. I don't know if having been punished as a child by being locked in a small hall closet or the dance on my bedroom walls of grotesque shapes caused by a street light shining through the bedroom window and back lighting a metal lamp were the origin of my fear. Every time I would crawl in bed I was afraid to look under it for fear of a monster and afraid not to look under it for fear of that same monster. It was unnatural but very real to me. My aunt's Negro maid, Sarah, told endless stories of haints, things that went bump in the night, and Soap Sally who boiled little boys who misbehaved in a big iron kettle and turned them into soap. I would cower under the covers on dark nights and often tremble until I fell asleep.

By the time I finally entered the basement that first night it was dark. It was a moonless night, and there was virtually no ambient light. I switched on the overhead light and quickly looked under the bed for anything out of the ordinary. There were boxes stored under the bed, so I knew that it would be impossible for anything or anyone to jump out from there once I got to sleep. Before I dead bolted the door, I turned on the light in the sub-basement to make sure it was empty of threats. I climbed into the bed and pulled the bed clothes up to my neck. I was too exhausted from the events of the day and the long bus ride to stay awake long. I no sooner seemed to have turned off the light when there was a loud banging at the door.

Bang, bang, bang. A loud booming voice coming from the direction of the door said, "Breakfast is ready." The voice was insistent. Bang, bang, bang. "Breakfast is ready; get your ass out of that bed, and come eat breakfast before I screw your plate upside down to the table," it said. "Watcha think, a bear gonna git you? You don't need to lock the damn door, this ain't Miami."

The voice was loud but good natured. I wiped the sleep out of my eyes, threw on my clothes, and was zipping up my pants as I hustled up the sidewalk to the side door. Bam! I let door fly. "Don't be slammin that door, boy," Frank said. "I already told you once! Sit down here, and get your breakfast before I feed it to the chickens."

Tennis and Pinky were already sitting at the table, the parrot squawked "hello, hello," and a deep voice coming from the console radio against the far wall delivered the news softly. The table was overflowing with more food than I had ever seen. There was a platter of eggs cooked hard, country style, with the edges of the white curled up. A waffle iron's sides steamed with the batter residue of newly cooked waffles that were piled in the center of the table. There were several jars of homemade jam and jelly and a large slab of butter. A large plate of bacon and sausage that Frank said was made from venison along with sliced ham shared the center of the table with the waffles. A toaster and a percolator coffee pot were perched in an open window separating the kitchen from the dining area.

"We are gonna fatten you up boy," Frank said. "It is time you put a little meat on them bones. You are too damn skinny," he said. "If I'm gonna work you hard, I don't want you to fall over in your traces. A good breakfast is the best meal of the day. A fella's gotta have energy to get his chores done."

We all ate slowly, and I savored the breakfast. Frank kidded Tennis about California ranchers. He said, "A couple of acres and two skinny horses rootin around in the dust and a Californian thinks he is a rancher. Tennis laughed and said he agreed but it sure was a great climate and a good place to be retired. He said he didn't live far from Santa Anita Racetrack, so he could get his horse fix from the many friends he had made during his working career.

"I just love the sounds and smell of the track early in the morning," he said. Lillie and Pinky spoke glowingly of growing up in the mountains and riding in sidecars with Frank and Tennis to Rocky Mountain National Park soon after it opened at the turn of the century. They told me how the house once housed motorcycles and was very basic.

"We used to park our machines in your bedroom and spend the night," she said.

"Have some more of them eggs," Frank encouraged, while he dipped another ladle of waffle mix and placed it in the waffle iron.

I was not only unaccustomed to eating breakfast, but I was not accustomed to getting up before noon, and even then I would often head to Jim's store for a sandwich and a Coke. My mother had established a charge account allowing me to purchase food but no candy or anything frivolous. I would often stay up until after midnight and occasionally my friend Jimmy and I would sneak my mother's car out of the driveway after she was asleep.

We once passed a police car performing a traffic stop well after midnight. The policeman didn't seem to know whether to come after us or continue what he was doing. His expression was priceless as he watched two sub-teens cruising by.

We had learned that the proprietor at a car lot located a few blocks away left the keys to the ignition in the floorboard of the cars on the back of the lot. After midnight we would race around in the gravel cutting donuts and racing one another. Somehow we never got caught while driving around the back of the lot, but unfortunately, Jimmy decided to take one of the cars home so he could pick up a couple of girls after school and drive them home.

The girls had no idea that the car was stolen from the car lot. It was a sporty convertible, so they could not resist. Jimmy intended to return it that night but was caught by the local police about a block from his house with both girls in the car. They were all transported to the local police station and the fear of God was instilled in them.

The day he was caught, I had been hitchhiking home. Jimmy stopped and offered me a ride. For some reason, perhaps a premonition, I refused. I was thankful that I did.

After breakfast we took the remainder of the uneaten waffles outside and scattered them in small pieces in the roadway. "For the turkeys," Frank said. He referred to the peacocks as turkeys and the chickens as "them bantys."

We helped Tennis and Pinky pack their car for home. The parrot was covered and placed in the backseat. Clothes were hung on a hanging rack that stretched from the left to the right side of the backseat, and a couple of suitcases were stored in the trunk. Frank had me open the hood and check the fluids and the tire pressure.

"Make sure that radiator is full," he said. I checked it, opened the radiator cap, turned on the hose, and filled it to the brim. I made sure to coil the hose remembering Frank's admonition to put it back the way I found it. Frank shook Tennis's hand, and Lillie hugged Pinky and then stood back on the walkway with her arms across her chest. "Next time, stay awhile," she said.

Frank told Tennis that he and I would be going to Freddie's ranch sometime soon and would give both he and Frances their best. "I'll tell him and Francis 'howdy' for you," he said. "Don't know if Freddie will join us to the cow camp, him bein sick and all, but the boy never seen a workin ranch before, so it ought to be interesting. We will be just in time for hayin and movin the cows to the high country. We are goin to head up to the headwaters of the Troublesome River to the cow camp and do a little fishin.

"Be careful on them roads, and watch your speed; them patrolmen sure will pinch you quick for speedin around here," Frank cautioned. The car moved slowly down the lane and disappeared around the mountain. As the dust began to settle in the roadway, Frank said, "Better get to work cuttin back that brush down by Grandma's hole, because I want to go on to town.

"First, let's feed the chickens." He pointed to a barrel in the shed next to the garage. "Chicken feed is in there. First thing every mornin you need to feed them chickens, and put a little somethin out for the 'turkeys.' Do it every mornin right after breakfast so you won't forget. It will come to be a habit. It is important that you develop good habits and learn to do the essential things first. It is a good idea to do the things you don't like to do first. Lots of folks fail in life, because they put off the essential and tend only to do what gives them the most pleasure. Feedin them chickens ever day at the same time doesn't seem a big thing but gettin into the habit of doin somethin right is. Developin good work habits will take care of you later in life. The first thing a fella needs to take a mind to do," he said, "is learnin to work and develop good work habits. If you don't like somethin, don't just walk away, look for somethin better. No one respects a quitter. Layin in the bed in the mornin will never serve no good purpose."

I was sure he was reminding me of all the times when he would show up early in the morning to help me with the rebuilding of my scooter, and I would still be asleep. "I feed ole Smokey and Tuffy in the evenin," he said.

"Let's get to cuttin down that brush and loadin it on the pickup, and I will show you what to do about them horses when we get back from town this evenin."

We worked together and quickly cleared the brush from the path leading to the island. He got a rotary lawn mower out of the basement and led me around the yard to point out the sprinkler system he had just installed. "Be careful about them sprinkler heads," he said. "Go easy around them and cut down to the fence line along the river. As soon as you're done, we will load up and head to town. I gotta check on the pump and make sure them screens are clear. I been havin trouble with the system gettin fouled by grass and debris coming from upstream," he said. "When the water stops siphonin, the pump runs dry, overheats, and shuts down. I get all of my water for the sprinklers directly out of the river! Oh, and don't you be drinkin that river water. Drink out of the hose. It looks mighty clean, but there have been a lot of cows pissin upstream of you. And don't forget to put lime in the crapper. Oh yeah, one last thing, if there is any cussin to be done, I'll be doin it. There is no need for you to be swearin 'cause I fairly well have got that covered."

He left to check out the pump and its obstruction. The grass behind the house was sparse, so I finished it quickly and started mowing on the steep incline up the mountainside. I mowed around the outhouse and was surprised that there was no smell. I had never used an outhouse before and couldn't help but think about the spiders and bugs that lived in dark places.

I was accustomed to mowing lawns, because I had a regular customer base in the neighborhood at home. I bought a lawn mower with the money I had raised washing windows; I charged two dollars a yard for most yards. One neighbor who owned an apartment complex built in an H pattern across the alley way from my house always tried to beat me down when I finished. It was a big yard, so I learned to ask for more money than I expected when I finished. Ivan, the owner, would always laugh and reduce my asking price, but I didn't mind, because he would give me a ride in his Austin Healy and let me use his tools to fix whatever I had that was broken. It seemed something was always in need of repair.

I had finished mowing the grass behind the house and had begun cutting the terraced area in front of the house where the sprinklers were. The grass was thick and green unlike the grass on the mountainside. I had made a couple of passes when suddenly the lawn mower blade struck something in the lawn with such force that the mower stalled.

Damn, hope that wasn't a sprinkler head, I thought. *I hope it was a big rock,* I wished to myself. *Damn, it was a sprinkler; I can see the pipe sticking out of the ground. Now what,* I thought.

What was the very last thing Frank told me not to do? Don't hit the sprinkler heads, be careful, he cautioned. *I can't do anything right,* I thought. He had said, "Pay attention and do things right the first time, and you won't have to do it over." I had not only sheared off the sprinkler head, but the mower had hit it with such force that it had been launched, and I couldn't find it.

I finally saw something in the middle of the road twenty feet away that looked out of place. *Yep, the damn sprinkler head,* I thought. It was halfway between me and the river lying in the middle of the road in plain sight. *How is it possible that Frank had not heard the noise?* I wondered. Evidently, he was either in the basement or in one of the garages and had not heard the mower stall. *Whew,* I thought, *that was some luck. Now what?* I picked it up and realized there was no way to repair the damage. *Damn, damn, damn, just what he'd told me not to do! Why hadn't I been more careful,* I berated myself. *Oh well, I will hide the damn thing, and maybe he won't catch it, or maybe I can deny cutting it off. It could be a mystery,* I opined. I threw the severed pipe and sprinkler head into the bushes, restarted the mower, and kept cutting as if nothing had happened.

He had obviously not heard the noise of the strike or the mower stalling so maybe, just maybe, with a little time I could think of an explanation. I knew he was having trouble with the water pick up in the river, so maybe it could take all summer to fix, and I would be long gone before it was discovered. Maybe we would have rain the rest of the summer, and maybe we would not need to turn on the sprinkler.

I finished cutting the lawn and carefully put the rotary mower back in the garage. I noticed the old Dodge was parked in front of the elevated gas tank. I thought, *Give me a little time, and I'll figure this thing out.*

I heard the kitchen screen door close quietly and heard Frank's footfalls as he rounded the corner. "Put some gas in her," he said, "check the oil, check the air in them tires, and sweep her out a little. There is a whisk broom under the seat. A fella's got to take good care of his things if they are going to take care of him.

"You can drive boy," he said. "Do you know how to handle a clutch? This here is a four-speed shift. 'Grandma', that's first gear, which is way up to the left, and the rest of the gears are in an H pattern. Second gear is down and to the left, and third is up and to the right. Fourth is bottom right. See that H pattern on the shifter, that'll tell you how to do her."

I slid behind the steering wheel and waited for him to close the passenger-side door. Once his door was closed, I very confidently turned on the key. Nothing happened. He grinned and said, "Put her in neutral or hold in that clutch and press that hickey on the floorboard next to the foot feed. That'll start her." I pressed the small pedal extending out from the floor and depressed the accelerator with one foot while keeping my other foot on the clutch. It was awkward, but the engine finally started. I moved the gear shift lever up and to the left and released the clutch—the truck bucked twice and then stalled.

Frank said, "You put her in 'Grandma', we only use 'Grandma' on steep hills and such; she's a real low gear, and a fellow's got to get used to startin out with her; pull the shifter down and to the left, and she'll be ok." I managed to put the shift lever in second gear after a little grinding, released the clutch, and the pickup lurched forward.

"We call this Cedar Cove," he said. He told me the names of the several people who lived along the lane and said that most of them live in the cove part time. "Our place," he said again, "used to be a motorcycle barn when my folks were alive. We didn't move up here until I retired in forty eight."

We pulled out onto the highway and immediately passed a field he pointed out on the driver's side of the truck. "When I was a boy, my mother operated a root beer stand right over by that big pine. She would sell root beer to the tourists durin the summer. The barrel ain't there now, but if a fellow were to look, I'm guessin he will find a few old barrel stays scattered around. I think Ray and his brother Walt chopped up the barrel for firewood that hard winter he spent in the cabin up on the hill," he said. "The well has some of the coldest water in these parts. She would use the water in the well to make her root beer and sit there all day under that tree waitin for customers."

We entered the west end of the canyon just past a small restaurant and a water diversion. Frank cautioned that I needed to take it kind of slow in the canyon. "Them damned highway engineers must have taken a drink or two when they designed the road. There is a reverse curve about halfway down," he said. "If a fella isn't real careful and has a little too much speed on, he'll run right into the mountain. Several people have died in that corner. They get to drinkin up in them honky-tonks in Estes and fly down this mountain in the middle of the night. When we hear the ambulances in the middle of the night, we know for sure what happened. You'd think someone would know to fix that damn curve."

Just about that time, I felt the pickup pull to the right. We had entered Dead Man's Curve. I could clearly see that had I been driving a little faster, it could have been dangerous. The truck drifted to the right into the wall as if guided by an invisible hand. "Now you see why we call her 'Dead Man's Curve,'" he said. "It has earned its name over the years. Sometimes we hear them ambulances once or twice a week." We drove through the entrance of the canyon, passed the Dam Store on the left and ascended a small hill. Just as we reached the top of the hill, he asked me to stop the truck. I stopped, and we got out and climbed through a two-wire fence. We climbed over a couple of large rocks before he pointed out one with a perfectly half round center. He said, "This was where them Indians camped. The Utes. They settled in this valley, because the grass was good, and it was protected from winter snows. Snow would mostly just blow over the hills and settle out in the plains. Them Indians were a hardy bunch! That smooth, rounded part in the center of that big rock was their grist mill. They would grow their corn in this valley and them Indian "Janes" would sit up here for days grinding it into flour. Their villages and campgrounds would extend all the way to the flat irons."

We continued east on the state highway toward town. Frank pointed out his brother-in-law's former family ranch, Rock Ridge Ranch. Farther up the road, he pointed to a rocky field that once was an Indian village. "Wouldn't think them Indians would survive on that ground would you—it's mostly rock and hard-packed ground."

He continued to point out the homes and businesses of old friends and other points of interest. "That there is old Hansen's motel on the right," he said. "He is a Swede. I been knowin him for fifty years. Them Swedes are hard-workin people. We went to school together. He stayed on to graduate, but I dropped out in the third grade. Never did like school much," he said. "Me and him rode motorcycles together in the twenties. He and his wife operate the place. She keeps up the rooms by herself, and he does the maintenance. They are a good team. It takes a team to keep a marriage alive in these times. They are gettin up in years but work every day. She won't let another Jane on the place. She has tried a couple of helpers but always run them all off; their work never suited her. She thinks no one can care for the place the way she does and don't want the boarders to be disappointed. Some of them tourists been stayin in the same room every summer for thirty years. It is kinda like her extended family," he said. "They never had no kids. Old Hansen really got him a good one in that Jane. A fella can't sit down for her cleanin up around you or asking to get you somethin from the kitchen. She was a hasher years ago. She worked in them restaurants before they were married.

"When you marry a gal, you need to find yourself a good hasher; they all know how to take care of a man, and they know how to work. Make sure when you are a courtin that you show up at the back door once in a while, kinda unexpected like. A fella can never tell about a person if he just shows up when he is expected and always shows up at the front door. Some a them Janes," he said, "shit in bed and kick it out with their feet."

He complimented my driving. "You know, boy, I can always tell a fella that has ridden a motorcycle. He don't fly up on them corners and slam on the brakes, and he don't try to hit every pothole in the road." Just about the time he finished his sentence I hit a pothole. "I guess we can't miss them all," he said. "I thought you might be able to drive okay."

The late morning sun was almost directly overhead, and the sky was cloudless and deep blue. I listened as Frank continued to point out things along the way. "That place on the left belongs to old Swenson." He's got one of them Dodge power wagons. Damndest truck I ever drove. The thing will go up a mountain like a billy goat. It'll take a mountain like a knife cutting hot butter. There ain't nothin like them Dodges. They put old Henry Ford to shame."

CHAPTER FOURTEEN

We passed a large lake on the driver's side of the truck. A wooden speedboat pulling two skiers turned sharply, creating a "rooster tail." One of the skiers jumped the wake. A family was sitting at the water's edge watching the boaters and enjoying a picnic. "The lake water is so goddamn cold, it will freeze the balls off of a brass monkey," Frank said. That was a new expression to me. I had never thought about a brass monkey or its balls freezing and didn't know until years later that the expression evolved from a device on a sailing vessel that contained cannonballs. "I don't know how them kids stand the cold," he said.

I had learned since arriving that Frank's language was colorful. He cursed in a matter-of-fact way and had made it clear that he would do the cursing for both of us. He was living up to his promise. "Been a lot of cars lost in that lake over the years. The law put up signs tryin to stop people from drivin out on it in the winter, but I guess it is just too much of a temptation. Them fool college kids from Fort Collins snuck out on the lake a few winters ago, thinkin the lake was froze solid, and the car just fell right in. I think there was three or four fellas and one girl that died. It was weeks before their bodies come to the surface. I'll bet if a fella were to look, he'd find a half dozen old cars at the bottom of the lake. Wouldn't be easy, though; that lake is really deep. You would think by the time a kid got to college, he would have better sense than to drive out on a frozen lake. The cars just broke the ice and fell in. Too damn bad. It ain't only college kids, but they seem the worst."

We passed a small park and tennis courts on the right, crossed a railroad bridge, and turned right down a divided parkway bordered by homes. "The shop's down here about a mile or so. I used to live in that house there on the right, second one from the corner. I could either ride my bicycle or walk to work most of my workin years. The town sure has grown over the years. It started out as a railroad town and just sprung up. Was a time I knew just about everybody in town, but it's gotten too damn big now. Think there is about two or three thousand people spread out over the town. Lots of them used to work in the sugar beet plant out east of town; the rest farmed and worked in the stores and banks and such.

"I worked at the sugar factory back when they paid a dollar a day. Even back then I saved my money," he said. "A fella needs to pay himself first. If you ever plan to have anythin in life, you need to pay yourself first. I don't mean a fella shouldn't pay his bills, only I mean, he should put aside some for hisself. Don't be countin on someone takin care of you. It is a fella's responsibility to take care of hisself. I mostly tried to put away ten percent of all of my pay. If a fella can pledge ten percent to his redeemer, I suppose he can pledge ten percent to hisself. Keep that in mind boy: a fella that pays hisself first and puts a little somethin away over the years will have a little somethin someday. I ain't braggin; I got a few nickels. It didn't come easy; it just came a little at a time. There are too damn many folks out there that thinks the world owes them a livin."

We turned right into an alleyway separating two buildings. The building on the right housed a hotel above a drugstore that extended for the entire block. A sign illuminated above the street read "Arcadia Hotel—rooms by the day, week, or month." "This here is the shop," he said. "Started out this is where my dad had his bicycle shop. It was just a wooden buildin then. I would help him in the back every chance I got. As soon as motorcycles come around, he changed from fixin bicycles to repairin motorcycles and then we started sellin Dodge, Chrysler, and Plymouth automobiles.

"I used to know Walter Chrysler by his first name. Ben Davis owned the Chevrolet garage across the street. He was kinda a big shot; half the time he didn't have two nickels to rub together, and he'd be drivin around in a Cadillac. At first we had to teach a lot of them buyers to drive to make a sale. One time I spent days with this preacher. He finally got the hang of it and then went across the street and bought from Davis. He'd ride by ever once in a while and toot his horn and wave just as if nothin happened. You gotta be a little careful who you trust; can't even trust them preachers. Sometimes I think they are the worst. They think they can do about anythin they want as long as they show up on Sunday and ask forgiveness. I think a fella ought to do right even when ain't nobody lookin. I never did hold it against old Davis; he just sold the fella a car. It's that damn preacher I have had a hard time forgivin. That don't mean all preachers are that way. It just shows a fella that doin right or doin wrong ain't confined to you and me. You can't tell about a fella until you see his actions," he said. "I believe in actions, not words. It is just like goin in the back door when you're courtin a Jane; you need to learn how a person is by his actions, not by his appearance. That damn preacher finally got run out of town. I think they found him slippin around with a Jane in his congregation and him bein married!"

We entered the shop through a side door. The outside wall was lined with windows that opened at the top. The shop was large and clean with three hydraulic lifts in a row. Frank pointed to Spot, a tall, thin man, who was changing the oil in a grey Plymouth sedan. A second man was bending over the fender of a truck in the second stall. I saw him look up as we entered, recognize Frank, and hurriedly stamp out a cigarette while blowing smoke out the side of his mouth. He wore a grey uniform with "Chili" stenciled over his left breast pocket. He had a round cherubic face, dark eyes, and a shock of coal black hair. He looked to be in his thirties.

The place smelled of oil and gasoline and stale exhaust but was spotlessly clean. Tools were arranged meticulously in open cabinets, and everything seemed to have its place. A large yellow–and–black sign over the door read, "We do not loan our tools—so don't ask." A lighted clock on the far wall read 11:45 and had a huge AC Sparkplug advertisement on its face.

Spot was dressed much like Chili and was replacing the oil plug in the Plymouth. His hands were covered with oil, and he wore a brimless hat to protect his hair from the dirt, oil, and grease that had accumulated on the undercarriage of the car. A red rag protruded from his rear pants pocket.

"This here is the boy I told you about," Frank said. Spot grunted a hello and continued screwing the oil plug into the oil pan. "Gotta get her finished," he said, "no time to jaw; this car belongs to our banker, and I promised it by lunch time. Talk to Chili over there; he never seems to have much to do." Chili laughed, but I could tell there was a little rivalry between the two.

Chili wiped his hands with a shop rag and extended his right hand to shake mine and said, "Glad to see you made it safely. Frank told me you were coming for the summer. He has been telling us about you for a month or so. The old man will shape you up," he said. "He sure busted my ass as a kid, but I learned something. Sure didn't seem like it was fun at the time. Maybe he has mellowed," he said as if in passing. "That bus ride was a long one. I rode the damn Greyhound bus back from San Francisco when I got out of the Navy. Don't think I will be doing that again soon. If it wasn't for a bunch of other sailors and an all-night poker game, I'd about gone crazy. I'll finish up here in a minute and you, the old man, and I can head over to the pool hall for dinner."

Dinner for me was always the last meal of the day, but dinner in farm communities or at least in most small towns occurred in the middle of the day. I had heard Frank refer to what I had always called "lunch" as "dinner" ever since I had met him. It still seemed strange to be eating dinner in the middle of the day.

Frank leaned over the other fender and removed a handful of leaves from the engine compartment of the truck. "Pick up that whisk broom over there boy," he said. "You might as well sweep out this truck while we're waitin for Chili. Ain't no sense in just loiterin. Soon as you are done, we can head over to the pool hall."

Chili finished what he was doing. I swept out the interior of the truck while he and Frank washed their hands in the utility sink against the wall. Chili said, "Wanta join us, Spot?" "Nope, the old woman has dinner on the table. I better get on home if I know what is good for me. Soon as I finish up this Plymouth I am a headin to the house." "Let's get out of here," Chili said. "It's been a morning. I still got lots to do before quitting time!"

CHAPTER FIFTEEN

The pool hall was about a block away on Fourth Avenue. We all sat in a booth against the wall. A diminutive, middle–aged, dishwater-blond woman brought us a menu at a trot. "Open-faced hot beef sandwich, potatoes, and gravy are today's special," she said.

"Damn, Alice," Chili responded, "hot beef is always your special. Don't you think you could get old Arch to come up with something different?"

She laughed and said, "It don't matter what Arch comes up with, I am the cook around here. A hot beef sandwich is the easiest to prepare and serve. I can get you a burger. We ain't gonna change what works, Chili, you want the special or not?"

Everyone laughed and Chili said, "Well, if you put it that way I guess I'll take the special."

"The special it is. Now what will you have, Frank? How about you, young man?"

Frank ordered the roast beef and suggested I do the same. I asked for a glass of iced tea to drink. The waitress said, "Where you from boy? No one asks for iced tea around here." I told her I had come from Miami, and she said, "Figured you were new here about! I can do her; we'll just heat up some tea in a cup, and you can put some ice in it. How will that do ya?" Not waiting for an answer, she laughed and said she thought I'd want some milk and hurried away to call in our order.

The room was divided by a half wall with a case opening on opposite ends. One led to the bar, which was in the dining area, and the other gave access to a large open room that was dimly lit and home to six or seven regulation-sized pool tables. A sign over the entry door read: "You have to be 18 to enter. Don't make me ask." There was a long polished bar with round stools bolted to the floor filled with patrons conversing animatedly. A loud disembodied voice came from the backroom asking for a beer. "Give me a couple of Coors, Arch," the voice said. "I got this fool on the run." And then laughter.

Centered over the pool tables was a double wire running the length of the table that was some sort of scoring mechanism. This was the first time I had ever been in a pool hall. The tables were lit from above by a rectangular fixture that threw a pattern of light onto the green surface and kept the surroundings in darkness. Players were leaning over the tables with cigarettes dangling from their mouths or standing back from the table with their cues resting on the floor and the business end facing the ceiling. There was a lot of laughter and jostling going on. Pool balls clicked loudly as they careened around the table. Occasionally I would hear a dull thud as a ball dropped into a side pocket followed by loud voices of approval or disapproval and then more laughter. All of the lamp shades were printed with "Coors" in the center, and smoke hovered over the tables like early morning fog moving in off the coast. The back wall was lined with chairs and an illuminated sign which portrayed a flowing mountain stream and the words "Pabst Blue Ribbon." "3.2 beer, Five cents" read another sign.

Brass spittoons were placed strategically around the room, and a jukebox that bubbled rainbow colors played country music. Lighted cigarettes balanced on several of the tables, and one man had his tablemate in a friendly choke hold. This was all new to me. Florida law did not allow anyone under twenty-one in a bar or any establishment that served alcohol other than at the dinner table. A pool hall was out of the question. I felt so grown up.

During the meal Frank said, "I never did smoke them cigarettes or take a drink. Since I was the youngest, my mother would occasionally have Cliff and Fred look after me when she had things to do. She didn't learn, and I never told her that they would take me to town to the pool hall and make me sit outside for hours while they drank beer, smoked them cigarettes, and shot pool. I hated it. Swore I would never do that to anyone. I told myself I would never take up them cigarettes, and I never did. Some of my friends tried to encourage me in the Army and when we were racin, but I never saw the point in it. Boy, don't be takin them cigarettes and beer up; it just don't do nobody any good."

Frank's comment caused me to think about all the times I would be asked to retreat to the car and either sleep or listen to the radio while my mother and her man friend had a few after-dinner drinks. I didn't care much for waiting in the car except on those occasions when I could listen to the *Lone Ranger* or *Johnny Dollar* on the car radio. I would often lay low and find something else to do to avoid going out to eat with her and her friend. The last time it was insisted I go was when I deliberately left the radio on and the car battery died. That created a stir!

Now I understood why Chili was so careful to hide his cigarette when we entered the shop. He told me later that he got "hooked" while in the Navy but tried to hide his smoking out of "respect for the old man."

After Chili returned to work, we drove out of town the back way. Once again we passed the high school, crossed the small bridge over the river, and passed the old faded shack that Chili had lived in and the feed lot. The pickup was loaded with debris, so we turned into the city dump. As we did Frank said, "I want you to meet this fella. Like I have told you before, life and people ain't nothin about appearances.

"The old boy that operates this place come here about ten years ago from Oklahoma with his entire family. He didn't have a job, so he took up runnin the dump," he said. "It ain't a glamorous job, but he runs this place like a fine watch. Everythin is in its place, and he always has a smile on his face. A fella can learn a lot about life from folks like him. He don't choose to cry about the hard work and dirt of his job. He just chooses to do his best and don't ask for no handouts. That is what this country is all about, boy. Get up in the mornin, don't lay in bed, don't complain, and strike out and do your best."

When we turned into the dump site, Frank pointed out a man standing next to a trailer full of brush being emptied into the green water of a small pond. "That's Wild Bill," he said. "I never did learn his last name, have always just called him 'Wild Bill.'" He had said during our ride down First Street that the man would take a drink, but it never seemed to affect his work. "He was on the dump every day before daylight and rarely left before dusk. He is a hard worker!"

He knew that the man had a family and said he had a "mess of children," but he had no idea where the family lived or what the circumstances were. He only knew he liked the man and admired his work ethic. He commented that the whole bunch had come to Colorado from Oklahoma about ten years ago. The man was looking for work and thought Colorado was the "Promised Land." "I been knowin him ever since he took over the dump site," he said. "Before he come people just threw stuff out and drove off. It was a damn mess around here, and it caused all kinds of disturbance at the feed lot. Couldn't keep the flies down, and half the time the damn fools would dump on my property. I caught one fella dumpin once on that lane next to my hay barn and scared him so bad

I think he left the county. When the city hired old Bill, I was a happy man. I think he gets a small salary and all he can scavenge."

"Wild Bill" was a small man wearing soiled, blue denim overalls and a faded, plaid shirt ripped at both elbows revealing a union suit or some kind of long-sleeved undergarment. His right suspender was loose and dangling at his side, and one high–top, laced boot was untied. He stood with one foot perched on the trailer loaded with brush, and dust swirled around him as he talked to the driver. He was deeply tanned and wore a ball cap at a rakish angle. He more resembled a football coach calling plays than someone managing a city dump. It was obvious from his wide grin that he liked what he did and enjoyed the people who came in to his life every day. Stitched on a small patch centered in the middle of his overalls between the pockets was the word "Payday." Both pockets were filled with pencils, a pen, a wrapped cigar, and an open package of Camel cigarettes. He had a toothless grin and a welcoming look in his eye so genuine that I could feel the warmth of his soul.

He was pleased to see Frank and waved us over to the edge of the dump. "Put her over there fella. Just back her in, whoa not too far; you could get up to your axels til Sunday if you ain't careful," he said to the man with the truckload of brush that he had been speaking with when we arrived. "Don't fret none; I ain't gonna let you back too far. That there shoulder is a little soft, so you might just have to drag that brush a few feet. You can be sure I'll stop you before you fall in. I don't want to have to start that tractor to pull you out, but even worse, I don't want to have to jump in that cold water to save you either," he said. "Don't know what a fellow will find in there. Actually found a dead body in the pond once." He said it all with a smile while directing another truck entering the site with his arms. There was order to Wild Bill's dump site. It was his fiefdom.

Frank introduced me as the kid from Florida he had told him
about. He removed a worn leather glove and extended his right
hand. "So this here is the boy that rode on the bus all of the way
from Florida," he said. "Glad to meet ya, boy! Old Kunce here
been telling me about you. Seems like he was looking forward to
you getting here. I am sure he would never tell you so!" We talked
a little about the beautiful Colorado afternoon and the warmth of
the day, and he commented that "Chili had been down a few days
ago with a truckload of them five-quart oil cans. He and old Spot
keep me busy selling them cans to the nursery. I sure am thankful
that they quit using that bulk oil. How do you like Colorado over
Florida?" he asked. He said he had never been east of Oklahoma
City but had heard about the palm trees and beaches of Florida.
"I bet it's a pretty place," he said. "For a youngster you sure are
getting to see a lot of country. Weren't ya scared riding on that bus
all by your lonesome?"

About twenty yards away, an old black Ford careened around
and around in circles. The car body leaned twenty degrees to the
left. Each time the driver's door passed, I could see a boy about
my age leaning hard against the door post with long dark hair
covering one eye. "That's my youngest," Bill said. "He is showing
his ass a little. I wanted him to clean some pot metal, but he had
other plans. He goes by James, and if you call him by anything
but James, he'll want to fight. He is the damndest young un I
have. He is a good boy really, but his mama has spoiled him so."

The old Ford continued to pirouette around in the dirt creating
a huge cloud of dust moving in our direction. "He is a little high
spirited, but other than the silliness like you're watching, he has
never give us any trouble. Says he is going to quit school when he
is sixteen, onced he gets them license. Hell, he been driving since
he was twelve, don't know why a license is so damned important.
We live so far out of town, we couldn't be carting his ass around,

so his mama just bought him that old Ford. He's a working on it more than he drives it, so we don't worry too much about him getting in any trouble. One of these days he's a gonna get pinched for driving, but so far he stays out of town mostly and keeps to them dirt roads. We don't let him drive to school, so he is pretty safe from the town police. They come out here at night all the time to shoot at the rats, so I suspect they'd just take his keys away from him and come find me. Me and them cops are all good friends. I think they come out here most every night, a shooting them rats when they are suppose to be patrolling. I think sometime that patrolling all night gets tiresome."

About that time the young driver straightened up the wheel, flashed by us, and catapulted up on to the roadway. The rear tires squealed, and the car fishtailed on the dusty road for about twenty feet. "No point in me fussing at him if he breaks the car cause his mama will just give him her egg money to fix it," he said. "It is funny how them women do with their youngest. The oldest girl run off at fifteen cause she didn't want to take no direction. Now she got three young uns, another in the oven, and don't have time to worry about taking no direction.

"Things have their place here," he said. "I can't let people put ordinary household garbage where the pot metal goes. A fella's gotta watch them all the time. It makes it harder to sort stuff out later. Them oil cans gotta be where we can burn off the oil. The trailer factory dumps all of their sweepings on the other side of the pond so that when we burn I can send my boys down to get the copper. It brings eighty cents a pound these days, you know. Highest it's been. Me and the boys pick that copper clean and sell it to the junk man."

I saw a small shed lined with old car batteries and stacked miscellaneous cast iron and aluminum pots and pans and discarded furniture. There was an old frayed, overstuffed couch and a couple of chairs under the shed's extended roofline. "There is money in all that stuff," he said. "A person just can't believe how much ordinary folks throw away every day. America sure is a rich country; why them people down in Mexico would work for a month just to have what many folks in this country discard every day."

Frank and I backed up to the shoulder of the dump and dragged the brush from the back of the old Dodge pickup. I swept the truck bed and saw Frank stuff a few dollar bills in the dump man's pocket. He grinned, winked at me as I got back into the driver's seat, and restarted the truck. "Let's head on to the house," Frank said. "Spot made me a hickey to repair that pump, and I want to get the damn sprinklers workin this afternoon cause that lawn is awful dry. I noticed them flowers along the fence that Lillie planted were lookin a little peaked." *Oh damn,* I thought, *the sprinkler.* I started the truck as we both said our good-byes to Wild Bill and turned onto the road in the direction of the old black Ford. *I guess I'm going to have to face the music!* The beautiful mountains loomed in the windshield, but I was not thinking about them. I was thinking about how I would explain the gusher of water we were soon to witness. *Oh well,* I thought, *better make the best of this ride home.*

CHAPTER SIXTEEN

I left the main highway and turned down the lower road into Cedar Cove. There were two access roads paralleling one another. One was short and smooth, and the other was longer and full of potholes and swales. I thought it would be fun to see if I could navigate the lower road and stay out of the potholes. The road had a gentle rise of soft sand in the center and was narrow with very little shoulder.

"Slow her down a little," Frank said right after the rear right tire slipped off the roadway onto what little shoulder there was.

The edge of the road was only about two feet away from a barbed wire fence and a forty foot drop to the river. He didn't seem to panic. We intersected the two lanes, and he pointed to a house on the left and commented that the woman living there was a widow, but a "fine Jane." "Her husband just fell dead of a heart attack, but she has been keeping up the place as if he were still alive. I've seen her out there cutting them willows along the river with a sickle and standing in water knee deep."

Just beyond the widow's small corral and across the old truss bridge was a beautiful cedar home nestled in the trees. "That's Harrigan's place," he said. "He is one of them guys who was born with a silver spoon in his mouth. He grew up in Brussels carpet up to his ass and acts like he is just a little better than everyone around him. He really don't know sheep shit from Arbuckles coffee but to talk to him you'd think he was the Duke of Mush.

He inherited most the land between here and Cedar Park. It is a damn fine piece of property.

"We never have gotten along. I have no use for the man. If he is talkin to you, he is always lookin around for someone he thinks is more important to talk to. He is really shifty eyed. He is such a big shot that if he were in the middle of that damn river dyin of thirst, he wouldn't drink unless someone gave him a glass. His old man was a banker but unlike Foote, he foreclosed on every farm and ranch in the valley when times got tough. Them poor ranchers and farmers never had a chance. The whole damn time he was big in his church and giving to any charity that would print his name in the newspaper. I don't normally hold a fella responsible for his ancestors' actions, but this guy took after his father just like a toupee to a bald head."

The ranch-style home extended from the hillside to the river. It was fronted by a swimming pool that was made of rock and blended into the natural landscape. Water diverted through a spillway next to the pool creating a small rock waterfall. Obviously, I did not want to be on Frank's bad side. He had some very strong opinions and a homey way of describing those who did not measure up to his standards. He had made up his mind about the man, and it was obvious that it would take a lot to convince him that he was wrong. I thought it interesting he thought so much of the dump man, spoke so highly of his integrity and work ethic, and had so little good to say about the rich man. He just didn't seem to care what a man had accumulated or how much influence he could bring to a discussion; he was interested in his character and his actions, not his words. He didn't think Harrigan met his test of character.

"The damn fool been married three or four times," he said. "Once them Janes figure out what a phony he was, why they'd head for the hills. I think a few of them got off with some of his daddy's money. Keep in mind, boy, that a man's circumstances often reveal him; wealth ain't a measure of much of anythin. If a man can keep his word, if he treats all people with courtesy and respect, and if he makes that extra effort all the time, he is my kind of guy or gal. This Harrigan, he just ain't my kinda guy.

"I been wantin to build a small bridge across Cedar Creek for years. He's been fightin me about it. He throws up every obstacle. At first he said part of the bridge was on his property and that buildin it would cause his house to flood. It weren't even goin to be on his property. I had an engineer take a look and see if it would affect his house—the man said it wouldn't have any effect on his ground.

"In the spring it is almost impossible on some days to get to town. The creek rises, and a car would get swept away if a fella wasn't careful. Been lucky so far that nobody's been hurt. Sometimes in the spring there will be a wall of water gush down that creek six feet high. You and I gonna build that damn bridge this summer.

"The fact of the matter is I think Harrigan just don't want to have to pay any part of the thing. Well, it ain't on his damn land, and it ain't goin to hurt nothin, and I'm a goin to pay for it, so we are gonna build it. Some of the older folks in the cove can get stuck for days without being able to get out. That ain't healthy... Hell," he said under his breath, "I don't like drivin through that creek when it's high myself! Yep, you, Fred, and me are going to build that bridge before the summer is out."

I drove through the creek and down the winding dirt lane to his house. We passed a house with a pine tree growing through the center of it, and he pointed it out to me.

"Ever see a house with a tree growin out of the center?" he asked. We passed Fred's place; he was still sitting on the metal chair by the front door just like yesterday with the rifle in his lap.

"Got one of them little bastards," he said. "Damn near got the mama cat, but she skittered away. She is a tricky little varmint, that one. I'll get her though.

"Melvin showed up right after dinner, said he was headin up to the park, and he would see you in a few days. Told him about the boy sleeping in the basement, but he didn't seem to care. He said he'd sleep in the huntin truck."

Frank didn't comment on the cat killing or the man named Melvin, instead he just said to Fred, "To hell with old Harrigan, me and you and the boy goin to build that bridge this summer."

I parked the truck, and Frank went into the basement to get some tools. He disappeared over the embankment next to the pump house. I could hear him muttering something to himself and the clank of metal on metal. When I looked down the embankment, he was kneeling over the river twisting a long galvanized pipe with a pipe wrench.

"Get that hickey Spot made from the back of the truck and throw it on down to me." He told me it was a short piece of pipe with a number of holes drilled and capped on the end.

I retrieved it and handed it down. He quickly assembled the two pipes and tightened the long length of pipe extending out of the water. "That ought to do her," he said as he pulled the lever to start the pump. I could see water rising twenty-five feet in the air from where I stood. As he climbed up the embankment, he too saw the gusher and said, "Oh damn, shut her off boy! What the hell? What the hell happened? Just get one damn thing fixed, and another is broke."

I turned off the pump, and he walked to where the gusher of water had come out of the ground. I heard him grunt as he bent over to examine the pipe. His neck turned red as he turned to me and said, "The pipe has been cutoff at the ground. Did you cut this damn thing off?"

Without waiting for my response, he said, "Damn it to hell I told you to be careful! I told you to watch for the damn heads. What the hell were you thinkin? What's wrong with you, boy, you got your head up your ass?"

I didn't know what to say. I stood on one foot and then the other. It was obvious he knew what had happened. It was also obvious that I had not been as careful as I should have been. I wanted to please him so badly. Tears immediately welled up in my eyes, and I began to feel worse. I balled up my fists at my side as if I expected a fight. *I hate it when I cry*, I thought. *What is the matter with me?* No matter how hard I tried, the tears just kept coming.

My next thought was to just run. I had always been able to run in the past. "That blubberin ain't goin to help boy," he said. "You can do better than that. You need to put your mind to what you're doin. Now you have gone and made twice the work for both of us. If a fella don't have time to do it right, when does he have time to do it over?"

"It was an accident," I said.

"It weren't no accident; I told you about them sprinklers; I told you to be careful. You need to take responsibility, and you need to fix it. If I hadn't told you the damn heads were in the grass, you might say it was an accident, but you knew they were there, you were told to watch for them, and you chose not to. It was a choice, and you were careless. I ain't interested in no goddamned excuses," he said, "more important if you do somethin wrong, own up to it. I don't mind a kid being a little careless. I was a kid once, but I won't have a sneak or liar on the place. Own up to your mistakes."

I turned on my heels and stalked back to the basement. My suitcase was open on the floor near the bed. I threw the few dirty clothes that had accumulated into the old bag, snapped it shut, and dragged it to the door. *I'll show this bastard,* I thought. *He isn't going to yell at me. It was just an accident! I didn't cut it off on purpose. Who the hell does he think he is anyway*, I thought.

Frank rounded the corner of the house with a determined look on his face and entered the basement door. He glanced at my suitcase but did not look at me. When he emerged he had a handful of wrenches, a hack saw, and another sprinkler head. He kept walking and said to me without looking, "Go out to the garage and get yourself a shovel and get back here and help me. Don't be just standin there with your face hangin out; it ain't the end of the damn world," he said. "You cut the damn thing off, and you are goin to learn how to fix it. If you want to go home to your mama, you need to do it after you take responsibility for what you did and not until after you help me fix it. I make enough mistakes of my own without you addin to them. Life ain't a free ride. No one owes you anythin. You cut the damn sprinkler head off being careless, and you are goin to fix it."

I retrieved a shovel from the garage. I started digging around the riser, and he softened a little. "I think you are a good kid. I invited you here, because I wanted you to come. I actually think you're a kid that will listen. You ain't a damn smart aleck or know-it-all, and I think if you will listen, I can teach you somethin this summer, but if you are goin to have an attitude, if you're goin to make excuses, or if you're goin to bow up, I can't help. It is entirely up to you, not me; you decide to stay or go but no matter, we are goin to repair the damage you have done before you leave. We are goin to dig the damn thing out, and if nothin else happens when you get back on that bus, you will know how to repair a broken lawn sprinkler. If you want to grow up and be responsible, if you want to learn, and if you will take a little direction, you are welcome here. If you don't want any of that, then you might as well just get back on that bus."

I continued digging around the riser while he stood and watched. Once the underground pipe was exposed, he used a pipe wrench to disconnect what was left of the riser and asked me to connect a new one and screw on the sprinkler head. He tightened it with his wrench. His anger had subsided, and I was beginning to calm down. I didn't want to go home, but I didn't know how to express to him my own disappointment in myself for being careless. I really liked him and wanted his approval but had learned that anger and rebellion had always worked in the past. It didn't seem to work with him.

We worked quietly for a few minutes. I shoveled dirt back around the hidden pipe and new riser while he walked toward the embankment and the pump house. He disappeared over the embankment again and suddenly the sprinklers came on all around me. I started to get wet, and I could see that he had started to laugh. I started to laugh with him and returned the shovel and tools to the garage and the basement without him asking. I picked up my suitcase and dragged it back into the basement. He said, "Come on, let's feed the horses." I followed him to the edge of the river and knew that this crisis had passed.

We crossed the narrow footbridge that spanned the river. The water was high and washed noisily over the concrete piers that supported the bridge. The horses waited expectantly and wide eyed on the other side.

Frank owned the property that fronted both the river and adjoined the highway to Rocky Mountain National Park. It was bordered on the east side by a dirt road that led to his brother's cabin and his brother-in-law's two-story home. There were several other homes and a fenced pasture along the lane. A small animal path was carved in the grass leading to a frame house—a cabin really that was set into the hillside. It opened into a shed in the front and dirt fell away from the rock on which it was perched. It had been someone's home once and housed the memories of another time.

Once inside the small two-horse stall, I could see the house was full to the ceiling with hay and gunny sacks full of grain and sweet feed. Frank said, "The iron grey is called Smokey and the Palomino is Tuffy. Both them horses will carry a fully dressed elk off a mountain as if they didn't know it was there. Like grease through a goose.

"Both them old boys are gettin long in the tooth, but they are the onliest two horses I'd trust in them mountains. A fella can shoot off their backs, and they won't even blink. It is as if they enjoy a hunt just as much as the hunter. I have ground tied both them boys and slept through the night and them not be ten feet away when I awoke in the mornin. Tuffy is a little shy around his face cause some bastard used to slap him around when he was a colt. Freddie bought him from the fella and gave him to me years ago just to get him out of the county and away from that bastard. I hate a fella that will mistreat an animal."

Smokey was a draft horse. He was at least seventeen hands at the shoulder and had a full mane and tail. His tail touched the ground, and his mane had a tangle of knots and one small pine-cone embedded in it. His color was dappled with shades of light and dark grey. The other horse was smaller and fawn colored with a white blaze on his forehead and white socks. Both were grass fat and high spirited.

It was obvious that Frank had a fondness for them, and they for him. He slapped them both lightly on the rump, and they pulled their lips back and showed their teeth in what appeared to be a smile. "Get up there, and go give them a couple of flakes of alfalfa and a scoop or two of grain and sweet feed," he said. "Shake that hay good cause you don't want to colic them. Don't let any hay get on the ground either, or they will wind up swallowin that dirt. A horse with colic is a pitiful sight. If they get to hurtin, they will roll around on their back, and before you know it, they will tangle up their insides, and there ain't much anyone can do to save them. Cows are much easier to keep than a horse; they are a lot smarter too. Bet you never seen a cow step into a cattle grate across the road. Damn cows are smart enough to know better; a horse, hell, he'll just walk on in and break his leg."

I cut open a bale of fresh hay and shook out a few pungent smelling flakes of alfalfa into the divided trough beneath the open window. Dust swirled up in the stall as Smokey nipped at Tuffy who whirled and kicked in retribution.

"It is a game they play," Frank said. "Can hardly separate them except at feedin time and then they act as if they don't even know one another. Animals, like people, have their own personality. There are some grumpy, wide-eyed ones, and there are some slow and easy ones. It is all how they see the world and the people around them."

I opened a barrel and reached into the darkness for a coffee can scoop. A small mouse jumped up onto my bare arm, hopped onto the feed trough and then into the grass beyond. My face must have gone white, because Frank started to laugh and said, "Hell, that varmint were more afraid of you than you were of him. Them damn mice get in the feed even if I screw the top down and nail it shut. It is the damndest thing I ever seen.

"This here is where that Buster's ole man and his brother lived that one cold winter. It was just before the war, and times were not too damn good. We had a real bad winter. There ain't been one quite like it since. It wasn't a good time for me, but I give them this place to live in, and they looked after the cows. They insulated the house with all that cardboard you see stuck up on them walls. Since neither of them boys had jobs in those days, and I had a herd of cows up here, it just made sense that we accommodate one another.

"I still had the shop back then, and I couldn't get up here every day to look after them cows. Hell, the snow was so damn deep, couldn't get a car up here at all for a week or so. It was good to have them boys, and I think they were happy to have a place out of the weather. Times just weren't good; people couldn't find any work and sure couldn't buy nothin. We had to do a lot of mechanican and repairin on credit or trade for somethin. We might have lost more cows than we did that winter if them boys were not here to put out feed and watch for stragglers. Walt," he said, "soon after joined the Army as a private in the rear ranks and come out years later as a colonel, but Buster's old man, well, he just drifted around tryin one thing and then another. He drank too damn much and couldn't stay away from them juke joints and them Janes. It is funny how a family will have one child who makes somethin of himself and another never amount to nothin. Same blood, same house, different result. That just tells me that it comes from the inside. All that stuff on the outside don't make for a hill of beans. If a fella believes in himself and wants to make good, he most generally does. That don't mean life is ever easy, but it gives a fella hope when he knows that if he does right, keeps his eye on the ball, and keeps on a movin, generally things will work out. Most losers want to make excuses and blame everybody but themselves. It's a damn shame. Buster is a good boy. I don't have any idea what would have happened to him if Georgia and Don wouldn't have taken him in. He might have had to live on the county."

CHAPTER SEVENTEEN

Buster and Jimmy were my closest friends. They were as different as night and day. Jimmy, like me, had been left to fend for himself. Buster had been sheltered by his aunt and uncle who monitored his activity very closely. He had to be home when the street lights came on. He had very little freedom to roam the streets, and although his primary interest was in girls and clothes like most adolescent boys, he was more attentive to his studies and showed little interest in motors and getting grease under his nails. He worked part time in the local grocery store stocking shelves and bagging groceries while Jimmy and I were more apt to scrounge returnable bottles, wash windows, and cut grass to create income. He was well liked by most and had an easy way about him.

We met when he was eight. His aunt and uncle purchased the small apartment building next door to my mother's home. I was just a few months older than he. He was a little overweight and not very athletic. He had the darkest shock of black hair and the blackest fluid eyes I had ever seen. One eye displayed a rust colored spot on the white of his eye. We met the day he moved in and became fast friends.

His father, like mine, had just walked away and abandoned him. He told me that he thought his biological mother had died in a fire yet he really wasn't sure. He was passed from family member to family member until he finally wound up in Florida with his father's older brother and his wife.

They made a place for him on the enclosed porch. He wasn't allowed in the house except to bathe. His bed was a small divan under the front window that served as a couch for guests when he was not in it. He never had a room of his own. He did have a small desk and lamp next to the divan to use when he studied, yet I never remember him complaining. I think he was just happy to have a place to sleep and eat.

He enjoyed having a little freedom and relished sleeping over with me. I had no restrictions on my activity and often had the entire house to myself.

His uncle suffered a massive heart attack and died soon after we met. Buster was with him and witnessed him fall. His aunt, now finding herself alone and responsible for a child, overreacted and became more harsh and restrictive. Buster often found ingenious ways to circumvent her authority. When she was absent, he would rebel.

He was a clever actor and could play any part required of him in order to get along. He was not a bad kid. He had spent the summer in Colorado with Frank the summer before, but since he had no interest in getting his hands dirty or working any type of manual labor, he and Frank were not a perfect fit. He did tell me what to expect and informed me that there was a girl about our age who lived in the cove that was pretty randy. I learned later that he was just a little reckless with the truth. (An expression I picked up from Frank.) He wasn't a liar and never meant any harm, but he would exaggerate—things were always larger than life.

Frank told me that he would be visiting his father soon for the remainder of the summer and asked if I wanted to spend a few days in the neighboring town with him. I was delighted and expectant. His aunt was visiting relatives in California and planned to leave him with his father during her stay. She planned to pick him up when she returned to Florida at the end of the summer. I looked forward to seeing him.

During late spring, a year earlier, Buster and I had been riding our bicycles along a country road east of town. Our community was bordered by canals that had been excavated to contain the runoff from the Everglades. The town was developed by Glenn Curtiss, an early aviation pioneer, and consisted primarily of re-claimed swampland.

When money permitted we would ride our bikes the four or five miles necessary to visit the local dairy farm. It had a creamery with fresh ice cream. We would cross a small drainage canal at the edge of town, peddle through the Florida East Coast Railway right of way, and cross the rock pit property and old dump site before getting to the main highway that led to the dairy. The highway was narrow, yet it accommodated a lot of automobiles going north and south to avoid in-town traffic.

We would often stop at "bare-assed" beach on the way to the dairy. South Florida summer days were so hot and humid that it didn't take much to convince any of us to strip off our clothes and dive in. On one occasion we heard the "tee hee hees" of several of the local girls and discovered we had an audience. The dairy was only a mile or so from the "beach" on the banks of the FEC canal.

One Sunday afternoon in late spring, we decided to ride to the dairy. The afternoon sun was bearing down on us, and it was intense. We wanted an ice cream and thought it might be fun to stop by the canal on the way home for a swim. Once we got to the dairy and purchased our double scoop, we headed down the highway in the direction of the beach. The sun was low in the sky, the clouds dappled the landscape, and it was extremely warm and humid. There was a slight breeze, and the sun was setting at an oblique angle to oncoming drivers. Cows stood indolently in the pasture with white birds on their backs. A drainage ditch full of water and cattails paralleled the roadway. In some places the water was actually on the shoulder of the road. I had been pedaling while holding an ice cream cone in one hand and steering with the other. I was only inches from the drainage ditch, and occasionally, had to move up on to the roadway to avoid the water. Buster was riding behind me, and cars were streaming past at highway speeds. Suddenly, Buster yelled, "Watch out!" I looked over my shoulder and looked back just in time to see the brake lights flash on several cars ahead of me. Several feral dogs had crossed the highway causing the cars to slam on their brakes. There was a chain reaction. Buster had seen the dogs and had tried to warn me, but no sooner than I had turned my head, everything went black—no more dappled landscape, intense sun, or cows. There was just darkness.

A driver behind me hit his brakes, and the car fishtailed. The large fin on the rear fender of the Plymouth struck me with such force that it launched me off the bicycle, and I flew across the water-filled borrow ditch. I landed spread eagle inches from a metal fence post, facedown in the shallow water. I blacked out for a few seconds but was revived by the water in my face. I remember waking up soaking wet with a complete stranger looking down at me. He was totally blocking the sun.

His face was ashen, and his brow so furrowed that his eyes were just slits. He helped me sit up and muttered, "Thank God. You okay, kid? Anything broken? Can you stand up? Damn, kid, it happened so fast, I just couldn't stop in time. I saw you both, must have averted my eyes for a second, and then a car was stopped ahead of me. I just reacted. I am so sorry," he said. "When I saw you lying there with your face in the water, I thought I'd killed you."

The man helped me to my feet. A short piece of trim that had penetrated my thigh fell to the ground. I had been struck with such force by the flat blade of the rear fender that it must have looked like a cricket bat striking a ball—flat, smooth, and hard. I was lucky. I was dizzy, soaking wet, and felt a little pain in my right thigh, but I was in one piece. I knew that had the car hit me head on, I would have been seriously injured. Once I realized how serious it could have been, I was thankful.

Buster was looking over the driver's shoulder wringing his hands saying, "I saw it all! Two dogs ran out in the road, and the sun was in the driver's eyes." I told the driver I felt fine, but I didn't think I would be able to ride home. He asked if I wanted to go to a hospital. I said, no, I only wanted to go home.

The police never came. We loaded my bike in the trunk of the driver's car, and he secured it with his belt. As we pulled away, I saw Buster heading in the direction of home, pedaling at full speed. When I got home, my mother looked me over, took down the driver's name, his telephone number, and sent me to the couch. I heard her tell the driver that she was sure I would be fine and sent him away. It wasn't long before I was fast asleep. Morning came, and it was time for school. My leg was sore, and I was stiff all over, but my mother made it clear that skipping school was not an option.

"That scratch is a long way from your heart," she said. "I will drive you to school today, but don't plan on milking this thing forever. I'm sure you'll be able to get to school by yourself tomorrow." We left the house and walked toward the car. Just as we did, Buster stepped out his back door, leaning heavily on a cane. He was limping noticeably. My mother laughed and said, "Raymond, you are going to be a famous actor some day. You weren't even scratched, but it looks as if you were the person hit by the car." He didn't go to school that day. I don't have any idea what he told his aunt, but my mother laughed about the incident for years. She never failed to kid him about his injury.

CHAPTER EIGHTEEN

The summer days passed quickly. Every morning I would be awakened by Frank banging on the door threatening to screw my plate upside down on the table. Although I had stopped dead bolting the door when he and Lillie were home, I often would lock it when they left for the dog races at night. Every morning we would eat breakfast, and I would feed the chickens. He would always find something for me to do around the place until it was time to go to town. We drove to town every day except Sunday. He would often have me whitewash rocks and move them from one place to another. I would cut the grass, carefully avoiding the sprinklers, trim bushes, and pick choke cherries for Lillie. If Frank couldn't find anything else for me to do, he would have me sort out nuts and bolts that he had accumulated over the years and put them in common-sized jelly jars. I would clean out the several garages and always seemed to have a broom in my hand. I would help him spread used motor oil on the road to keep dust down, stack lumber and wood, and wash or clean something around the place every week. He kept me busy every hour, every day.

I didn't realize until later that I had moved some rocks back to their original location by the end of the summer. When we visited the shop, Chili would tell me about his experience with Frank as a child. "The old man has mellowed," he would say. He told me about how he and Melvin had worked at the feed lot, in the hay, and at the shop when they were my age.

I still had not met Melvin. He had told Fred that he would be back in a few days a week or so ago. He was Frank's nephew. He was the only son of Lillie's sister and brother-in-law. He had seen some of the harshest fighting in Korea I had been told. Although he had not been physically wounded, he had spent some time in the Denver Veterans Hospital for some sort of "hysterical" injury. "The government put old Melvin in the hospital after he returned from Korea," Frank said. "He has never been right in the head since.

"The boy wasn't slow when he was a child but just real sensitive. I think all that shootin and dyin just got to him. He spent his whole tour in Korea in the trenches. It was just too damn much for him. I was in the Army during the first war, but I never had to shoot at someone I hadn't been formally introduced to. I don't hold it against him, hell, I like the boy. He is a damn good worker, and he can be trusted. He is a man of his word. If he tells you somethin, you can put it in the bank, but I never know when he might show up, and I never know when he might leave. He might just take a notion to head to Alaska and if the chores are done, he'll be gone. Last time he took off, he was gone for over a year. Hell, his folks never had no idea where he was or when he was comin back. He just showed up at the house one day as if he'd never been gone. He sure is a strange one. He come back one time, and he was pasty white and skinny as a rail. He ain't a heavy fella anyway. He can live on scraps. Some folks thought he had served a little time, but he said no; he been up to Seattle working as a 'pearl diver' in some restaurant and helping fight fires in the mountains when they'd have him. He said he worked on one of them Alaska fishing boats for a spell, and when it got cold, he would just come on home. He is a funny sort of fella. He would just stick out his thumb or ride the rails if he has to. He has never owned a car and except a short time before he went to Korea and was married, never really had any responsibility.

"I can't say the boy's had a bad life. Not too damn much seems to worry him," Frank said, "and he sure as hell ain't worried about the price of a bushel of corn! Damndest fella I know. Just come to show you everyone is different, and that is the way it should be. It would be awful borin if we were all alike. He just shows up, and I take him in.

"One night last summer he was stayin in the basement. He had appeared a few days before, didn't say where he had been or where he was goin. Suddenly, the second night he was here, there was a tremendous explosion—a gunshot. We were already in the bed, and it sounded as if the roof was goin to come off the house. I threw on my clothes and raced down to the basement. There he was, sittin on the edge of the bed with a stunned look on his face, a 30/30 rifle across his lap, and his face as white as that wall.

"Then he said to me, 'It just went off, Uncle Frank. I sure am sorry, but I thought I would clean it for you. Onced I got finished, I noticed a box of shells and thought I would check the action. Worked fine, only, I guess I didn't get the last one out of the chamber. I pointed it at the floor and pulled the trigger. Sure did scare me. Damn near wet my britches. Sure am sorry about that mess I made in the floor. Must of made a lot of racket up in the house. I sure am sorry. I know better, guess I just wasn't careful, sure glad I didn't hurt nobody.'"

Frank said he gave him a little hell in a good-natured way and went back to bed.

"Next mornin," he said, "I came down to raise him for breakfast. He had cleared out; there wasn't a sign of the boy except a faint smell of cordite and a hole in the floor. Ain't seen old Melvin since.

"Fred told me he'd come by this week so he is around somewhere. If he shows up, we'll just put some more water in the soup. Hell, he'll walk over a mountain flat footed and keep on a goin. I truly like the boy; he served in that damned mess in Korea. He ain't reckless with the truth, will work all night if necessary, and don't make no damn excuses for hisself or anyone else. He's Lillie's sister's kid, so he's blood and that is important. They say he was shell shocked in that war, but I think he has always just liked being in the woods. He knows what he wants and goes about it without askin anyone's permission. The boy seeks his own counsel, and I admire that. He'll show up one of these days soon, and we'll just put him down in the huntin truck until he is ready to head out to Australia."

Our routine didn't change on Saturdays. Feed the chickens, throw out the remnants of breakfast for the "turkeys" and stay busy. It seemed that no matter what Frank decided to do, the first hour was devoted to fixing, sharpening, or repairing whatever tool we needed. He had built a grease pit in the lower garage. If he couldn't find anything else for me to do, he would have me grease one of the cars or trucks, change the oil, and when I finished he would say, "Sweep her out and put her back where you got her." After I had finished and locked the garage, he'd say, "Did you air up them tires?" There was no down time with him. The old aphorism, "Idle hands are the devil's playground," was not lost on him.

Since the shop was open until noon on Saturday, in the mornings we would often stop briefly and then go to the livestock sale and flea market. Frank never purchased livestock. He just seemed to enjoy sitting in the stands and watching the animals come under the auctioneer's gavel. He would comment on the confirmation or disposition of a horse. He would identify with one horse or cow and comment on how it looked like one he had had in the past. He would call attention to others in the stands watching the proceedings.

He seemed to know everyone and have some understanding of their backgrounds and personalities. "Now that fella over there, the one with the Stetson, well, if he tells you somethin, you can take it to the bank. Don't think I would try to out slicker him, though; he knows his horses. I've knowed him to sell a fella a horse and take it back a year later for full price just because the new owner didn't want it no more. He's done well, but there ain't many like him out there."

The auctioneer would shout, "Who will give me twenty, now twenty-five! Who will give me thirty!" The cow, horse, or sheep would be led around the center of the arena, white eyed and trembling. "You gotta watch some of these fellas, though," he'd say. "They'll doctor an old horse or cow so that a fella won't have any idea what he is a gettin. It is important that we have to trust folks. But you gotta remember in this life that some folks don't have it in them. Honesty that is. If they would fill their time with doin people right, they wouldn't have time to cheat and steal. Sometimes it is just their nature. Sometimes a fella will fool a person, so keep your eyes open, listen, and don't be talkin. The bad in a fella will always come out, and if you keep your mouth shut and listen, you will soon be able to see it. In this life a fella's circumstances reveal him.

"See that tall lanky fella standing by the corral?" he asked. "You can't trust him as far as you can spit. He been sellin horses around her for years. He'll speed em up or slow em down. A fella will get the damn old horse in the trailer and back to the house, and he'll tear the place down.

"See that fella in the red shirt and bib overalls? He's biddin' on his own stock. There are a bunch of shills in the crowd. It ain't just here where a fella's got to pay attention. There are plenty of good folks in life, but that one bad apple will ruin your day. About twenty percent will ruin things for the rest of us. This here sale is just a little bit of life!"

Following the sale we would cross the highway and eat lunch in a small smoky café filled with farmers and ranchers. Later, we would walk through the flea market that adjoined the sale barn. Frank would pick up and look over just about every item and make a comment about its use or origin. He would identify a headlight from a Model T Ford and a hickey to tighten spokes in a motorcycle or bicycle. He had a story to tell about every item.

We would stop along the way, and he would introduce me to someone he knew. He never treated me as a child. Although I had little to say, I was always allowed to be part of the conversation. As we walked away, he would say something like: "That Russian has been workin his place for nearly fifty years. He's the kinda person who if you shake his hand, he will honor an agreement ten years from now. Unfortunately, a lot of this new crowd just ain't like that. A handshake don't mean much anymore.

"Remember that, boy, if a man's word don't mean somethin, there ain't much to him. If you can't believe what a fella says, why would you want to be around him? A liar is as bad as a thief. He'll steal a man's trust as quick as he will steal a man's pocketbook." I had heard that before.

CHAPTER NINETEEN

Saturday afternoon was a time for me to ride the old Cushman down the lane and through the old canyon, fish in Grandma's Hole, ride the horses in the pasture, or follow the mountain trails to the several abandoned gold mines for exploration. There was always plenty to do.

Sunday was truly a day of rest. Most of my Sundays were filled with enjoying the beauty of the mountains, exploring the canyons and back roads on the scooter or bicycle, riding the horses, or fishing. Since there was no one my age in the cove, except the girl I had never met, I was virtually on my own. Once or twice that summer, we all went to town for dinner, but most Sundays I had the day to myself. My only responsibility was to feed the chickens and "turkeys" in the morning and the horses late in the day. Frank made it clear that he wasn't going to ask me but once to perform these basic duties.

There was a church camp above the highway that I would visit occasionally but all of the residents were children. I would spend much of my time talking to the counselors so I wasn't drawn to the place.

I would ride a bicycle down the main highway occasionally through the canyon and back, and once I hiked to the top of "Pole" hill where I could see for miles in every direction. When I rode the scooter, I would have to pass Fred's house. He would look at me with a glance so severe I thought I might be his next target. The dust created in passing was an annoyance so once I left the property, I would try and stay away until it was either dark or time to put the scooter away.

One Sunday afternoon I was returning from the electric plant at the entrance of the old canyon road and came upon a tall man walking down the side of the lane who had a long face and neatly trimmed, wavy blond hair. As I approached him, he stepped into the middle of the road and motioned me to stop. He didn't seem threatening, just matter of fact. He asked me, "Is that is Frank's Cushman?"

I said it was, and that he had let me ride it.

"I thought it was," he said. "There ain't many around like it. I have put many a mile on that thing myself. You must be the boy that come from Florida to stay with Frank. I been hearing good things about you. Would you mind giving me a lift to the house? I'm Melvin, Frank's nephew," he said. "I've been walking since Drake and starting to drag a little."

He was dressed in blue jeans and a long-sleeved denim shirt, open at the collar. The bottom of his pants was tucked into a sturdy but well-worn pair of high-laced work boots. He had a cased knife on his belt and held a small canvas bag over his left shoulder. He had no other luggage. He stuck out his right hand and said again, "I sure could use that ride."

"Sure, climb on," I said. *So this is Melvin,* I thought. He looked exactly like I had expected him to look. I wondered who he could have spoken to about me.

We rode together silently down the lane, across the truss bridge and through Cedar Creek. I felt a little safer passing Fred's house with my passenger. Fred didn't even look up. We stopped under the lone pine tree in the middle of the road in front of the metal glider Frank had been napping on. His hat was in his lap and his eyes were closed, yet he had a slight grin on his face. I could tell he wasn't sleeping.

When he opened his eyes and saw Melvin, his grin widened, and he said, "Well, I'll be damned if it ain't old Melvin. You look like you been down the road apiece. You are just in time for supper. Go tell Lillie hello, wash up a little, and we will put another plate on the table." The elusive Melvin was back, and it was clear to me that Frank was happy to see him.

Supper was animated, but we learned little of Melvin's whereabouts the past few years. He admitted to fighting fires in Montana and spending time on the West Coast. He seemed more interested in my bus trip and childhood than in talking about himself. He said that he had never traveled any farther east than Omaha. He had delivered some livestock there for a rancher once but otherwise had never been any farther east than Wiggins, Colorado when helping Frank on one of his farms. He told of returning from San Francisco after mustering out of the Army. I don't remember whether or not he said he had been in the Army or the Marines, but Frank referred to every branch of the military as the Army. He had ridden the train both to and from San Francisco. He had been drafted, he said, trained somewhere in the West and then on to Korea. He left the subject with his arrival in Korea. He did not comment any further about what he saw or how he felt about the war. He merely dropped the subject. That was the extent of his discussion of it. He spent a little time at Fitzsimmons Army Hospital, he said but almost as an afterthought and mentioned that President Eisenhower was also a patient during his stay. One of the president's first heart attacks, he thought.

"Them doctors and nurses were jumpier than a cat in a room full of rocking chairs," he mused. "I've been west mostly. Spent some time in California during the big fires of '56 and then I thumbed up to Oregon and later to Montana. That Oregon is sure beautiful, but Montana suits me better. It sure has earned its name, Big Sky Country. It is a lot like Colorado of an earlier day, only they mostly use silver dollars and not paper money. Walking around with all those silver dollars makes a fella think he's rich. I'd have to hitch up my belt to keep my britches from falling off," he said with a laugh.

"I worked in the mines for a while, but it finally got so damn cold, my nose would freeze up, and I would be up to my ass in snow. Colorado ain't the banana belt, but it seemed subtropical compared to Butte. Onliest place I think I was colder was in Korea, but there I was so damn busy keeping my head down and thinking about going home, I didn't have time to think about the cold.

"Have you ever done any fly fishing?" he asked.

I admitted I hadn't, and my fishing experience was limited to bobbing a hook in the canals and rivers around Miami. I did tell him how once my mother had taken Jimmy and me to a fish camp on the Tamiami Trail and how one of the locals knocked her off a foot stool inhabited by a water moccasin. The rivers and canal were infested with all sorts of snakes and waterborne creatures. It was not uncommon to scare up an alligator at the swimming hole. I told him that I would like to sit under the bridge crossing the Miami River on hot afternoons and fish for brim, but I had never had anyone teach me much about fishing. I rarely caught a fish, and most of the time, I would spend shooting at the water snakes and minnows with my BB gun. When I did catch a fish, it was usually so small that it wasn't worth considering for dinner. I couldn't imagine what kind of reception I would have received if I had come home with a smelly bunch of fish. I did it primarily to stay out of the house and amuse myself. The spot under the bridge was cool, there was always a slight breeze, and the cars traveling overhead created a cadence I enjoyed.

"Come on down to Grandma's Hole," he said. "I will show you how to catch a mess of fish before dark." He retrieved a pair of hip waders, two fly poles, and a creel from the basement. "Don't think you oughten to start wadin' in the river yet, but I'll teach you some before I head out. Grandma's Hole is the best spot on the entire river to catch a mess of trout."

We walked down the path beside the lower garage, pushed through the brush and choke cherry bushes that remained, and crossed the small wooden footbridge to the island. A breath of coolness enveloped us as we crossed. There were lots of green apples on the trees that had been planted by Frank's mother years before.

"Them are some of the best apples I ever ate," Melvin said. "They will be ripe soon, but if you eat some, don't eat too damn many, or they will give you the squirts." He laughed and handed me a fly rod with a fly already attached.

"If you lose that fly, I will show you how to tie another one on. It is easy, but a fella's got to do it right, or he'll lose all his damn flies. Sometimes these brambles and bushes eat more flies than them fish do."

The river rushed over and around the rocks, and late afternoon bugs and water spiders covered the surface. The spiders looked exactly like the fly tied to the end of the line on my pole. "Live bait will work out here sometimes," Melvin said, "but it is much more fun to catch a trout with a dry fly. Watching them rise to a fly will give a fella chill bumps every time."

The spider-like bugs scampered across the water in the gentle eddies and pools along the river bank. I saw the occasional flash of a trout and watched a bug or spider disappear. A sliver flash and the bug was gone. My first effort resulted in a loss of the fly. It never reached the water but got tangled in the briars across the stream. Melvin showed me quickly how to attach another and set out down the river to catch some fish. He said, "You're on your own, boy. Don't fall in 'cause you'll be in the canyon before I can retrieve you."

Before he departed he showed me how I should hold the pole in my left hand and the line in my right. "Just lay that line in the water and let it flow out with the river. Don't be trying nothing fancy; just let her out and float the line in those pools around them rocks. There are plenty of fish in this river, so if you don't catch none tonight you got plenty of time. Summer is just startin."

After a few demonstrations and the loss of another fly or two, it did not take me too long to figure out that I had better take his advice. If I didn't want to run out of flies and spend the night untangling my line from the trees and bushes, I had better just let some line out and let it float with the current.

Melvin stepped into the waist-high waders, threw the creel over his shoulder, and entered the river. Water flowed around him about knee deep until he reached the center, where it came to his waist. I saw him slip once and steady himself before seeming to plant himself on the river bottom.

His line snaked out thirty yards and landed at the edge of the river downstream in a quiet spot. It wasn't thirty seconds and a trout struck his line with force. The fish broke the surface of the water and fought him all the way to his net. The man was a wizard, I thought. No sooner than his line hit the water, he was playing a twelve-inch rainbow trout. He adeptly removed the fish in one motion, dropped it in his creel, and his line shot out again to land in another quiet spot.

It wasn't long before he had another and another and another. It seemed he merely called, and they came. I didn't have any flies left. My feet were soaking wet, and daylight had turned into the long shadows of twilight. Within about forty-five minutes he had caught his limit of fish.

He waded back to where I was standing, trying to untangle my line from a tree. He laughed and unsheathed his knife at his waist. "They are all keepers," he said. "Let's get em cleaned. I'll show you how.

He slit the several fish from the underbelly in one motion, just below the tail to the gills. In another motion he removed the innards and then used his thumb to remove some sort of bloody membrane along the spine. The blood had an acrid smell. In minutes all of the fish were clean and ready to eat. He left the heads on but said he didn't like them looking at him when he fried them up, so he would cut them off later.

He told me we were lucky, because Frank would have the State Department of Fisheries man stop off about once a week and stock his portion of the river. "I think he slips them a few bucks," he said. The fish he had caught were all rainbows and native to the river. The stock fish were browns, and there wasn't one in his creel.

As we walked back toward the house, he said he had been married once but that when he learned that his wife didn't like to fish, the marriage was over. He laughed and said, "That weren't all of it. She was a good girl, and when we met it was pretty hot. Turned out she liked to dance and carry on more than she liked to stay home and clean house. She was pretty, but real high strung. I'd wanta go fishin' or huntin' with the boys, and she wanta go to them juke joints. It was just as well," he said, "we just sorta drifted apart. I see her once in awhile around town when I visit the folks, but I like to travel and wander.

"Folks tell me she is a hairdresser and married again. I say, 'good for her, it ain't for me.' When we agreed to split the sheets, there was no hard feelings. We are just different people. She might be better now that she has growed up a little, but I don't think I could ever just settle in one place. A fella needs to know that before he falls into something he can't get out of."

He told me that he had worked at the garage for awhile with Spot and Chili, but that just wasn't for him. He had worked in a hardware store, but it was boring waiting for folks to come in and buy something.

"A fella's got to do what makes him happy in life," he said as we walked back to the house. "I saw all the dying I'd ever need in my lifetime while I was in Korea and made up my mind that if I lived, I was going to spend my life doing pretty much as I liked. My wife and I drifted apart before I left, but she asked for a divorce while I was gone. Didn't matter, didn't think I'd make it home anyhow! Good thing really; I didn't want to be married anymore no how."

He handed the fish to Frank who said he would put them in the freezer and turned in the direction of Fred's house and the old hunting truck down the lane in the darkness. He looked over his shoulder and said, "See ya early, boy." He began to whistle quietly as he slowly walked away.

He slept in the truck for the rest of the week. He was up every morning before dawn and sitting with Frank at the table drinking coffee when I was called to breakfast. He said he felt at home in the old truck.

It was a former beet truck, and Frank had mounted a corrugated box shell on the bed. The interior was insulated with fiberboard and accommodated two bunks against the far wall. It was accessed by a ladder that slid out from beneath the chassis. There was a small gas cooking stove on one windowless wall and a propane heater under the one tiny window on the other wall. It smelled like the canvas that covered the bunks and had the dates of the recent hunts etched on the wall in pencil. It was spartan but the perfect vehicle to take into the mountains during hunting season. Its engine was powerful enough to haul Smokey and Tuffy, and it would accommodate four people if two were willing to sleep on the floor.

That week Melvin joined us for meals and rode with us to town. We ate together at the pool hall and visited Wild Bill at the city dump. He never stopped talking about wanting to go west again. He thought he would head for California soon and maybe down to Old Mexico.

He said, "I have never been to Old Mexico, so I kinda want to look her over. I heard them Mexican senoras will crawl up the steps of them big cathedrals with a chicken to give to the church. Seems like an interesting place. Poor as hell, though."

He talked about fire fighting and pearl diving in some waterfront restaurant in Seattle—a term I learned, for dishwashing. He didn't seem to worry about money and said he received a small disability check from the government. He didn't own a car, and the only luggage I saw was the canvas bag he carried over his shoulder.

During our conversation one afternoon driving home from town, Frank mentioned that Buster's aunt would be arriving in the next week or so for a few days to visit and that she would be leaving Buster with his father for the summer. I spent the next week with Buster and when I returned to Cedar Cove, Melvin was gone. He left that summer, and I never saw him again. I learned he returned once to go hunting with Frank but disappeared a few years later and was never heard from again.

CHAPTER TWENTY

Buster was astride the yellow line in the middle of the street waving wildly with both arms as Frank and I approached his father's drive-in restaurant. Fortunately, the street was deserted as he seemed oblivious to his surroundings. He must have focused on the red pickup almost as soon as we crossed the horizon. He knew I was coming, and his expectation was great.

Almost before we stopped moving, he said, "I've been picking up 'cig butts' in the parking lot all morning, glad you are finally here. Park over there next to the Ford."

He recognized Frank's old Dodge from the summer before. Frank told me that his driving skills had "left a little to be desired," but by the end of his stay, he no longer feared for his life.

"Didn't think you would ever get here," he said. "Sure good to see you. Hi, Uncle Frank! You letting him drive the Dodge, huh?"

Since the name of the town began with "Fort," I envisioned a stockade arena with a grass common on which a platoon of Calvary soldiers would be drilling in cadence and horses hitched at rails around the perimeter would be drinking from glistening wooden troughs. Instead, I found a small college town with oak tree-lined streets. "Old Main" was settled back on the expansive lawn of the university, and cars were parked in both directions in the middle of the street in the downtown area. Low-rise brick buildings with yawning glass fronts and an occasional multi-storied office or bank building announced the date of construction, with carvings over their doors.

Since it was Sunday and college classes had adjourned for the summer, the downtown area was nearly deserted. There was an occasional bicyclist and a few couples strolling hand in hand, but otherwise, it was quiet. A few street lights were blinking amber. The "fort" I was expecting to find did not resemble anything I came to expect from the Saturday afternoon matinees at the Circle Theatre. To say I was disappointed was an understatement. I had just assumed a town whose name was prefixed with the word "Fort" wouldn't have the audacity to present itself in any other way.

We had passed a huge "A" created from an assemblage of rocks and stones on the side of one of the foothills west of town. Frank told me that the large "A" represented the A in Agriculture College or "Aggies" as the college was historically known. Evidently, every fall the newcomers, or "frosh" he said, would trudge up the hillside and whitewash the rocks in celebration of the new college year. Aggies had quite a tradition, but the college had recently become a part of the Colorado University system, and now was referred to as Colorado State University. Frank thought the tradition of whitewashing rocks would soon be forgotten, and if the faded "A" was any indication, it already had.

Ray's father was standing just inside the door of the restaurant at the cash register as we walked up. He said hello to Frank and acknowledged me with a nod. After a few pleasantries with Frank, he said, "I have things to do, so you boys might as well head on home and get your jawing done."

Although I did not see a customer in his store, he emphasized how busy he was and suggested we get on with our boyish foolishness before morning, because cherries were in season, and if we wanted to make our board, we had better be ready to head for the orchard by morning.

So much for idle hands. He said, "Raymond, the closest place to pick is three miles north of town on the Cheyenne Highway. You boys need to be there early."

He didn't suggest how we were going to get there or who we needed to see about employment, only: "Be there. You can't miss them places to start picking if you head north to the 'Y' in the road and take the right fork a little piece. It's the road heading toward Cheyenne. I don't have enough work for both of you boys, and if I did, all you'd be doing is playing grab ass. There sure ain't no use in you two strapping boys laying up all day. Nope there ain't no future in that at all. Be here in the morning when I open up, and I'll have some lunch made for you both."

He and Frank spoke for a few minutes, and Ray and I climbed into the cab of the pickup. Frank soon dropped Buster and me off in front of a small residence a few blocks north of the restaurant near the entrance to the college. Buster told Frank and me, "My dad's new wife thought that the house would be too crowded if I stayed with them." He didn't say "stepmother" or mention her name, just "my dad's wife." Buster then said, "The entrance is around back. I eat with them when I am not at the restaurant, and I sleep here." He suggested that he didn't mind sleeping in the basement of a stranger, but I knew he did. We had been confidants for many years now, but I also knew he, like myself, needed to disguise his hurt.

"Ray was, after all, my father," he said. "I am sure glad you are here, though; some nights are long. There are no guys my age in this neighborhood, and I haven't met one girl. Most of the college kids are gone, and those who are still here have already made friends or have roommates. Ray works all of the time, so if I want to spend any time with him, I have to go to the restaurant."

The truck was still idling at the curb, and Frank promised to return the following Saturday to bring me "home." As he disappeared down the street, I followed Buster down the driveway and around the back of the house to an entrance leading into the basement.

It was a small Craftsman-style house with a lonely one-car garage set far back on the lot. The garage appeared to have been converted into living quarters, but there was no evidence that anyone currently resided there. The basement entrance accessed two small apartments connected by a hall and an adjoining bath. Ray was the only tenant at the moment, and his quarters were more a small sleeping room than an apartment.

There must have been another entrance to the basement elsewhere, because the door on the other side of his room led to the shared bath, a small hallway, and a stairway that led upward to a door in the approximate center of the residence above. Across the hall from the bath was another door leading—Ray told me—to another small room that had not been occupied since he arrived. The homeowner, a widow, rented rooms by the month to college students. The windows were small and high in the wall allowing for very little light. The room was dark even in mid-afternoon and had a musty, though not unpleasant odor. It smelled a little like the basement room at Frank's and was of similar size. It was spotlessly clean, and there were two small single beds. There was one on each wall that was about the size of an army cot. An old tattered multi-colored carpet covered the grey painted floor, and a few small framed pictures graced the walls. A photo of a covered bridge and a large red barn appeared to have been cut out of a magazine. The room was certainly spartan but more than Buster was accustomed to at home and seemed very private.

There was neither a radio nor television in the room, and the landlady strictly forbid smoking. Lighting was offered by a couple of small lamps and a naked overhead bulb in the ceiling. A large bathroom containing a huge footed tub, a pedestal sink, and several towel bars served the two sleeping rooms. Its floor was tiled with small one-inch tiles that reminded me of the floor at Stadnick's Soda Fountain at home.

We talked until about midnight. Buster asked me how I was getting along with Frank and if I liked Colorado. He reminded me of the girl he had met in Cedar Cove the previous summer and told me she lived in a small trailer next to her parent's house, just beyond the Cedar Creek crossing. He couldn't remember her name but wanted me to remind her of him if I did see her. He had evidently met her while riding the Cushman down the old canyon road. Unlike me, he was a little homesick.

He couldn't wait until his aunt returned, so he could get back to Miami. "Colorado just isn't for me," he said. His father was distant and not easy to talk to. Most of his summer had been spent picking up cigs, washing dishes, or mopping and sweeping up. None of this was his idea of summer fun. He had not come to know his stepmother. They had very little to say to one another other than "pass the butter," or "would you like another helping of beans?" His father didn't seem to have much to say to her either. She was his fourth or fifth wife.

I told him about the children's camp, riding Smoky and Tuffy, and how I had occasionally walked to the entrance of the canyon to drink coffee in a small café that had two teenage waitresses working in the evenings.

That seemed to get his attention. And he wanted to know more about the girls. I told him that I had only just met them and that one was a little chubby for my taste, but the oldest had gotten my attention. Unfortunately, she was not the one that paid any attention to me. It was the chubby one that seemed to take notice.

The girl who did not seem interested in me was a year or two older than I was and had a boyfriend from town that showed up about twice a week in an old Ford. She was going to be a senior in high school that fall. I would be a freshman.

He laughed at my misfortune and bad luck with women while talking about all of the girls he knew back in Miami and all of his adolescent conquests. I remembered what Frank had recently said, "You gotta watch that, Buster. He is a good boy but just a little reckless with the truth." Sleep finally overcame us. Cherry picking time came early.

I seemed not to more than settle deeply into the small army cot when the sound of an alarm clock and clattering silverware in the bottom of a small metal washbasin pierced the darkness and startled me awake. A sliver of light shining under the door from the hall cast a faint line on the wall opposite the door. Grey- and mauve-tinged shadows lit the high windows surrounding the room and the noise of the small clock and rattling silverware stirred up a cacophony hostile to the just waking ear.

I could make out the white blur of Buster's jockey-shorts-clad body diving headlong across the room to stop the clock from ring- ing. Just as his hand connected with the metal bowl, he slipped on the rug, and silverware was rocketed everywhere.

"I just wanted to make sure we woke up," he said. "Sometimes I can't hear the clock, and I wind up getting to the store during the morning breakfast rush. Ray hasn't been all that understand- ing when that happens.

"He told me last night that if we didn't get to the store before the morning rush, we would just have to go without lunch." He laughed. "I think it would be a long day without anything to eat but sour cherries. The silverware was insurance. Someone told me it works, and it sure does. How the hell could anyone sleep through that racket?"

We both threw on our clothes and raced out the door. A milk truck was idling at the curb, and I could hear a delivery man rat- tling bottles somewhere close by.

Buster had scrounged an old bicycle from the landlady that had belonged to one of the former tenants. He sat on the front handlebars, and I peddled as fast as I could. We arrived at the restaurant just as his father was turning the key in the front door.

The store was dark except for the lights in an old jukebox on the back wall and the trembling neon light of a Merita Bread sign that didn't want to start.

Ray's dad quickly prepared two turkey sandwiches, slathered on mayonnaise, and stuffed them in a brown paper bag along with a yellow apple. I was surprised when he went to the register and rang up twenty-five cents apiece. *What a guy*, I thought. *Times must be really tough.* While I had not expected a free ride, I thought at the very least Buster would not have to pay for his meals.

"Just take the Y to the right when you get to the Cheyenne Highway," he said. "You can't miss them orchards; they are up on the hill about a mile or so beyond the fork. There will be plenty of folks hanging around and a bunch of cars and old pickup trucks parked around the place."

There was no traffic that morning, so we were able to breeze along riding double down the middle of the highway. I tried to keep the front tire on the yellow line as if I were crossing a high mountain stream over a narrow bridge. The sun had already come up, and we could tell that it was going to be a hot, dry day. The sky was cobalt blue, and there wasn't a cloud anywhere.

A few cows and horses were grazing behind two strand barb-wire fences, and bales of deep green hay were neatly aligned for stacking. The morning was exhilarating and smelled of newly mowed grass. As we rode we would occasionally penetrate fresh pockets of cold air as if the morning spirits were riding the high-way with us. The sun was well over the horizon when we arrived at the first orchard.

It was already a beehive of activity. There were entire families of migrant workers on ladders and gathered around the bases of trees busily picking cherries. Children from the age of five to twenty-five were gathered with their parents, and an occasional grandparent filled boxes with the bright red fruit. Several babies were wrapped in blankets and nestled in baskets and boxes under the trees. One child was screaming at the top of his lungs while no one seemed to notice.

After asking several of the pickers what we were expected to do and who we needed to see to get started, a girl about ten years old pointed to a wagon at the end of the row of trees.

A man was sitting on the tailgate watching all of the activity. It took us several inquiries until we realized that virtually none of the pickers spoke English. I think the workers were surprised to see two Anglo teenagers in the grove. The wagon had high wooden wheels and was already partially stacked with wooden lugs of cherries. The man asked if we had ever picked before and explained the process.

"We will pay you fifty cents a lug for as many as you can fill," he said. "You can stay as long as you like as long as you leave by dark. I go home when you can't see to pick anymore. Once you fill a lug," he explained, "bring it to me, and I'll give you a chit. I will redeem all of your chits for cash at the end of the day or the end of the week, whichever you prefer. Don't be putting no dirt in the middle of them cherries to make it look as if you filled the lug when you didn't. I'm on to that! I'll just make you dump them all out, wash them, and start over."

The man handed us both a galvanized pail and pointed to a stack of wooden crates at the beginning of the row of trees. "Start in any row you want but stick with it. Don't be jumping around thinking you can pick more. I'll be stopping by occasionally to make sure you ain't leaving too many cherries on the trees. I don't mean every last one, but I don't expect to find many. I'll send you both back to finish. Pick every tree clean before you head to another. We got plenty of trees, and you got plenty of time. Grab yourselves a ladder each out of that shed, and put it back when you are finished.

Best way to clean them trees is start at the top, but if you two work together maybe one can pick the bottom, and the other can pick the top. It can be a long day standing on them round rungs. If it were me, I think I'd kinda alternate picking one tree at a time, top to bottom, bottom to top. Now that is what I'd do, but you boys do it how you want; just don't leave any cherries on them trees. Don't matter though, 'cause I am only going to pay you fifty cents a lug so pick em however you please. It usually takes about two weeks to pick this orchard. You boys have some good fortune since all the moisture we had this spring has produced a real good crop—just enough, not too much. Some years past we'd barely get a lug off a tree. This year each tree is yielding two or three lugs. Good picking."

He told us there was plenty of water in the barrel on the side of the wagon, and it was for everyone. "We ain't stingy with the water. Don't need no heat stroke out here. Make sure you drink plenty 'cause it is going to be in the high eighties today and dry. There ain't a cloud in the sky! I've known a person to topple out of one of those trees 'cause he got too heated up. He didn't listen. Oh," he said almost in passing, "since this is your first picking, don't be eating too damned many of them cherries, or you'll have the squirts for a week."

The first tree we chose was in a row of ten or twelve stretching up the contour of the hill. The trees were laden with cherries. I started by leaning the ladder against the interior of the tree and balancing it against several limbs. I was a little shaky and unbalanced at first, but it didn't take long to get the hang of clinging to the ladder with my knees and legs while picking with both hands. I dropped a few worm-eaten cherries on Buster, and he immediately threw them back at me. It didn't take long to figure out that wouldn't work.

The migrant families seemed to swarm over a tree and fill their lugs quickly. Two Spanish-speaking girls about our age were clothed head to toe so that we could only barely make out their faces under floppy, wide-brimmed hats. They wore long-sleeved shirts and baggy pants. It was hard to tell that they were actually females except for their high-pitched voices. They certainly were not particularly appealing, but they giggled and laughed a lot as they went about picking the tree adjacent to us bare in about half the time it took us.

A boy about five years old was working around the base of the tree, and the girls were both on ladders sweeping the tree clean. While they worked without much conversation, we caught them looking furtively our way every few minutes. When they did their voices would rise, and they would laugh. If they saw us looking in their direction, they would avert their eyes and speed up the pace.

Their pails consistently filled at twice the rate of ours. By noon they were two or three trees ahead of us and hadn't yet slowed the pace.

My arms were tired. My feet ached. The round ladder rungs created impressions on my feet and hands, and my fingers stuck together. Occasionally, I would look down and see Buster heading for the water barrel.

On a couple of occasions, he attempted to engage the girls in conversation by sign language and pantomime—they kept picking, and the lugs at their feet kept filling.

We stopped to eat our lunch and sprawled out under the wagon, which was the only real shady place we could find. I don't recall seeing the girls eat lunch, but if they did, they managed to do so without interrupting their pace.

By mid-afternoon the back of my neck was red and sore from the intense sun. My arms were bright red, and I could feel the part in my hair tingle. My shoulders ached, and my calves cramped from constantly reaching up to pick more cherries and trying to prevent dropping the galvanized pail. On one occasion I did drop the entire pale just as had I finally filled it to the brim. Cherries flew everywhere.

My knees and legs ached, and my calves felt as if someone had driven a hot stake in them. The girls kept moving.

As the shadows of the afternoon began to grow longer, all I could think about was heading back to the small apartment, taking a bath, and climbing into my cot. I wasn't looking forward to riding the bicycle double the several miles we needed to cover, eating supper, or doing anything other than washing the stickiness off my body and climbing into the small cot.

By this time the girls and their little brother were about two thirds of the way down another row of trees. I saw them pick up several last lugs overflowing with cherries and head toward the wagon. Several other older children and two adults approached them from several directions in the grove as if on cue, and I watched as the man in charge totaled up the chits and handed an older man a handful of dollars. He counted the money carefully, seemed to question the others, and then stuffed the money in his right front pocket.

"Quitting time!" we both said almost simultaneously. We poured what we both had picked from our pails into the wooden lug at the base of the tree, stepped to the next tree, and quickly filled the last box of the day.

There was some daylight left, but we were ready to go. If the truth were known, we had been ready to go home for hours but couldn't permit ourselves to admit we were worn out and wanted to quit. We especially didn't want to give up until the two girls quit. I thought they might work all night.

We cashed in our chits, walked about twenty yards, and collapsed on a grassy hillside. The girls and their family came out of a packing shed where they apparently had changed clothes and had cleaned up. The two girls were wearing Levi's and tight blouses and western boots with the bottoms of their pants tucked inside.

Buster and I looked at one another as if to say: where did they come from? All of a sudden, they looked pretty good. As they walked by laughing and giggling, they looked over and said something to us in Spanish and giggled some more. They looked as if they were going to go out dancing, and we looked like a couple of dead cockroaches. They did not even seem tired. We had just finished our first long day of picking cherries and had earned six dollars apiece.

By the time we had ridden back to the apartment, we were both too tired to eat supper. The landlady came down the inside staircase just as we opened the hall door. Buster introduced me as his best friend from Miami and told her we would be sharing the apartment for the week.

He said, "We picked cherries north of town today. Neither of us has ever worked so hard in our life." He told her about the Mexican girls and how they picked two or three lugs to our one. "It was embarrassing. They worked us into the ground. Their little brother picked almost what we did and skipped over to the packing shed. Boy, what a day! There were entire families working in the orchard—mothers, fathers, brothers and sisters, and even some grandparents. It was brutal. It just about killed us."

The landlady laughed and went back upstairs. "I think she likes me better than the college kids," he said. "She tells me that she is always having to get after them about loud noise and misbehavior.

She is tough old dame. I think she must have been in the Army once, maybe a first sergeant. Or a drill instructor. She won't take any guff. Doesn't bother me. I am not here much anyway. After all it's her house."

We both took a hot bath and went to bed. When the alarm clock sounded the next morning, neither of us could hardly move.

The soles of my feet ached, and my back and shoulders were stiff and painful. Buster told me that he had had a strange dream. He said he had dreamed that his fingers were stuck together all night. He couldn't even pry them apart. Surprisingly, I had the same dream. I dreamt that my hands were sticky, and all of my fingers were stuck together.

The second day was bad, but we loosened up around noon and didn't seem as tired. We gained a little on the girls, but they continued to pick two lugs to our one.

One morning we secretly latched on to the back of the milk truck as it pulled us down the highway to the orchard. The week passed quickly, and every day the work became easier. We had a great week together. We repeated the refrains of "Ninety-Nine Bottles of Beer on the Wall" until it became monotonous, and we fell asleep every night just after dark.

We learned that stoop labor is difficult and tiring and that neither of us aspired to pick cherries for a living. We also came to admire the girls and their siblings who never seemed to tire or complain and turned their earnings over to their father at the end of every day. By the end of the week, it was clear that Buster was ready to go back to Miami, and I was ready to go back to Frank's.

CHAPTER TWENTY-ONE

I was waiting at the curb when Frank arrived Saturday morning. He said he would be there at 7:00 a.m., and I knew he would expect me to be ready to leave. Buster and I said our good-byes and laughed a little about the week's experience. "Uncle Frank," he said, "you wouldn't believe those girls. We could never keep up with them; we tried."

"That ought to tell you guys somethin," he said, "a fella never knows what he is up against in this life. Don't be taken in by appearance or by someone else's opinion. Learn to make up your own mind about things. Sometimes it is not the size of the man in the fight; it is the size of the fight in the man. What you see is not always what you get in this life. Them girls knew what they needed to do, and they went on and did it. You two may have learned a few good lessons."

Frank slid over to the passenger side of the truck and told me to get in and drive. "Go ahead," he said, "but don't be flyin up on no corners and slammin on the brakes. We are goin back around Horsetooth Lake and through the buckhorn; it is all dirt road," he said. "The river was dammed up about ten years ago by that Army Corp of Engineers. I think it was sometime around 1948 or '49. They did it, they said, in order to control the water in the entire valley. The reservoir is six or seven miles long and has a shoreline of twenty-five or thirty miles.

"There once was a town at the southern end of the lake by the name of Stout, but that is all history now. They moved all them folks out and flooded the whole valley along the river. They even dug up the bodies in the cemetery and moved them to higher ground. When the water is low, a fella can still see remnants of the old stores and houses and the foundation walls. It is kinda spooky knowin there used to be a town under the lake where people married, raised their kids, and lived and died for generations. It is all gone. The lake is called Horsetooth after the solid rock mountain on the west side that has a shape of a horse's tooth."

I drove south on College Avenue and turned west toward the foothills. The road changed from asphalt to dirt as we climbed up the first of the foothills to the top of the reservoir. Once on the top, the road paralleled the shoreline for several miles. The view of the valley was spectacular. It overlooked the town, and I could see farms and ranches off in the distance. Frank said he had raced motorcycles on these roads in the twenties and thirties.

"That was long before the dams were built, so occasionally when the river was high, we would have to ride through it. I laid a Harley four valve down in the middle of the river one time on a hot summer day. Them roads would be real hard-packed in the summer with a thin layer of sand across the top. Lots of them riders and their machines would wind up with the cows during those races. We didn't race much in the winter, because them roads would turn to mud as slick as owl's shit after a snow or rain."

A large jackrabbit crossed the road in front of the truck followed immediately by a coyote at a full run. I could hear a "yip, yip, yip" over the noise of the engine as the coyote chased the rabbit. Frank laughed and said, "Them jacks are real smart, and I suspect he is only foolin with that coyote. Once he is tired of the game, he'll just run off from that coyote like grease through a goose. A coyote has to get up pretty damned early in the mornin to catch a jack. See that shale ledge across that field? Soon as that jack tires of the game, he'll disappear into the mountainside, and that coyote will never find him. Them rabbits got burrows and tunnels all back in the mountainside."

We continued to drive around the lake and passed several large barns full of hay and smaller ranch houses. Cattle grazed along both sides of the road, and occasionally, there would be half a dozen or more crossing from one side of the road to the other. We came upon a couple of ranch hands on horseback with a small herd of cows and watched briefly as their dog kept the cows together.

"This here is open grazin land," Frank said. "It is up to you to get out of the way of them cows and not the other way around. Speakin of which...I spoke to Frances Grimes yesterday, and she said Freddie is feelin better, so this may be a good time for us to head over to the cow camp. He and the boys are in the middle of the first cuttin of hay so he won't be able to join us, but one of his neighbors and his boy need to tend to some cattle in the high country and plan to be at the cow camp. The kid is about your age, a real horseman and loves to fish. He is a good kid and works along with his dad all day—from daylight to dark. When he ain't workin, he is rodeoin and showin them animals at the fair. I like the boy. His dad thinks he hung the moon. You two ought to get along fine."

CHAPTER TWENTY-TWO

There was a sign at the summit of Trail Ridge Road. Printed in small letters were the numerals "12,004 Feet" with the suffix "Above Sea Level." The air was thin, and the clouds were high and wispy, stretching for miles. It was July, yet the snow was piled deep in places, well above my head. The wind howled, and the cold pierced my old bomber jacket.

Frank had removed the canvas doors from the jeep before we left and seemed to wish he hadn't. He didn't say a word about the cold, but I knew he was anxious to get to the other side of the range. We stopped briefly at the warming house on top of the pass and then started down the other side.

It was difficult for me to relate to the thinness of the air or the fact that many flat-land automobiles could even operate at this altitude. Frank told me earlier that many cars driven from lower altitudes would stall or flood unless adjustments were made to the "jets" of their carburetors. "The air is so thin and the summer is so short, hardly any vegetation will grow," he said.

It wasn't long before we passed through a community, a wide spot in the road, named "Never Summer." It was aptly named. Summer departed almost as quickly as it came.

I tried to envision the early road builders and their horse-drawn and steam-driven equipment laboring at altitudes where I could hardly breathe. Other than my time in New York and the Empire State Building, the highest elevation I had ever experienced, before coming to Colorado, was the top floor of the old Flagler Hotel in

Miami overlooking the expanse of Biscayne Bay and the fishing fleet in Bay Front Park. We were over two miles above sea level. My breath was short, and the views were taking what little breath I had remaining.

The old army jeep had managed to slug its way up the mountain at an average speed of twenty miles per hour. At times, just when I thought we were about out of horsepower, Frank would downshift and the jeep would lurch forward. We had passed through canyons of snow and had stopped to drink from a spring with water so cold my teeth ached. We never stopped again. We just chugged and hiccupped along until we reached the summit. Frank and I talked about a lot of things, especially the lessons I learned picking cherries with Buster.

He told me a little history of the building of the road. His brother Fred had actually worked on one of the original crews. He told me about the great flu epidemic that destroyed so many lives in the early part of the century and how he thought he had avoided it, because he was in the Army and isolated from the city where it flourished. He talked about his early life and mentioned a woman named Stella that came into his life and left with great pain. He spoke briefly of his father and mother and asked about my family. He was interested in whom I was and what I wanted out of life.

If we passed anything along the way he thought might be of interest, he told me about it. He pointed out trails that Indians had used to cross the divide generations ago. He told of a fighter pilot during World War II who had collided with the glacier and was never found. He described the fires that had created Match Stick Mountain and the disease that had ravaged the forest over the generations.

He showed me where he had hunted elk and deer and big-horn sheep in the past, and he described the changes that had taken place in the road over the century. It had been dirt once and very narrow. The little jeep purred as we descended and rounded the sharp hairpin curves on the downside of the mountain, and the sun warmed us through the open doors of the jeep.

When we finally exited the national park and reached the plateau, we passed a beautiful western town situated on a deep blue lake. He referred to the range of mountains we saw on the horizon as the "Mummy Range." The description seemed appropriate to the silence and grandeur of the place.

We left Grand Lake and passed through Hot Sulfur Springs before arriving at the outskirts of Kremmling just before noon. We had already stopped in the park to eat a late breakfast of bean sandwiches and Vienna sausages.

Kremmling is a small ranching community on the western slope of Colorado. There is no way to get there except to cross over one of the several high mountain passes blocking its entry and protecting it from the urbanization of the Front Range.

It seemed almost as if we had not only driven a hundred miles but had lost a hundred years when we arrived at the ranch. Entering the gate, I watched fields of hay being mowed by horse-drawn mowers and rakes. Ranch hands were riding on sleds drawn by mules, and manpower was being used to stack hay twenty feet in the air and fifty feet long.

Freddie's Troublesome Ranch was on the outskirts of a dusty little town with low -rise buildings and little traffic. The ranch consisted of one hundred twenty thousand acres of leased federal land and privately owned property. Men on horseback tended to cattle on land with grass so sparse that it often took twenty acres to feed one cow. The best grass and the most water were usually found at the higher elevations.

We were going to visit the summer grazing lands of the ranch at the head waters of the Troublesome River. Frank told me that the cow camp was situated fifteen miles from the main house in a fertile valley just below timberline surrounded by snow-capped mountains at the ten-thousand-foot level.

Freddie was a lifelong friend who Frank had known as a child. He had retired from training and racing thoroughbred horses for others. He and his wife, Frances, had returned to their roots from southern California where they had spent most of their working lives.

He was a short man, not much over five feet tall in his high-heeled western boots, and she was "a tall drink of water." She had sharp features, and he had a cherubic face with rosy red cheeks housed beneath one of the largest Stetson hats I had ever seen.

They raised cattle in the high country during the summer and lived quietly on the plateau during the rest of the year. Their only family appeared to be the cow hands and kitchen help on the place.

We arrived about noon. Frances had prepared a ranch-style dinner for Frank and me and the several hands that were cutting and raking hay and tending to the horses and animals on the ranch. The house was very modest, but the dining room was large with a long table with serving platters piled high with food. There was a large pitcher of milk, still warm from the cow.

Ranch hands were dusty and grimy from the morning work, but they were polite and respectful addressing Mrs. Grimes as "Miss Frances." They removed their hats when they entered the room and cleaned their boots at the door and ended their sentences with "yes sir" and "yes ma'am." They acknowledged me but said very little during the meal.

The foreman, who was clearly in charge, spoke when asked a question but said little. He told us about the condition of the cow camp since winter and suggested one route over another because there were downed trees and debris on the trail. He said there was plenty of firewood but that the outhouse had blown over and needed some repair.

Freddie said that a neighboring rancher and his son had left before daylight on horseback with a couple of pack animals carrying supplies. Most of what we would need for eating and fishing would be at the camp. The only way into the camp and the only way out would be either by four-wheel drive vehicle or by horseback. Horseback was usually the quickest way in, because the trail was occasionally obstructed this time of year. The camp was a one-hundred-year-old homestead acquired from the descendants of the original settlers of the valley. It was built by a family early in the nineteenth century who had crossed the mountains with all of their worldly possessions and only a dream. I would not understand the difficulty of their journey until I arrived at the homestead and saw the culmination of a life spent there.

The Englishman looked the part. He wore a plaid, wool sports coat and gabardine slacks with a long–sleeved, button-down white shirt. I could only guess his age but thought him to be in his seventies. He was a distant relative of Frances. I learned that his wife had recently passed away and that he had been visiting the ranch in an effort to console himself and to enjoy the fresh, clean mountain air of Colorado. He had been living with his children in Los Angeles and felt the need for a break. He was tall, gaunt, and pale with thin grey hair and had a thin stark white mustache perched on his upper lip. He spoke with a very pronounced and correct tone. His language was impeccable. Every word seemed almost the beginning of a mantra enunciated clearly and almost poetic.

Frank, on the other hand, wore his usual payday overalls, sprinkled his speech with descriptive profanity, and graphic idioms. While he never deliberately spoke with vulgarity in the presence of a woman, there was an occasional slip up in the course of a strongly held opinion. He had strongly held opinions on most every subject. He wore brogans and a long-sleeved shirt and looked as if he was born to the mountains and the countryside. For the most part, his sentences were short and to the point. I never knew him to use words of more than a couple of syllables, and he rarely spent more than a few sentences on any subject matter. Although they were contemporaries in age, there was no comparison in style or demeanor.

The Englishman moved slowly and breathed heavily even at the lower altitudes. He spoke very deliberately and painted a picture by word and syntax. Frank, by comparison, moved very quickly and his action and his reaction to events was always quick, forceful, and to the point. He wasn't wordy and rarely repeated himself. He seemed to be in charge and know what to do in every circumstance. He could not be intimidated, yet he did not intimidate. He merely spoke plainly and clearly without subtlety.

I rode in the back of the jeep, and the two older men rode upfront. Frank drove. Driving was not an option for me on the narrow roads and animal trails that served as thoroughfare on the way to the cow camp. The canvas doors were still removed from the jeep and had been sitting on the floor in the back with the rest of the supplies: camping and fishing gear and the generator Frank had constructed to provide electricity at the camp. The jeep was full, and the contents were continuously shifting.

We crossed the highway at the entrance to the ranch, passed the haying crew, and crossed several cattle grates as we continued up the mountainside for the first mile or so. In the beginning it was easy going, the jeep was handling the roadway well, and I was relatively comfortable in the back.

We crossed several creeks with gravel beds and a small river before starting our ascent up the mountain in earnest. We entered the tree line and dodged deadfalls and boulders until the trees started to fade behind us. I frequently had to jump from the back of the jeep in order to remove obstacles from our path. We drove around and through copses of trees where the road was no longer navigable.

We were finally above timberline, and there were patches of snow on the ground and on the mountainside around us. The streams glistened with the reflective light of the afternoon sun, and the mountainside was covered in places with beautiful flowers of all colors. The sky was a stunning Columbine blue. Summer cumulus clouds floated over the valley below, and the surrounding mountains were snow covered. Mountain streams traced silver and gold and came in and out of view as the jeep lurched heavily to one side and then the other. At times the jeep seemed like a lonely sailboat on a starboard tack in a heavy wind. The boulders and deadfalls that had toppled and rolled down the mountain during the winter continued to hinder our forward movement.

As the day progressed and the shadows lengthened, Frank finally had me walk ahead of the jeep and remove obstacles and point to the less restricted track. Dust swirled and danced in a cloud behind us, and the sky seemed streaked with silver assaulted by a brown mist. Frank and the Englishman aged before my eyes as dust speckled their glasses and settled on their faces. The jeep was no longer green but brown with a light coating of dust.

While I rode I held on with both hands and pressed my legs against the side of the jeep. The craggy mountain range on the horizon glistened with the reflected light from the snow, and the streams descending the far mountainside seemed like slivers of broken glass attacking the lake below.

Frank pointed out elk wallows, gave names to the many mountain flowers, and identified the distant mountain ranges by name. I heard him speak reassuringly to his passenger and told him that he had made this passage many times before.

The Englishman was clearly agitated and seemed to be breathing more heavily than when we left the ranch. The altitude was clearly affecting him, but he also seemed to be frightened. Frank said, "We'll be there soon. We've only a mile or so to go, and most of it's downhill." I continued to hold onto the side of the small truck bed mounted on the back of the jeep while being jostled between the camping supplies, canned goods, and shopping bags full of clothing. I found a way to wedge myself between the camping gear, fishing poles, and bags that eased my ride.

Suddenly, the jeep pitched forward, and the engine raced. All four wheels were spinning and throwing mud, small rocks, and water the consistency of tar several feet in the air behind us. We were stuck. We had lost all forward movement, and the tires were just spinning as we settled deeper into a bog. None of the previous crossings had stopped us, but now we were dead in our tracks.

Several cow elk and their calves crossed the road nonchalantly a few yards ahead of us as if we offered no threat. It seemed that they knew we were stuck, and they were amused. They were the first elk I had seen on the mountain all day. Frank raced the engine again and muttered a few obscenities under his breath before he said, "Better get out, boy. We are stuck up to our axles."

Get out, I thought, get out to where? There was a sea of mud stretching about twenty feet in every direction. *What could I do,* I wondered. We were above the timberline, and I figured the closest wrecker would be in Kremmling, twenty-five miles away.

Frank turned off the ignition, and I heard his passenger say breathlessly, "I can't help push. I am not really that strong, you know, and this altitude has taken virtually all of my strength." His voice was becoming shrill as he admitted his fear to Frank. "What are we going to do?" he asked. "How are we going to get help? Do you think anyone is at the cow camp? I can't walk that far."

Frank tried to reassure him.

"I know, but I had a heart attack about a year ago, and I'm just not that strong." He told us it was his third heart attack, and he didn't have the strength of a kitten. "I knew I shouldn't have come along; I am just a hindrance. My daughter told me I was an old fool. She said this could be dangerous. What can I do but sit here like a damn bump on a log. It is hell getting old."

Frank continued to try and reassure him and said again, "Better get out, boy. Time to go to work."

I heard the Englishman say, "I just shouldn't have come; this has been a dream. I don't want it to become a nightmare."

The afternoon shadows began to lengthen, and the air cooled. Frank was already out in front of the jeep by the time I pulled back the canvas and jumped down into the mud. I could see that there had been no way to get around the bog. It was clear that frontal assault was the only answer. I wondered how we would get out. I tried to move toward dry land and felt the mud suck the tennis shoe off of my right foot. Reaching to save my shoe caused me to fall with my right arm fully extended. I was reminded of Brer Rabbit in the childhood story of "Uncle Remus."

The mud had me in its grip, and Frank was laughing. This caused the old Englishman to smile, and the tension seemed to break.

"We'll get her out," Frank said. "When you grow tired of playin in that mud, get that pick and shovel mounted on the side of the truck box, and let's dig us a hole. Get that block and tackle out of the back of the jeep."

"What's a block and tackle?" I asked.

"It is that hickey with a couple of wooden pulleys and some rope wound about it that you been sittin on since we left the ranch. If it were a snake, it would have bit you. Look just behind the generator at that pile of rope—that's it—plain as the nose on your face. Get it out here, and let's get to work; ain't no sense in jawin 'cause it will be dark before we know it. Dark comes quick in the high country. It especially comes quick when a fella ain't in no hurry for it."

I climbed back into the jeep, removed the block and tackle and pick and shovel from their mounting on the side of the jeep. I had never noticed them mounted there before. By the time I jumped out of the jeep a second time, I was covered in dark sludge. I had a dark streak down the side of my face where I had swatted at a deer fly with the back of my hand. My Levi's were crusted with mud, and I had fallen a second time with my left arm, and it, too, was coated with mud up to my armpit.

The floor of the bog was a couple of feet deep. Frank had a grin on his face a mile wide, but I didn't see the humor in the situation. By this time the old Englishman thought my being covered in mud amusing, and the atmosphere had changed. He, too, had a smile on his face. "Dig me a hole right about here," Frank said pointing to a spot in the center of the trail.

I started digging. The ground was rocky in places but soft in others. After I had dug a foot or two, the first hole was obstructed by a stone, so I moved a couple of feet from the original spot and started digging again. This time the digging was easy. I was soon reaching into the post hole at arm's length removing dirt and small stones.

Using the old army trenching tool, I soon excavated a hole four or five feet deep with a circumference of about eighteen inches. "That ought to do her!" Frank exclaimed. "Put that shovel down, and go find us a deadfall. We need one about this big around," he said while using his hands to demonstrate the circumference, "and about ten feet in length. I remember passing a pile of dead trees off the trail a few minutes before we got stuck. That will be a good place to start. We'll wait right here," he said with a grin, "but hurry; I don't want them bears to get you, plus them boys at the cow camp will have caught all the fish if we hang around here too damn long."

Frank was straddling a large boulder with an impish grin on his face, and the Englishman was dangling his legs outside of the jeep on the passenger side as I struck out to find a deadfall. I soon found several that would work; some seemed long enough but too brittle to support any weight. I finally settled on downed lodgepole pine that had broken in several pieces. The section I chose was about twelve feet long and easy enough to drag.

Frank had given me a small band saw to use, but it wasn't needed. I dragged the pine back to the jeep, and with Frank's help, placed it vertically in the hole. I packed the hole with gravel and soil.

It took about an hour to find and retrieve the pole and fill the hole before we were ready to try and move the jeep. We gathered stones and brush that we placed in front of and under the four tires. By this time I was covered in mud.

Frank tied a rope to the front of the jeep and attached the block and tackle to a loop he had created. He started the jeep and asked the Englishman if he knew how to operate a stick shift. "Oh yes," he said as he moved to the driver's seat in order to operate the clutch and shift the gears while Frank and I pulled with all we had. I secured the rope around my waist, and Frank threw me a pair of gloves.

"Put her in gear, and give her a little gas. Mash that foot feed." He shouted over the engine noise for the driver to take her slow and said, "As soon as them wheels catch, we will be off to the races."

No sooner had he spoken than the jeep began moving forward slowly. Once the wheels touched solid dry ground, we knew the jeep was free. The Englishman's face lit up, and he exclaimed over the engine noise, "Jolly good! I thought we were buggered for a moment or two."

The late afternoon shadows continued to lengthen as we started down the mountain on our last leg of the trip. Two predator birds circled high over the jeep taking advantage of the afternoon thermals, and a cool breeze crossed the mountain and through the doors.

We entered the tree line again and crossed another rocky-bottomed stream. The last vestiges of sunlight streamed through the trees as we made our way down the mountainside. It seemed almost an afterthought as we crested a small rise, and the trees parted, revealing something out of a dime novel.

Below us in the center of a beautiful valley was a building constructed of logs with a tin roof about sixty feet in length. The main building was surrounded by smaller buildings in varying states of collapse and decay. There were two horses and a couple of pack mules grazing unfettered close by.

"That's her," Frank said, "that's the cow camp, boy! Ain't she a beaut? Looks like old Jim and his boy are already here. That's their horses yonder. Let's get this jeep unloaded, and start lookin for somethin to eat. Them fish don't wait around much. We will get up early in the mornin to outwit em." I noticed the Englishman grinning from ear to ear.

Jim Logan and his son, Mathew, had just finished chopping wood behind the long log house. A small creek separated them from the barn and the pole corral. There was an outhouse leaning precipitously to the left with its open door dangling from a leather hinge. The door had jammed in the tall grass that had grown up around the small building and seemed to be preventing the entire structure from collapsing.

Jim, the father, was a heavily built man of medium height with short, cropped hair and a three-day beard. It looked as if he had shaved part of his face since his mustache was full and droopy, and his beard was lighter on his cheeks. He looked intimidating in his Levi's, rolled-up shirt sleeves, and bulging forearms. He caused me to think of the outlaws I had seen in the Saturday afternoon matinees.

His son was about my age with a heavier build, a cow lick, and dirty blond hair with a tinge of red. His face swarmed with freckles. He wore leather chaps over his blue jeans and western boots, a belt buckle the size of a small saucer, and the tail of his belt hanging down his front. He was shirtless, and his deeply tanned face faded to a milk-white chest just below the ring around his neck. He obviously had not enjoyed the Florida sun the way I had.

My complexion was tan, dark tan, due to the black Irish influence on my father's side of the family and the long hours I spent outside in the sun.

Matthew and his father had cut and stacked a cord or more of wood. There was a large two-man saw lying on the ground next to pine poles forming an X that held a horizontal tree limb. Frank referred to it as a "man killer." There was a stack of pine poles adjacent to the stack of wood.

They had sawed several larger poles into small sections, so they could split them with an axe. "Gotta have a lot of wood to fry up all of the fish we are going to catch," the man said as he stood there hatless with a smile and hand extended to Frank. I noticed his face was deeply crinkled around his eyes, and his forehead was as white as a baby's rear.

Two crumpled and sweat-stained cowboy hats lay on the ground beside the wood pile, and a denim shirt hung from the sawhorse. Frank turned to me and said, "Say hello to Jim Logan and his boy."

"Hi," I said.

"These two are the hardest workin owl hoots on the western slope," he said. "I been knowin Jim since he was his boy's age. Thought you might want someone your age to fish with while we were here, but first, grab yourself an armload of that firewood, and get it up to the house."

The boy stuck out his right hand and introduced himself, "I'm Mathew. Glad to meet you."

I quickly shook hands with Matthew and his father and picked up an armload of wood to take into the house. Frank held the rear door open as I entered. The inside of the door was painted pink with the handwritten words inscribed, "titty pink." There was a large pot-bellied stove in the middle of an open room and a wooden box filled with wood. I added my contribution to the box and looked around.

A large table extended the width of the house on one side, and an overstuffed couch and chair lined the other wall. There were about a half dozen straight-back chairs scattered around the room, a washtub on a counter under the window that served as a sink, and a large cook stove. Kerosene lamps were scattered around the room, and one was positioned in the center of the table while another hung from a ceiling joist.

The floors were wide wooden boards with what appeared to be hand-woven rugs at the door openings and other strategic locations. On one wall was a standup piano with a lever-action rifle leaning against it. The walls were all chinked log, and the ceiling was open and dark from the years of stove smoke.

Two large bedrooms were situated on each end of the house. The room Matthew and I would share had several bunks and a large double bed deep in quilts and covers. There were no sheets, only blankets and old quilts. The bunks were piled high with olive green army blankets, and there were large stones at the foot of the bed wrapped in yellowed newspaper. Frank explained that they were used in the winter to heat the foot of the bed. They were heated on the cook stove and placed near the feet of the sleeper in the harshest of winter.

"Snow can be over the roof in a bad winter," Frank said. "A fella had to literally dig his way out to feed the animals. Only way to the crapper is to dig a path."

I had noticed there were some strange looking bowls and pitchers in the bedroom that I didn't think were used for drinking.

"The people who homesteaded this place in the middle of the last century come in on horseback and wagon. The woman of the house taught the children, and they growed or raised everthin they needed to survive," Frank said. "They were a hardy bunch. They would be lucky to get to town a few times a year. The Missus taught the children their lesson's and they all worked the ranch. She played the piano and taught her girls to play. There weren't no radio or TV up here, so they had to amuse themselves by readin and singin around the piano. The fact they were able to drag that old piano over them mountains surprised the hell out of me. I have a lot of respect for them people. They, and people like them, are what the origins of this country are all about. They were tough, no nonsense, hard-workin folks that don't take no for an answer. Word is the original family consisted of the father and mother and seven children. All the children were born in this house. A couple of them died here too. Freddie told me that the father stayed up in these mountains into his nineties, even after his wife died and the children left for other parts. Word is he died in a big snow slide while tendin to his cattle one winter. He weren't found 'til spring. There were cows all over this valley for a while till they were rounded up.

"Them were tough folks in those days. There weren't no roads or telephones or hospitals close by. The only doctor was in town, and if the woman was to have a baby, one of her neighbors would come up to help with the birthin. Lots of them Janes died in childbirth."

I had grown up in a city on a bus line. Although we only had one TV channel, my mother had purchased our first big Emerson console a few years before. We had always had a radio to listen to at night and a grocery store somewhere close by, but most importantly the bathroom was down the hall. I could not imagine having to dig my way out of the house in the winter, raise my own food, and not buy my jeans at J.C Penney. I think what struck me most was the piano. I had never wanted something so badly that I would have considered making such an effort. What amazing people these were. I wondered where the children had gone and how their lives and their children's lives had changed since leaving this valley.

I awoke in a cocoon of blankets to the smell of bacon cooking. I could make out the deep guttural voice of Matthew's father and the high nasal tone of the Englishman. The room was pitch black. There were no windows, and the only ambient light came from a small seam of light pushing under and through the cracks in the door.

What time is it, I wondered. I had slept in my jeans, but the room was cold after the warm bed. I sure did not remember a time like this in Florida, even in the middle of winter. I would find myself opening the kitchen stove to heat my backside on the coldest days, but they were nothing like this.

As my eyes became accustomed to the dark, I could make out Mathew's form huddled in the blankets in the bunk against the wall. "Are you awake?" I asked.

He muttered something as I heard his feet hit the floor. "Ohhhhh, good thing I have my wool socks," he said sharply, "this floor is cold."

I wasn't prepared. I was still wearing my Florida clothing: thin summer socks and a pull-over shirt. I now had an old sweater that Frank had discarded. It was much too big, but I was glad to have it this morning. The old bomber jacket that Wild Bill gave me came in handy, too. I really wasn't prepared for the cold mountain nights.

The days were warm, but the nights were brutal. I had arrived in Colorado with three pairs of denim jeans, a similar number of short-sleeved open shirts, some light pullovers, socks and underwear, and a dungaree jacket. I had only one pair of shoes, sneakers, and could only expect to replace my allotment at the beginning of each school year. I did have a pair of penny loafers, but I had left them in Miami. They were my favorite footwear.

Mathew and I entered the living area of the house where Frank was cooking bacon and venison sausage in a cast-iron pan on the wood stove while drinking a mug of black coffee. Frank had set a half bottle of creamy milk outside the night before and asked me to bring it in so that Mathew and I could have some with our breakfast. I had learned to drink coffee early with a friend, so I asked for coffee. He seemed surprised since this was the first time he had seen me drink coffee. My first experience with coffee was awful, but I had grown to like it. I felt so "adult."

Mathew joined me at the table, and we waited while the eggs cooked. The Englishman, Trevor, I believe was his first name, was explaining the British love of fox hunting to Mathew's father. "The little devils can outwit the best of us," he said. "It is more of a social event than a roundup like you American chaps have. It really isn't hunting after the first experience," he said jokingly, "after that it is revenge." I had heard that expression before.

I was beginning to feel more comfortable with Mathew's father. Not unlike Frank, he appeared gruff but was really thoughtful and treated both Mathew and me with courtesy and respect. I could tell that Matt loved and admired his father deeply and always said "yes sir" and "no sir" when he was asked a question by any adult. He never seemed to hesitate when asked to perform a task. Mathew's dad laughed when he told us that he and Frank had a job for us after breakfast.

"Before you boys head out to the beaver dams, someone needs to dig a new hole for the crapper. Me and Frank here have elected you."

The pit under the outhouse was nearly full and that needed to be remedied. "This here would be a good time for you boys to dig a new hole, fill the old one, and move that crapper. Don't think we need to be using it in the condition it is in."

Matthew and I fed the horses and mules. We worked together and dug a new hole for the latrine. The ground was wet and soft, so it did not take long. We filled the old hole with the dirt from the new and pushed the outhouse end over end until it was aligned over the new hole. We chinked it with river sand and stone and found an old piece of leather to repair the missing hinge. We laughed about the "crappy" day we were having and finished up about noon.

Frank outfitted me with a creel, an old fly rod, and some waders patched with bicycle patches, and Mathew and I headed up the river to the beaver dams. The open meadow glistened with moisture, and the ground was soft and easy to hike. Elk and deer had made paths through the meadow and along the riverbed, and the crossings were shallow and rock bottomed.

Occasionally, we would break through the tall grass and brush to throw out a line. I caught a rainbow trout within minutes. Fish were attracted to anything shiny. By the time we reached the beaver dams, we had already caught and released a half dozen of the smaller trout. I caught and released more than twenty in the first couple of hours. It was amazing. I had never caught so many fish so easily in my life. It was almost as if we were fishing at a trout farm.

Mathew and I lay back in the tall grass and talked about ourselves and our lives. I told him how I had met Frank and how I had ridden the bus for days to get to Colorado. I told him about Jimmy and his mother and how Buster and I had been worked into the ground by a couple of Mexican girls the week before. We laughed and told a few of the only off-color jokes we knew.

He said he had rarely been out of the county. He and his father would attend the Denver stock show once a year, but his knowledge of the world was limited primarily to ranching and western Colorado. He loved to hunt and fish, and he and his father had killed an elk every year. He laughed, though, because they could kill an elk in their backyard virtually year round. The damn things had eaten his mother's garden, and it had to be fenced. He looked forward to bagging a big-horn sheep this fall and told of his dad killing a mountain lion when he was his age. He loved to work cattle with his dad and hoped to own a ranch of his own some day or take over for his father. He had never seen the ocean, never ridden a motorcycle, or worked anywhere other than on the family ranch. He didn't particularly care for school and thought it a waste of time. His dad didn't encourage him. He liked girls but had little time for them. His cutting horse, Maverick, was his best friend, and other than his dad, he had an older sister who had already married and left home. She was not a big part of his life, because she had moved to Grand Junction and had two children of her own.

We were up early every day and fished until we were tired of fish and then he let me ride Maverick while he rode his father's horse. We raced across the meadow and high grass bareback and threw off our clothes and jumped into the freezing river when the afternoon sun was at its highest. We sat silently along the riverbank and watched quietly as a bull elk and three cows crossed ahead of us. A coyote watched from the edge of the meadow, made a shrill sound, and then turned and headed back into the brush as if he knew better than tangling with the elk. We could hear the sound of beaver tails slapping the water as they worked on their dams and watched the predator birds circling for their dinner.

The sky was so blue and water so clear it was hard to describe. Rainbow trout lay on the bottom of the river silently or cavorted among the rocks and boulders as we watched from the riverbank.

Matt wanted to know more about my friend Jimmy's mother and asked several times if she really was a stripper. "Have you seen her without her clothes?" he wanted to know. "What did her tits look like? Were they big?" he asked. He had seen a picture once of a naked woman. "Her bush showed and everything," he said.

I embellished facts a little and told him about Buster and I inviting a couple of girls over when my mother was gone one weekend and going all the way. It was a lie, but it sounded good. I don't think he believed me, but the girls did come over so it wasn't difficult to stretch the truth a little. Buster had taken Jenny into my bedroom, and I had taken a girl named Cathy to the middle bedroom. I got nowhere. "Were there really pictures of Jimmy's mother around the house without her clothes?" he asked again. "I don't think I could take my clothes off in front of a girl," he said.

It was a fun week. We ate fish with every meal. We rode bareback until my butt was sore and arm wrestled until our arms were shaky. Mathew could mount Maverick by running from the rear, placing both hands on his hind quarters, and leaping on his back. As soon as he mounted, he would race across the meadow holding only the horse's mane. He called it a "flying mount."

Every time I tried it, I would hit the ground with a thud and roll into a ball, laughing. It was a wonder that I didn't break my neck. We would both laugh ourselves senseless.

I had thought of myself as a good horseman until I met Mathew. I didn't hold a candle to him. He worked a cow while I watched. He and the horse seemed to anticipate the cow's every move. If the cow moved one way, they were there. If it turned another way, they were there. The cow finally gave up and returned to the herd at the far end of the meadow at a run. I had never seen anything like it.

Mathew and I had become friends and promised to write once I got home. He hoped out loud that Frank would invite me back next summer and that perhaps I could spend a little time on his parents' ranch.

Our week together seemed to be over too quickly. We said our good-byes and loaded the jeep. He and his father were going to move the cattle to another meadow, so the grass would not be over grazed. Mathew was excited. He rode with the skill of the best cowboy and wanted more than anything in the world to please his father. I watched him and his dad disappear as the jeep left the meadow and entered the trees. They both waved and turned toward the house. We stopped at the ranch and said our good-byes to Freddie and Frances. I shook hands with the Englishman and he wished me well on my bus trip home. He complimented Frank on his ability to get the jeep out of the bog and told Freddie he would never worry about riding with Frank in the backcountry again. Frank gave Frances about fifty freshly cleaned fish, and we left.

The ride over the pass was uneventful. We stopped and had an early dinner in a diner just outside of the park on the eastern side of the mountains. Frank commented that if I came back next summer, we should build a wagon to haul tourists around town. He thought it a good way for me to make a little extra money. We passed the imposing Victorian-style Stanley Hotel, built in the early part of the century and perched on the side of the mountain surrounded by huge rocks and boulders.

I daydreamed about someday going inside and staying in one of the rooms. The hotel had been built by the inventor of the Stanley Steamer, an automobile that operated on steam which was far ahead of its time. Frank remembered that Mr. Stanley had chosen the Estes Park Valley because his doctors had told him the high mountain air would lessen the effects of his consumption. He had come from somewhere back East after inventing the Stanley Steamer and built the storied hotel and a beautiful private home overlooking the valley.

We stopped and began unloading the jeep just outside the basement door. Lillie came from the house. Her face was dark, and her mouth was turned down at the corners. I had never seen such an expression. It was clear that something was seriously wrong. She looked at me furtively and then said quietly, "The boy was killed today."

What boy? I thought. I was not aware of any boys other than myself.

"Mathew."

As she continued to speak, my eyes widened and my mouth fell open as I tried to comprehend what Lillie had just said.

"Frances called just a few minutes ago and told me that Jim Logan's boy rode his horse into a big patch of brush just after you and Frank left the cow camp. He was trying to drive a cow out from along the river. The brush was thick, and it had some sharp branches hidden in the center of it. A branch pierced his heart. Jim thinks he bled to death almost immediately, because by the time he got to him from across the herd, the boy had passed. They have already brought the body down. It was one of those horrible freak things, chance in a million. Jim saw the horse run out of the brush back toward the house and knew something was wrong. Freddie just wanted you to know.

"They are just going to have a family thing so no point in go-ing back," she said. "He was a good boy, they say, worked like a man and very respectful. Just too bad!" She turned and went back in the house. Frank and I kept unloading the jeep. He looked at me solemnly and said, "Too bad, it's a damn shame."

After the house was settled, and as I lay in my bed that night, I thought about Mathew. I thought about the pain his family must be feeling. I thought about the soldier I had met on the bus and the Negro woman and her daughter who had sat next to me that hot night in Louisiana. I thought of the man on the Denver street, Clay Wells and his journey from North Carolina, and the Mexican girls and their little brother picking the cherry trees clean. I thought about the Englishman and the fear I saw on his face when we were stuck in the bog. Was I dreaming all of this: the bus ride, Frank, the beautiful fresh mountain valley? The summer had seemed so surreal. My living breathing friend was now only a memory.

I thought of how I had not known him for fourteen years and how he had burst into my life much like a tornado in the afternoon sky. I could still see his sea of freckles, tremendous smile, and hear his infectious laugh. I could hear the noises the animals made as we lay in the grass watching the clouds move across the sky. I could see the face of a first cousin I had lost to a drowning just a few years before. One moment he was here and with us, the next he was gone.

I thought about a classmate who lived down the street who had fallen from a storage building and died, and another who had hanged himself in his parents' garage. I thought of Frank's words, "Too bad." *Too bad, that's all, too bad,* I thought. I guess he felt there was not much else to say.

Strangely, I didn't cry. I don't know why. I had always cried easily; my emotions had always been close to the surface, except for that day. I guess it just did not seem real. It seemed only an instant before I heard banging on the basement door and the words: "Breakfast is ready; better get up here before I screw your plate upside down to the table." Frank never said another word about Mathew's death.

CHAPTER TWENTY-THREE

The next few weeks passed quickly. Frank and Lillie went to the dog races in Denver several nights a week, often not returning until the early hours of the morning. My fear of the dark had not diminished but the humiliation of his teasing kept me from locking the basement door every night. When I did he would always be up no later than six thirty banging on the door and asking if I thought the bears were going to get me.

Every morning we would have a hardy breakfast, and I would toss the remains to the "turkeys" and chickens. Saturdays were pancake days, and Sundays always meant waffles. The waffle iron would be dripping with batter, and a platter in the center of the table would always be piled high when I arrived. There would be bacon and sausage every morning along with country fried eggs and so many pieces of toast that I thought the toaster might melt down. I had gained about ten pounds by the middle of the summer.

Breakfast at home had been a Milky Way bar at Jim's store and a Coke. My mother's ritual was to stop at the liquor store down the street every night after work and replenish her bottle of ninety-nine-cent wine. After one glass of wine, her personality would change: her voice sharpened and her words were acerbic. She didn't seem like the same person.

"I am not your servant," she would say after a few glasses of wine. "Get it yourself." She rarely cooked but when she did, she did so with a flourish.

There would be spaghetti sauce all over the stove, crusted cooking utensils piled in the sink, and unfinished plates and glasses on the table. It was my job to clean up. On other occasions I would just disappear until she fell asleep.

Often the doors would be locked by the time I returned, and I would sleep in the front seat of the car. I would awaken in the morning, and the car would be covered with the morning dew, and there would be lines and ridges in my face from the fabric of the seat. I was just tall enough to stretch across the seat from door to door.

Frank would always find something for me to do before we headed to town. I would wash one of the cars or trucks—even if it was not dirty—move rocks from one place to another, cut brush, or mow the grass. I would pick choke cherries and apples for Lillie and paint anything she thought needed painting. We seemed to always have a load of tree limbs or brush to take to Wild Bill.

We left for town just in time to arrive for lunch. I drove, and Frank would point out people or places from his past or of historical interest. He generally did all of the talking, and I listened. He was not one to chatter idly, however, and always seemed to have a moral or ethical point of view. Right and wrong seemed very important to him. He didn't like phonies and was quick to say so. He was disdainful of most preachers and although he acknowledged that many who attended church were good people, he felt he did not need organized religion to "institutionalize his virtue." He commented on how often people would sit through a sermon on Sunday morning and "run you down in the parking lot" to get home.

He was a very practical and plain-spoken man. He had no agenda and did not hide his feelings or thoughts. If he liked what someone did, he told him. If he didn't like what they did, he told them. We passed a friend's business, and he commented, "Get yourself a hasher," he would say. "Them hashers are accustomed to pleasin the customer. They understand hard work and how to get the job done. Get yourself one like that Jane in the pool hall or old Skagle's wife. They work harder than two men and ain't that hard to look at either. They don't always have to be a looker, just sturdy; them pretty ones are not always the best ones. Some of them think they are doin a fella a favor. If you don't keep your eye on some of them, you'll find another fella sneakin up on you. A fella needs a helpmate; someone who isn't afraid to muss her hair or break a nail.

"Most of them Janes just expect a man to be honest. They don't expect a fella to be layin out at night and hangin around them honky-tonks. Those fellas find out pretty soon that while they are layin out, their wives have slipped off with another man.

"Chili married a looker when he got out of the Navy. Hell, they was a fightin before the reception was over. Can't say he was perfect, but I'm sayin don't jump into marriage until you know all about the gal. Marriage is a commitment. A Jane's gotta be treated with respect. Treat em like you want to be treated, and you will be surprised how good things can be. If a fella was to always be courtin, he would never be surprised."

We would stop at the city dump several times a week just to talk to Wild Bill. He would always flash a toothless grin and usually spin a yarn. "Did I tell you about the lawyer and the Doberman?" he would say. Frank would stuff a few dollars in his shirt pocket if we had a load to dump or occasionally buy a pint of whiskey and put it on the front seat of his truck. "Don't cost much to be nice to people. Some will take advantage, but most won't."

We often saw Bill's son working down in the dump picking out five-quart oil cans or scavenging for copper wire.

"That copper will bring eighty cents a pound from the junk man." He had given me the old bomber jacket before we went to Freddie's' and said it might be something I could use. "It's kind of an antique," he said. "The man that wore that must have been a little fella."

We would leave and head down First Street to the shop. I always had the special. The special never changed, and Art was always standing behind the bar with his white apron while his wife would continue to scurry between customers and the kitchen.

There were no other employees that I could see, yet I had never been there at night. I don't know who washed up the dishes and swept up the place, but if I had to guess, I would guess it was Art and his wife. Frank pointed to them and said, "Those two are what America is all about. A fella can work as little or as hard as he wants. Those people come here from Russia about thirty years ago with nothin. Hell, they speak the language better than I do and work six days a week. They open the place before dawn and close every night after ten. I don't know how they do it."

We often went back to the shop after dinner, and Chili would have me wash cars or run for parts on the shop bicycle. I would see Clay Wells walking the streets occasionally, and if he saw me, he would ask, "How's my fellow Tar Heel doing today? Frank keeping you busy?"

We stopped by the feedlot every afternoon, and I tossed a few flakes of hay to the burros. "Maybe if you come back next summer, we can hitch them jackasses to a wagon, and you can take them tourists for rides like we talked about the other day." That was the first time he had even suggested I would be invited back. There was an old motorcycle sidecar covered with dust next to the stacks of hay in the loft. "Me and old Foote won many a race in that rig," he said. "Sometimes old Foote's face would be so close to the track that it would almost shave him. We turned up some speeds on them dirt tracks. Sometimes it would be like a carnival, them Janes would be followin the riders around, and the bleachers would be full of folks yellin at the top of their lungs. The only sounds we could hear was the roar of them machines. One time I put one of them machines down and found myself passin it up on my backside. It was a fun time. Most of the races took place down at the fairgrounds, but occasionally, we would race on them board tracks in Denver. I liked the dirt tracks better 'cause they didn't get as slick from the oil and rubber from the tires. Old Lester, he liked the dirt tracks too. We would just fly," he said with a faraway look in his eye.

CHAPTER TWENTY-FOUR

It wasn't yet dark, but it wouldn't be long. Frank and Lillie had gone to Denver to the dog races, and I was bored. I liked to fish, but *it probably isn't a good idea to wade in the river with no one else around.*

The river was rushing and up to its banks due to a recent rain. I had felt the strength of the water a couple of times before, and it was running faster and higher that night than I had ever seen it run before. Frank had warned me to fish in the river with caution. He had known people to be swept away in an instant. "A fella could drown before he knew what hit him," he said.

Many late afternoons I would ride the Cushman, and occasionally, the antique Harley Davidson into the old canyon, but although Frank had never said it, I sensed that he preferred that I not ride when he was not on the place. I knew Fred would be happy because he would no longer have to contend with all of the dust the scooter raised.

The kids attending the summer camp on the hill were too young, and I wasn't old enough to hang around the Canyon Inn. I thought about the two girls who worked in the café near the entrance to the canyon. *Now that's an idea,* I thought. *At the very least, I could get a cup of coffee and talk to the woman who owned the place. She was always welcoming.*

The shadows were lengthening, and the air was cooling fast. I crossed the footbridge and tossed a few flakes of hay to the horses. Tuffy kicked up his heels and farted. I was reminded of one of Frank's frequent expressions: "Any old horse could fart in the morning, but it took a damn good horse to fart at night." I did not quite understand what he meant, because I never had any trouble farting at night.

The dirt road leading away from the small barn ran parallel to the state highway and was a safer way to hike down the canyon entrance in the shadows.

I passed by Cliff's house, Frank's older brother's place, past a few cottages that were weekenders' homes and the large two-story house on the river owned by Frank's nephew. He was a retired Army officer who I had only met once. The parking lot of the Canyon Inn was already starting to fill. I could hear loud voices combined with the twang of western music. Several men and women were seated at the bar, and one couple was already dancing a slow dance. Cigarette smoke was thick in the night air.

By the time I reached the highway, which was fifty yards from the café, it was dark. I had almost tripped over a porcupine crossing the road in no hurry. Two mule deer scampered across the highway lit by the headlights of an oncoming car.

The café was well lit, and the taller of the two girls was working that night. Both of the girls were entering their senior year in high school and lived for the summer in a small *I Love Lucy* trailer on the back of the property. The small café consisted of three tables for four, a built-in lunch counter with stools permanently bolted to the concrete floor, and the normal accoutrements for serving behind the counter-coffee urn, cooking surface, and a dispenser of soft drinks. It was empty when I entered. I would often sit on one of the stools and spin around in place while trying to keep up a conversation with the woman proprietor and whichever of the girls happened to be working that night.

Mrs. Watson owned the place and described herself as the "chief cook and bottle washer." Her husband worked in town as a tile setter and rarely got home until well after dark. I think the café was one way for her to fill up her time and keep from being lonely during her husband's long absences. He worked whenever he could and summer was a busy time. The couple did not appear to have any children and lived in a small building attached to the café.

I had met the husband one Sunday morning when Frank stopped in to discuss building a community firehouse sometime in the future. There had been a fire recently, and a cottage was destroyed by the time the volunteers got to the truck six miles up the road. Frank had located a truck he could donate to the community, but it needed a storage facility.

He seemed like a pleasant man but appeared much older than his wife. He was stooped and had a grey, stubble beard; and his hands had the coarseness of sandpaper. He wore Levi's, and his western belt supported his stomach much like the stays of a barrel.

While the girls were always friendly, they rarely paid much attention to me. The woman owner always kept my coffee cup full. I think they were all surprised that I drank coffee.

Mary Ann was working that night and seemed unusually attentive. Since no one was in the place, she sat next to me on the stool and spun one way while I spun the other. Something was different. During prior visits she was polite but rarely had much to say. She would sit at one of the tables when no one was in the café and write on a lined pad. That night she hummed as she moved around the café and started to clean up earlier than she had before, almost as if she was expecting me. She emptied the coffee pot and washed whatever dishes were in the sink. She filled several ketchup bottles from a large can behind the counter and refilled the napkin dispenser. She seemed to be watching the clock behind the counter and kept me engaged in conversation. I was delighted, because I knew Frank and Lillie would not be home until the early morning hours.

Suddenly, she casually asked me if I would like to go for a walk after closing. It surprised me at first, but I said, "Of course, I'd like that." Not recently having had company of anyone my age, I could not think of anything I would rather do. I did not know what else to say. She had never made such an offer in the past and had not paid very much attention to me. I had watched her leave a few minutes early on a couple of occasions and hurry to her trailer in order to change, so she could leave with her boyfriend at closing time. Evidently, he was not coming tonight. He drove an old black Ford that looked very similar to the car Wild Bill's son had careened around the city dump in a few weeks ago.

Mary Ann and I walked down the edge of the highway in darkness. The shoulder of the highway was rough and uneven, and the sound of the rushing water was soothing. The headlights of approaching cars projected our silhouettes onto the rock walls of the canyon. We stopped briefly and sat on a guardrail in the curve and listened to the sounds of the river.

Mary Ann wanted to talk. She told me her boyfriend had asked her to marry him on their last date. She asked me what I thought. I tried to evade the question. It did not seem to matter that I had not offered an opinion, because she kept talking. It was obvious she was uncertain about marriage but was working it out in her mind. She had accepted, she said, but I could tell by the change in the pitch of her voice that she was unsure. She needed someone, anyone I think, to listen to her. She thought I might be someone she could confide in. Someone who did not know her, her boyfriend, or her circumstances that would be objective, yet she never waited for my response. She didn't seem to notice that I had still not offered an opinion.

She had grown up on a farm east of town, she said, and had helped her brothers and sisters with farm chores since she was a child. She had cared for her infant sister when she was at home.

Her sister was the result of an unexpected late pregnancy that she thought might have resulted from one of the reconciliations her mother and stepfather had after their many fights.

She was afraid of her stepfather, not that he had ever struck her. He was gruff and demanding and seemed to hold her responsible for the many family disagreements. He told her she always took her mother's defense, and he was sick of it. She said she could not wait to get out of the house.

Her summer job was a pleasant respite from the bickering and the responsibility of her farm chores and the care of her siblings. Her older brother had left the farm early and worked construction in Denver and pledged never to come home.

She felt her stepfather resented her and that he harbored a deep-felt rage, because she was the child of another. Her natural father had been killed during the last fighting in Korea, and her memory of him was vague. Her mother always seemed to compare her dead husband with her current husband, and he would lash out, she said. They fought all of the time, and she felt as if she were in the middle. She wasn't sure her mother hadn't planned it that way. There never seemed to be enough money to pay bills, and the older children never lived up to her stepfather's expectations. "All of his attention was devoted to 'his children,'" she said.

Her younger siblings were always considered too young to work, yet she couldn't remember a time when she hadn't. "He drinks too much, and that is when the fighting always begins. He is a binge drinker and would go on a 'toot' for several days at a time." Her mother would argue, "You spend all the money on drink and your low-life friends." "It wasn't a very happy household," she said.

I told her my childhood had not certainly been perfect, and I was thankful Frank had come into my life. I didn't know if I would ever get married, I said, but I really had not thought about it much. There was a lot I wanted to do. I especially wanted to travel and learn something about the world.

Marriage did not seem like a happy event for her, but she didn't want to continue living at home. She said she, too, wanted to travel and had always wanted to move to California and live on the beach. She thought perhaps if she could raise enough money, she would go to a secretarial school or a teachers' college somewhere and teach school for awhile. She seemed to care deeply for her mother but felt that she was held captive by her bad marriage. Ironically, she saw marriage as a way out for her. We talked about the contradiction of her thinking and the absurdity of her jumping immediately into marriage. She laughed and took my hand. "Let's walk down to the pump station," she said. "We can sit behind it and avoid the car lights and talk."

While we walked she commented on how confusing life was. She really liked her boyfriend, but he certainly wasn't the man she had dreamed of. She didn't know whether or not she truly loved him. He had dropped out of the tenth grade and went to work in a local grain elevator and seemed very responsible, she said. His only interests other than her was hunting and working on his old car. She was seventeen, and he was almost nineteen. She had never had another serious boyfriend. She said she had had a few infatuations but had never more than kissed a boy before she met her current boyfriend.She said he was always pushing her to go further sexually, but so far she had been able to resist. Pregnancy seemed a big concern.

She asked me if I had ever had sex with a girl, "gone all the way," she said. I stammered a little and then said that I had been with several girls but no one special. The reality was that the only thing I knew about the female anatomy was the pictures I'd seen of Jimmy's mother and what I had discovered looking at the pictures in the *Crime Story* magazines that Melvin had hidden in Frank's basement. I had attempted some clumsy groping the weekend my mother was away. The girl was flat chested and clearly had no interest in my attempts. I told her how my friend Buster and I had some girls over one weekend, but I didn't finish the story. There was really nothing to finish.

She suggested she was cold and asked if I would put my arm around her. "Sure," I said. I would be happy to accommodate her. I shivered a little, but it wasn't because I was cold. She was a grown woman. She was seventeen and fully developed under her full skirt and light sweater.

We stepped over a small fence, and she led me to the back of a pump house on the concrete bridge that crossed the river. We were hidden from the lights of the cars. It seemed as if she had been here before. She pulled me to her and kissed my neck and then stuck her tongue in my mouth. I didn't know how I felt about that.

We were of similar height; she may have been an inch or two taller. She pulled me down to the concrete and moved my hands to her breast. "Unbutton my sweater," she said, "you can." By this time I was physically shaking, and my heart was racing. This seemed to only embolden her.

"Unbutton my sweater," she said again as she rolled on her side, arched her back, and moved my hand to the buttons up the back of the sweater. As I fumbled she helped me with the remaining buttons. She unsnapped her bra and let it fall free.

Oh my God, I thought. Her breasts were so soft. They felt like warm Jell-O, and her nipples were as hard as dried raisins. Buster and I had talked about walking barefoot on a sea of tits, but I never thought they would feel so good. She arched her back again and gathered her skirt above her waist and directed my other hand to her pubic mound. It was wiry and soft at the same time, and my youthful maleness was rigid and palpitating.

My thoughts were running together, and my breath was so short that I gasped. I really didn't know what was happening. It had happened so fast. We lay there for awhile, and I stroked the softness of her inner thighs and buried my face between her breasts. She kissed me and pressed her hand down hard on the front of my jeans. She put her tongue in my ear and kissed my neck.

Then she stiffened. As quickly as it began, it stopped. Her breathing slowed, and she arched her back again and pulled her panties back up under her skirt while rolling over on the concrete and connecting her bra. I don't know if I was disappointed or relieved. I was not sure what she had wanted to do next. I did not know what I wanted to do next. I did not know what to do next. It sure had not come naturally.

My pants were wet, and my heart was beating so fast that it was about to jump out of my chest. She sat up, pulled me up to a sitting position, and hugged me in a bear hug. She didn't say anything. We stood up, and the lights from a car projected our shadows on the canyon wall.

In the light I could see she had tears running down her cheeks. We held each other for a moment, and then she said, "I have to go home, back to the trailer; it's late. I have to work breakfast in the morning."

The small of my back ached, and while my breathing had slowed and my heart was not still racing, my voice cracked with every other word.

She held my hand and swept the hair that had fallen in her face with her other hand and quickened her pace. I walked along the road behind her with her hand extended back to me. While we walked the narrow edge of the road, she asked me over her shoulder if I would ever consider marrying her. Did I think she was pretty? What did I think about marriage? Did I want children and how many? "Where do you want to live?" she asked. "Colorado?"

She wanted to know if I had ever thought about going to college or joining the Army.

It was almost as if we had not spoken before and had not covered some of this ground earlier. I am not sure she was talking to me. It was as if she didn't expect an answer but was asking rhetorically, as if she wanted to be filled that night with information about a boy, a stranger, that didn't really matter and who she would probably never see again.

We lingered a few minutes in the darkness in front of the café, and the light from the clock inside cast a shadow on her face. Her tears had dried, but their tracks remained in the soft light. She turned toward the trailer and took a step in its direction without releasing my hand. I was a little off balance and stumbled toward her as she caught me and kissed me lightly on the cheek. She released my hand and walked toward her trailer. She looked back again and then entered the trailer and disappeared.

I walked down the highway, crossed through the Canyon Inn parking lot, and crossed the footbridge over the river. I heard sounds of the horses and saw them drinking from the river. It was moonless, and no cars had passed on the highway while I walked down the dirt road. I sat on the metal glider next to the river. The river continued to course past me, and the night breeze stiffened.

My thoughts were on Mary Ann and the suddenness of my experience. My emotions were raging; my chest was still tight. I could hear the anxious rustling of the peacocks in the trees and took in the night sounds. The birds seemed to be warning me of something. Suddenly, a light struck the top of the tree above me. It moved down the tree and grew so bright that I had to avert my eyes as it moved closer. A car had entered the gate and was moving slowly past Fred's house toward me. Its tires crunched in the gravel, and the lights from the windows in Fred's house glowed orange. I could hear the high pitched squeal Lillie's car's fan belt made as it decelerated and moved closer. The crunch of the tires grew louder and a peacock let out a piercing 'Help' Earlier, Frank had told me that Fred's wife of sixty years often read until the early hours of the morning. The car stopped next to me, and Frank leaned across the front seat and rolled down the window.

"What you doin boy?" he said quietly. "It is almost three in the mornin. Aren't you afraid them bears may get you out here in the dark?" He chuckled. "Better get in that bed; it will be mornin soon. This ain't Miami. We don't lay up in the bed around here. I gotta find us some barrels so we can build that bridge over Cedar Creek. Get on to bed."

I entered the dark basement, threw off my clothes, and slid under the blankets. I was comfortable and warm, but my senses were still overloaded with the experience behind the pump house. I could still feel the softness of her skin and the texture and silkiness of her pubic hair. My hands still held the faint scent of her femininity. I thought about how powerful the experience had been and how my body shook. *What did she think? Did she think I was just a child? What did she feel? I wondered if she had expected more.* I hadn't known what to do. It had all happened so suddenly. Why was *I so frightened?* I thought. Just before I fell asleep I realized that I had nothing to do with the night. I had had no control. She was in charge. The entire experience had been in her hands, and it had nothing to do with me. It wasn't real.

I saw Mary Ann a few more times in what remained of the summer, but she worked days primarily and left with her boyfriend in the late afternoon. Her roommate was nice, but I had no interest in her. I thought often about that night we were together and the pleasure I had experienced.

I visited the café a few more times before I left for Florida. She was always friendly and playful, but it was different. It was as if our encounter had never happened. She never mentioned that night or our time together. She never suggested again that we go for a walk or that I was anyone other than the kid from up the road. She looked different, less animated perhaps or only just more resolved.

Just before I left, I stopped in the café briefly, and she told me she thought I was a good guy and how nice it had been to get to know me. She wished me safe passage home and almost as an afterthought said, "Oh, by the way, did I tell you I have decided to quit school and get married this fall? My boyfriend has asked me to marry him. We have planned a fall wedding. Isn't that great?!" It was almost as if we had never spoken.

CHAPTER TWENTY-FIVE

Darkness came quickly to the mountains. While the temperature in town would often top ninety degrees in the middle of the day, there was rarely any humidity, and the heat would retreat once we entered the canyon and approached the cove. If there was even a slight breeze down the river canyon, there could be a five-degree difference in the temperature between the highway and the house. Often the temperature along the river in the cove would be ten degrees lower than it was in town during the middle of the day. I always slept under blankets, even in August. Temperatures many nights would be in the low sixties and rarely much over seventy degrees. I loved the pungent scent of pine comingled with the faint smell of alfalfa and dust rising from the roadbed when we entered the lane every afternoon. I understood why Frank had retired to the mountains. The pressure of the day seemed to melt away.

Frank could not understand my need to shower every day. He said I was going to fill up his septic tank. In Miami I slept under a single sheet with the windows open and a circulating fan at each end of the bed. Air conditioning was not common, and the house always had a dank, musty smell. Very few houses had air conditioning. Often it was too hot to sleep in mid July, and my bed clothes would be wet, and the night air would be saturated almost to the dew point. Automobiles would be covered with a morning sweat, and a trip through the grass would soak my tennis shoes. It wasn't difficult learning to cope with the Colorado summer climate.

Except for the rustling of the peacocks on their perches in the trees and the sound of the river as it coursed down the mountain, it was as quiet as a graveyard at the end of the lane. I didn't miss the bus noise, the sound of aircraft engines being run up, and the shriek of emergency vehicles in the night. Some nights in Miami, it was difficult to sleep, so Jimmy and I would roam the alleyway behind the apartments on my street in search of soda bottles to redeem. Occasionally, we would try and slip into the parties around the pool populated by the airline people living in the many apartments. On some nights we would see a police car cruising, and we would attract the attention of the cops and then run in separate directions. We had no routine and no discipline. Frank's routine never varied: we went to town, we came home, we ate and slept all night, and it began all over again every morning.

On our trips to town, Frank shared his homey philosophy with me. He spoke well of most people but the common denominator was hard work and thrift. If a man put on "airs" or denied his family, he was quick to have contempt. The worst was a man who abandoned his family or ran from his obligations. He was quick to praise the industrious and especially those who reached out to others, but if someone crossed him, lied to him, or was generally "reckless with the truth," he would never forget. He especially did not like the man who lived upstream from him. He said he and his family had made their fortune foreclosing on local farmers during the Depression while sitting in the first pew in church every Sunday. He loathed hypocrites. He had a concept of divinity that few people who had spent a lifetime in a church understood.

What he could do to help or reach out to others, however small, was his credo. He would give a basket of food to people down on their luck, pay a rent or utility bill quietly for someone, and if he shook a man's hand or gave his word, there was nothing that could change his position. He said, "If a man's word has no meanin, his very life has no meanin."

He didn't like politicians very much and would go out of his way to avoid the local ones he knew. Women were to be honored and appreciated for their contribution to the family and society in general, and he would say, "All I can say is they are different. They ain't better; they ain't worse. They are just different." He cautioned, "Don't be cynical just keep your eyes and ears open. Don't always be doing the talkin, and if a fella starts to braggin, start dividin what he says by two."

Some late afternoons I would ride the Cushman down the old canyon road, past Willie Papa's homesite and into the Electric Plant Park. I would sit quietly on the boulders and rocks lining the river and enjoy the cool breeze rising from the rush of water and wind following the river down the canyon. I was careful not to ride past Fred's house too often, because he would give me what Frank referred to as the "fish eye."

Other afternoons I would climb the mountain behind Frank's place and explore the open pit gold mine and its surroundings. When I climbed Pole Hill, I could see for miles in every direction. I sat on a rock on top that I discovered was inhabited by thousands of ladybugs. "Them bugs will bring you good luck in life," Frank said when I told him what I had found.

I had become a fair fly fisherman and often would catch a "mess" of fish, which I would clean and freeze for later meals. Nights were cool and the stars so ubiquitous that the horizon seemed like a sequin blanket. I knew it would not be long until I would begin my bus ride back to Miami. I was not homesick. I didn't want to think about the summer ending, and since we had not yet constructed the bridge across Cedar Creek, I felt I still had a reprieve.

We drove to eastern Colorado to visit one of Frank's dry land farms. The road was flat and straight and after about fifty miles, I could no longer see the mountains in the rearview mirror. *This could not possibly be Colorado*, I thought; it looked to me like pictures of the lunar surface. The highway shimmered in the mid-morning sun, and the horizon seemed to stretch forever. There were very few automobiles traveling in either direction, and tumbleweeds crossed the highway at regular intervals. Frank slumped in the passenger seat with his hat covering his eyes. Every once in awhile, he would look over at the speedometer and with a broad grin say, "You're inching her up a little, aren't you? Them patrolmen will pinch you."

We slept at the farm in a "doghouse" with two small cots, a wooden floor, and no other furniture except a potbellied stove in the center of the room. It was located a short walk from the tenant's house and was served by a "one holer;" that was what Frank called the outhouse we used behind the shack.

Frank snored like a freight train all night, while I covered my head with the pillow to try and get some sleep.

In the morning we 'pulled' a submersible water pump that had stopped working and repaired it; we loaded a truck with hay to be given to a neighbor, cleaned out a number of irrigation ditches, and restarted the flow of water to the fields.

We sat around after supper in the evening "shooting the bull" with the tenant and his wife. They did not own a television and retired right at dusk. "The five o'clock milking come early," the man said.

We attended the livestock sale and auction just about every Saturday and wandered through the adjacent flea market. Frank purchased several old bicycles and taught me how to repair them. In some instances we would start with four and resurrect three that I would sell at a small profit the next time we returned to the flea market.

"You need to be thinkin about your plans when you are grown, boy," he would say, "it won't be that long before you will be on your own." I did not realize how soon that would be. "Me," he said, "I never wanted to work for the other fella, but I never got a good education, so I had a little bit of a hindrance. I was always dreamin about fixin bicycles and motorcycles and never tended to my studies. I always had to noodle it out on my own if I wanted to fix somethin or find out about what the other guy knew. I never did take much interest in readin, but since Pinky Grimes been sending me those *Reader's Digest* books, I have been readin a lot lately. Times have changed, boy. Used to be a man could do well for himself without schoolin, but now the more schoolin you have, the better able a fella is to find a good job. While I am proud of what I have done, I want to encourage you to keep to the books. It will make a difference in your life, but don't be thinkin that you are too damn smart. The world is full of educated derelicts, and there are always those that are smarter than you. It ain't always what's in your head that's important; it is how you use your head. Good old common sense is the key to a successful life."

Every Saturday morning Frank's wife had an appointment at the beauty parlor. Frank called it a "hen party." "Blue hairs, all of them," he would say. That Saturday morning I fed the turkeys and chickens and performed all of the chores Frank had assigned me. I may even have moved some of the rocks I had moved earlier back to their original location. I backed Lillie's' car out of the garage and checked the oil and made sure all of the tires were inflated. I swept out the inside and washed the windows. The summer was coming to a close, and I wanted to do something special for her. The car wasn't really dirty, but I washed it anyway. Frank had never confirmed whether or not he was going to invite me back the following summer.

The Dodge truck was loaded with debris to take to the dump. Frank could never miss an opportunity to stop by and visit Wild Bill. He admired the dump man's industry and good humor. He made sure to remind me that "you cannot tell a fella by his clothing, his big automobile, or his fine talk." The measure of a man was found in his deeds.

We stopped by the dump for a few minutes and discarded the debris. Frank stuffed another couple of dollars in Bill's overalls pocket. As we turned left on First Street, Wild Bill's boy rounded the corner on two wheels and slid to a stop next to his dad. He was leaning against the car door, his hair covering his right eye, and there was a cigarette dangling from his mouth. The cloud of dust consumed the two as we headed up the street toward the center of town.

CHAPTER TWENTY-SIX

Saturday was our day to visit the livestock sale, but Frank said we needed to stop by his friend Rudy's farm that morning. Rudy and his wife lived on the outskirts of town in a small weather-beaten farmhouse that was grey in the morning light. We had met before, and he seemed to immediately like me. The house hadn't seen new paint in years; the yard was cluttered yet neat and well kept. Colorful flowers overwhelmed the small white picket-fenced yard. An old wheel barrow with a metal wheel lay on its side with a profusion of flowers seeming to scatter from it.

There were several old tractor seats mounted on tree stumps and a wooden swing hanging from a heavily barked tree. Someone had been working in the flowers, because a hoe and rake lay in the grass and a pair of fabric gloves was stuck between the pickets of the fence.

A small outbuilding housed an antique store. Frank called Rudy a "junk man." He loved to gather and sell antiques and memorabilia from the past. He had several old wall-mounted telephones hanging under the eaves of the building and an assortment of haying implements and horse collars with mirrors mounted in the center.

Rudy was standing in the doorway with a huge smile on his face when we pulled into the yard. "Women love to buy these old phones and horse collars," he said. "It is amazing sometimes what junk brings. Just about anything will sell if a fella is to hold it long enough. Hell, we used to haul this old harness and them collars to the dump, and now everone seems to want a set. That sure don't bother me none. Wish I had a thousand of em." Rudy was going to join us at the sale today.

"He hadn't farmed in years," he said, "scouting out and selling this junk is too much fun. A person will just about buy anything if it reminds him of his youth or something in his past. It is a fun business. Sure beats getting up before dawn every morning and milking."

His family was grown and farmed nearby. The only evidence of his past was an ancient goat and a black-and-brown spotted milk cow that was currently rubbing its neck on the barbed wire fence. "She hadn't given milk in years," he said.

"Old Bossy is sort of a member of the family." There were also about a half dozen chickens that had the run of the yard and the dirt road that passed in front of the house. "I keep that damn old goat on the place so I won't have to mow the yard. I named him 'Merciless,' because he will consume just about anything. Damndest critter I have ever seen. I'm not sure he won't eat a tin can and chew up the fence if I don't watch him. Don't be bending over either, cause he is a Billy and will butt you out of the county if you ain't careful. I gotta keep him out of the flowers if I know what's good for me."

Rudy was Frank's age, middle to late sixties, about five foot five in stature with dark eyes and a deeply tanned and weathered complexion. Like many farmers he wore bibbed overalls and a long-sleeved shirt even in the middle of the day. I had never seen him without his cap except when entering a building or when tipping it to a lady. The tan line across his forehead was stark, much like those I had seen on all of the working men I had met that summer.

Frank told me Rudy and his wife had come from Eastern Europe. They came to America with almost nothing but the clothes on their back and migrated with the work from the Midwest to Colorado. They had lived in what was now the antique store and what had also served as a barn in years past. There was no inside plumbing, and a pot bellied stove provided heat when they moved in. They had worked for years, Frank said, until they had saved enough to buy a small piece of ground of their own.

The farm had been owned by a former employer who had decided to retire to town and had sold the place to Rudy and his wife. When they acquired it, they also received the mineral rights. After years of farming and bare subsistence living, an oil company offered to lease the rights. Soon after they drilled the first oil well, it started producing enough oil to provide Rudy and his wife, Mary, with a small income. Frank said nothing had really changed. He discontinued farming and opened the "junk" store.

The house remained unpainted, Mary continued to cook and bake, and Rudy continued to go to the various sales around the state to buy merchandise for his store. They didn't travel, and they didn't eat out or change their dress. They didn't buy fancy cars or fine clothing.

Rudy continued to wear his old ill-fitting overalls and long-sleeved shirts, winter and summer. His cap, that he wore jauntily cocked a little sideways, looked as if it could use an oil change. Mary was no different. Every time I saw her, she had on a flowered dress that I expect she made herself and an apron with big pockets in the front. The pockets were always filled with cookies that she dispensed to just about anyone that wandered by. She loved to cook and bake and work in her garden.

Whenever Frank and I stopped at Rudy's, Mary would insist that we take home a paper sack full of vegetables, a bouquet of flowers, and a cake warm from the oven. She always admonished us, with a twinkle in her eye, to keep our hands off the cake. "It's for supper," she would say, "and there is plenty for Lillie too. I never seen such a scrawny-looking boy. This here cake and them cookies oughten to fatten you up."

Rudy said, "I found them barrels you been looking for Frank; they are them fifty-five-gallon jobs that will work perfect for that bridge you and the boy are going to build. That plant south of town has em, and they ain't sticky and don't smell bad. The wife of the manager stops in here occasionally to paw through my stuff and told me about them on her last visit. She tells me her husband will sell me all I need. I talked to him yesterday, and he said he would even load them up on a company truck and deliver them to your place. He is going to drop off fifty sometime middle of the week. That ought to get the boy started."

CHAPTER TWENTY-SEVEN

Sundays were quiet, halcyon days in Cedar Cove. It rarely rained that summer, and I could not remember a day when we had more than light showers. The real storms were often in the high mountains dark and boiling above the highest snow-covered peaks. Late afternoon showers usually passed quickly as the temperatures dropped and were just enough to keep the dust down on the road and offer the flowers and grass fresh nourishment. Many days were cloudless with skies of columbine blue. Cloudy days would produce wispy ice crystals that stretched across the sky above the mountains, revealing high mountain winds and faint rainbows.

I had not known Frank to attend a church that summer or ever for that matter, and if he had, he did not speak of it. It was not his way. He wore nothing on his sleeve. He rarely spoke of organized religion or the Bible, except in a very broad sense. He only spoke of good people and good works. He didn't diminish those who were not religious or members of an organized church. It was a controversy that did not seem to settle upon him.

I sensed he was a deeply spiritual man, but he did not speak in terms of an anthropomorphic deity. He never spoke of God or a supreme being other than using the term in a strongly felt epitaph. He felt the presence of something profound and ineffable and thought that there must be a divine plan, someone or something that put it all together. He did not believe in coincidence, and he acknowledged pain in the world. Whatever the plan, it was not one he understood, but he sincerely believed there was one.

The only religious service I ever remember him commenting on were those conducted at the funerals of his friends. He attended them all and felt it was his obligation to pay his last respects. "We all have obligations in this life, boy, and that is one of them."

Every day and every breath seemed special to him. He never spoke of self doubt and told me, "If you do not believe in yourself, how the hell could you expect a stranger to believe in you?"

While every day had meaning to him, Sundays were special, because it was the one day when he could shut down and sleep in an extra half hour, go fishing, ride his ancient bicycle, or just lay quietly in the metal glider on the banks of the river. He didn't seem to think about life's vicissitudes on Sundays. At times I would find him asleep on a couple of hay bales pushed together in the barn, or he would be stretched across the backseat of one of the cars or trucks with the doors open, allowing the cool river breeze to caress him. He would always have his hat on his stomach and frequently snored and sounded like a train in a mountain tunnel.

Sunday was clearly his day of rest and time to rejuvenate. It was also my day of rest. After breakfast I was on my own.

Buster and I would occasionally attend the Presbyterian Church when at home. We would dress in our Sunday best, which in my case was often too short in the sleeves and too tight in the waist, and walk to the church near city hall with a quarter in our pockets for the collection plate.

Meanwhile, Sunday was the day my mother would sleep off the pressures of her work week, the pressures of trying to raise a child with no money, and a day to try to assuage the demons of her drinking the night before.

Once Buster and I arrived at church, we would sit in the back with our feet on the pew in front of us snapping our chewing gum and snickering at the small glass-eyed dead animals adorning the shoulders of the ladies in the congregation. They looked as if they could leap to the floor and race through the aisles. *Wouldn't that be funny,* we thought. *It would be fun to chase them through the sanctuary.*

Neither of us understood the mysticism of the Trinity, the concept of original sin, or how God became man or vice versa. It did not seem to compute.

As our reward for sitting through the service, we would take the quarters designated for the collection plate and head for the police motorcycle barn across the street. *After all,* we thought, *it would probably be a sin to just spend the money and not attend the service.* We never attended the children's services. We thought that was for kids. Our most fervent prayers were that the Coke machine would not be empty, and that with a little luck, we would encounter one of the cops willing to regale us with the events of their last shift.

I hoped the deity the minister spoke of would forgive my transgressions and not realize that I had not left the quarter in the basket. I would even occasionally hit the basket with three fingers in hopes of fooling Him. I wondered why we even needed police if there was a God. I thought, *one would think he would punish the evildoers, and we wouldn't have to worry about it.* It worried me a little that he was watching me and that I had kept his quarter, but I was convinced sitting through the boring service would be repentance enough.

Frank, on the other hand, didn't think of a punishing God. That was comforting.

That particular Sunday morning, I was sitting backward on Tuffy grooming his rump with a stiff brush. It had become a ritual that summer, serving as a substitute for the Coke machine and the motorcycle barn.

Rudy had arranged for the barrels to be delivered that week. I could see them aligned along the dirt lane like soldiers in a frontal assault of some imaginary cemetery ridge. They were in a perfect row of ten, five deep. Frank said we would start construction as soon as I cut the bottoms out of each barrel. "Now the entire process was up to me," he said. It would be my job to cut the bottom out of every barrel with a cold chisel and a five-pound sledge.

Tuffy was a beautifully conformed palomino gelding that Freddie Grimes had given to Frank to be company for Smokey. He had been a lead horse at the race track in California and had served out his usefulness and wound up on the ranch. He was a little too fiery for children and didn't have the ability of a cow horse.

Smokey, an iron grey that stood eighteen hands at the shoulder and had hooves the size of saucers, was the mainstay of Frank's annual hunting trips. Frank believed he was lonely and said he would moon around the pasture, or at least he thought he did. Smokey could pack out a fully dressed bull elk with the strength of a locomotive and the ease of a gazelle, but he would not move without Tuffy at his heels. Tuffy would stand quietly while Frank fired his favorite.270 rifle off his back and carry any load, but neither would move without the other. They were a great team, but they would not work alone.

Tuffy was wary of strangers and would fight and do a defiant dance if someone new approached him. Freddie said a trainer sometime in his history had beaten him around his face. "I'd kill the bastard if I found him in a dark corner," Frank said. I didn't think he meant it literally, but I think he cared as much for animals as he did for humans.

I loved Sunday morning grooming and riding Tuffy bareback around the pasture with Smokey at a trot on our heels. The smell of the horses and the fresh alfalfa in the morning air was always intoxicating and served as my Sunday morning ritual and worship service. No one had to tell me there was a God when I felt the horse under me and the cool, fresh breeze off the river in my face.

I had learned early in life to love horses. My mother had shown gaited thoroughbreds for others all over the south before I was born. She kept the trophies and ribbons by the dozens in her closet. It seemed almost intuitive. I'd never had a fear of animals and learned early to cling to a bareback horse like a monkey on a stick. I would sit backward on either of the horses and feel the steady grind of the oats and sweet feed that I had just fed. I would dodge their long tails as they swept the air and their backs for flies and biting insects, and I would spend hours untangling their matted tails, forelock, and mane while avoiding the gentle nips they would try to take out of my legs. We had become friends, Smokey, Tuffy, and I.

I had purchased a Standardbred gelding with my portion of the settlement money from the auto accident Buster and I had been involved in. My mother had paid the doctor bills, kept a little for herself, and gave me enough to make up the difference between what I had saved and the cost of the beautiful buckskin gelding. "If I could buy a horse," I had said, "I would pay all of the board myself out of my lawn-cutting money." I had a regular route, and at times, made more money after taxes every week than she did. What I failed to consider was if I was riding my horse, I wouldn't have time to cut the lawns, so I rarely found time to visit him during the school year. The seller didn't mind, since I had given her permission to exercise him. Summer break was a different matter. I could ride my bike or hitchhike the fifteen miles to the barn and sleep in the tack room a few days if I wanted and still cut enough lawns to pay the bills.

I purchased the horse from a young woman by the name of Mary Donna. I quickly fell in love with the animal. It was gentle, had been taught a number of tricks, and was, by Mary Donna's definition, a "green hunter." He would sail over jumps up to five feet with ease. His registered name had been "Smoke Puff," but everyone called him "Smokey" for short. I thought it ironic that

Frank had a horse named Smokey, but then he had said there were
no coincidences.

As I groomed the horses, I remembered one late summer afternoon the year before. Perhaps it was my sermon for the day. My
friend Jimmy and I had been riding double through the palmetto
scrub and pine trees bordering the Everglades south of Miami not
far from where I boarded Smokey. The area was undeveloped and
largely consisted of small vegetable farms and an occasional fenced
pasture, plus a horse farm or two. It was close to the reform school,
where my mother often threatened to send me when she was
drinking, and adjacent to the YMCA. Riding was unrestricted.

The area was punctuated with rock quarries and gravel pits
and crisscrossed with manmade canals that served to drain the
surrounding swamp. The water in the gravel pits was deep, aqua-
marine in color, and great for swimming if the swimmer didn't
mind an occasional alligator or water snake. They were certainly a
magnet on hot afternoons for teenage boys.

One in particular, like the spot on the river, was also referred
to as "bare-assed beach." That day we were heading right to it.
Smokey was dripping sweat and streaked with lines of dirt. Jimmy
and I were soaked with perspiration. It was a hot, windless day,
with low cumulus clouds and sweltering humidity.

As we made our way to the swimming hole, we both smelled
smoke. Smoke wasn't a good thing, because if fire raced through
the Everglades, it could be impossible to outrun, even on a fast
horse. Then I heard the soft cry of an infant somewhere in the pines
ahead. The closer we came to the water, the more pronounced the
smell of smoke became. We stopped and both listened, and sure
enough, it was the cooing sound of a dove or the soft cry of a child.
We weren't sure—something strange—out of place. Jimmy heard
the sound too; it couldn't be what we both thought, but we both
heard something. It didn't sound like an animal or a bird.

"There it is again," Jimmy exclaimed, "a baby sure enough. It is coming from somewhere ahead near the rock pit. What the hell! There ain't no kids out here. Are we dreaming?" We were miles from a house or farm. "All there is around here is skeeters, possums, and water snakes. How can that be? There it is again! It is a baby. There is a baby out here somewhere," he said. "Hmmm, how can that be?"

We had been following a narrow sandy trail into the Everglades for several miles. A brief rain shower had rinsed the perspiration from our bodies. No one lived out here. We could hear the rustle of small animals as they scurried through the palmetto brush and the splash of frogs as they leaped off the canal banks into the water. The head of a water moccasin would occasionally glide by in the canal. We couldn't wait to strip and jump into the rock pit. Our Levi's had stuck to us like flies to flypaper around a kitchen light. If the humidity was any higher, it would be raining again. *Damn, I heard it again. A baby.*

I couldn't wait to ride Smokey into the water where he, too, would stand up to his belly and seem to smile. In this heat I am sure he enjoyed the water as much as we did.

Jimmy was a few years older than me, having emigrated from Cuba as a child and held back in school until he could speak English. He had the beginnings of a beard and would laugh at my prepubescence. "Hell, you are going to graduate high school before you have hair on your balls," he would say, "and I will be the only kid with a full beard and old enough to vote." We were great friends, and since he was much older than me, I rarely had to worry about the class bully. He was my defender, and I was his confidante.

A long slow-moving freight train crossed the trestle a hundred yards ahead and disappeared into the pines. We could still hear the faint clickety-clack of the wheels on the rails. Red-winged blackbirds swirled above us and around us landing on the pines and in the brush. Several large scavenger birds circled off in the distance identifying the death scene of some swamp animal. I caught a glimpse of the water's edge. There was smoke suspended a few feet above it.

I detected movement, and then the trunk of an old car came into view. It appeared abandoned and was perched on the bank of the quarry a few feet from the water's edge. The driver's side and the rear windows were covered with a bed sheet that was moving with the slight breeze. A young woman, perhaps in her twenties, came into view kneeling in the sand next to the car and in front of a small washbasin. The washbasin held a child, laughing and splashing at the water. The woman did not see us initially and was startled when Smokey hit his front hoof with his hind hoof making a loud clicking sound. She quickly picked up the child, wrapped it in a towel, and held it closely to her breast.

"Hello," I said, "we are just passing through." I asked how she was today, as if it was common to find someone living in a car at the edge of the Everglades. She said, "Fine, looks like it's going to rain some more" and then returned the child to the washbasin and continued the bath. We must have looked harmless.

There was a second child asleep on a mattress in the back of the car. Small buckets and children's toys were scattered in the sand. A fire smoldered in a pit surrounded by coral rocks just a few feet away. Several mismatched kitchen chairs and a small table were set up under a canvas that had been stretched between two small trees. A camp stove sat on the tabletop and a red-and-white Coca-Cola cooler rested on one of the chairs. I could see several books on the front seat of the car and an open book on the table. Canned goods, paper plates, and kitchen utensils occupied the passenger side floor of the car. The doors were open, and everything seemed to be tidy and in place. A wet roll of toilet paper hung on a limb of a tree, and an enclosure made from limbs, palmetto fronds, and woven swamp grasses served to protect the woman's toilet. It was obvious that the young woman had been here a while.

Jimmy whispered something about moving on as I dug my heels into Smokey's ribs. We sighed simultaneously as the horse picked up his gait, and the scene moved behind us. We had forgotten about swimming and just wanted to head back to our camp and the fresh water hose in the yard. Perhaps we could wash off what we had seen.

Once we got out of earshot, Jimmy gave out another sigh and said, "Can you believe that? I couldn't do that. It's scary out here. Wonder what happened to her husband. Damn, that was something!" I agreed, and we kept riding. "I'd be scared shitless. Damn, that was awful, and those two little kids. No one should have to live out in the woods alone. Whew, it sure does get dark out here at night, and all them noises scare the hell out of me." We continued back to the barn without much conversation.

When we arrived, I saw Mary Donna working her hunter on the jump course and her mother snapping peas on the back porch. Jimmy and I hosed down Smokey and brushed him to smooth out his coat. I opened the gate and turned him into the pasture. By that time Mary Donna had finished her routine and turned her horse out with Smokey.

We told the two women what we had seen in the swamp and walked over to our two shelter halves assembled in the willows at the edge of the pasture just as it started pouring rain. We had planned to sleep in the makeshift tent and listen to the crystal sets we had brought along. As the rain continued, the shelter started leaking heavily, and the water rose in the bottom of the tent. Red fire ants clustering on twigs, leaves, and flotsam invaded and started climbing on us. Our homemade bedrolls were soaked, and our primitive packs were floating.

"This is a frog strangler," Jimmy said over the sound of the rain. "Let's get our asses out of here. These damn ants are getting all over me," he said. "They burn like fire. Damn."

We abandoned the tent and ran for the barn. We made pallets in the center of the tack room, folded up a couple of smelly horse blankets, and went quickly to sleep. Just before nodding off, I thought about the woman and her two small children huddling in the old car, riding out the storm. *Was she able to protect herself,* I wondered? *Would she be soaked?* What a way to live.

I had slept in my mother's car many nights. Sometimes just because I didn't want to argue; sometimes because the doors were all locked, and it was easier than removing the jalousie and breaking in, but I never really had to sleep in the car. I just chose to. The woman in the swamp had to. That's not right. I could not imagine what she and her children were going through.

I learned a few days later that Mary Donna's mother had called the sheriff and the pastor of her church. His parishioners offered the woman and her children temporary food and shelter, and she moved into one of their homes. Her life in the old car had ended thanks to some charitable people who did good works and did not just talk about it.

A few months later, I rode through the same area and found the site. The washtub was half buried in the sand at the edge of the water and bent as if it had been stomped on with heavy boots. The fire pit had been destroyed, and the rock surrounding it was scattered in every direction. Burnt remnants of an old shoe and blackened wood were everywhere. The open doors of the old car were punctuated with bullet holes, and all the glass was broken. The tires and wheels were gone, and there was a gaping hole in the center of the dashboard, which was once inhabited by a radio. The mattress was gone, and the only evidence that someone had lived there was a solitary spoon sticking out of the ground.

I dismounted and opened the trunk. It contained a baby's shoe and a container of bobby pins in the wheel well. There were several letters tied with a yellow ribbon hidden under a flat tire. I ground tied Smokey and sat on the front fender and tore open the first of the letters. They were addressed to the young woman from somewhere up north and told quite a story.

I saw Frank approaching, crossing over the footbridge with his usual bounty of carrots and sliced apples. He had carrots sticking out of each pocket and was carving a green apple with a pocket knife.

Water rushed under the bridge and down the river throwing up a spray that created a rainbow downstream. It had rained in Cedar Park the night before, and the river was swollen and overflowing its banks. It was a torrent compared to its normal peaceful flow. It was no longer whispering but shouting, "I am powerful, and man is but a puny impediment."

I slid off Tuffy's back and slapped him on the rump leaving the impression of my hand as a tiny cloud of dust rose in the air. Tuffy spotted Frank in the distance, threw up his head, picked up his tail, and raced towards him. His body arched in a corkscrew as he bucked and farted. Smokey followed at a gallop.

When the two horses reached Frank at the edge of the pasture, they both crow-hopped sideways and playfully grabbed the carrots from his pockets with their teeth. He held the apples behind his back as he whirled around as they begged with their great lips parted and huge teeth flashing. It was a game they played every time Frank came to the barn. He always brought apple slices or carrots to taunt them. They would take the food delights from his pocket but were careful not to harm him. They would playfully nudge him with their big heads or turn their hind quarters into him gently or push him with their massive shoulders. He would dance in a circle withholding the apples just briefly enough to frustrate them. Once they had gotten everything he had to eat, he would hold his open hands out as if to say "see, nothing more" and rub their chests between their front legs or scratch their withers. They would respond by throwing their heads in the air and shaking their manes and their huge bodies. They had a great affection for one another, and it was obvious they spoke a language each could understand.

As we walked together back across the footbridge toward the barrels, I told Frank about the woman living in her car with the two small children. I told him how surprised Jimmy and I were to find someone, no less a young woman living with two very small children at the edge of the Everglades.

I told him about the letters I had found and summarized their contents. They had been written by the woman's mother and were in response to letters she had written about her life in Florida. The theme of the young mother's response in each she had received from her mother must have been the same: Things are great. Don't worry. She had a great life and had found an apartment close to the beach. The children swam in the pool every day, and the weather was wonderful...

She must have painted a picture, based on the response by her mother, of a carefree life in the warm Florida sun.

Her mother wrote how comforting it was to learn of the great apartment she had located. She said how she and the woman's father had always wanted to visit Florida. She especially wanted to visit her daughter and grandchildren, but she hoped her daughter would understand since the business was failing, and her father's health was not good. The time was not right.

He had suffered a mild heart attack, and a competitor had moved in close by taking some of the long-time customers by lowering prices. He sadly let some long-time employees go, and the writer thought the stress of his decision may have precipitated the father's heart attack. They wished they could do more for their daughter and still hoped to visit once things improved.

All of the daughter's missives to her parents must have been positive and upbeat. The mother seemed to glow in the knowledge. Their money was tight, and the winter snows were worse than any she could remember. Wouldn't it be wonderful if she and the father could visit Florida?

She was so proud of her daughter, especially following the bitter divorce. She had expected so much from her son-in-law, and he was such a disappointment. She had told all her friends of her daughter's good fortune, and they all sent their love and best wishes.

An old boyfriend had returned from the Army, where he had been stationed in Germany, she told her daughter. He, too, sent his best wishes and planned to start work at the glass plant south of town as soon as they called him. Work was hard to find. He was such a good boy—too bad Gary came along. That is just the way it is in life sometime. One really never knows.

The letters from the mother were newsy and chatty. It was easy to see she had no idea the young woman was living in a car at the edge of the Everglades, miles from the closest store and without having even basic sanitation facilities. The gist of the responses to letters written by the daughter was how happy the mother was to know her daughter's life was good and her wish to visit as soon as life improved for her and the father. It was a dream, she said over and over, to know her daughter had been able to escape with the children and leave the hard, cold, and dark days behind. She missed and loved her daughter and the children very much. They would visit as soon as they could. She wrote life didn't seem fair sometimes, and she had expected more by this age, but she was joyous in the knowledge all was going so well for the daughter and the children after the pain of the divorce. Her letters repeated this theme over and over. Her daughter's life was a work of fiction and must have been written only to spare her mother the pain of knowing things were not better but worse.

When I finished relating what I had read to Frank, he pondered the facts for a few minutes as we continued across the bridge toward the barrels. He threw a round stone into the river and looked back and said, "I doubt you will ever forget that Jane, a stranger who showed you what courage and strength are all about. A fella could write a book about what you learned that day. It is them kind of people that make the difference. She made up her mind things were tough, but she was goin to tend to it. She knew her folks had their own problems, and she had hers, based on choices she had made. She didn't paint no pictures or take out no ads in the paper to say she loved her folks, or she was strugglin and it was someone's responsibility to fix it or help her. Maybe she should have asked for more help, but instead, she took charge. She did the only thing she knew how to do in a strange place. She took responsibility. Action, not words—that is my motto. Maybe there was a better action, but what she did was certainly better than no action. She did the onlyist thing she knew to do to survive until help came. Lots of folks whimper and cry about their lot in life but not that Jane; she did somethin. That is a hell of a story, boy.

"Look at ole Wild Bill. He come to Colorado without a dime and took a job at the city dump when no one else would. I have never knowed him to complain about the heat or the cold. He always has a smile on his face. He goes about life with a grin. I think he has done okay. Some people will lay down in the street and just bellyache. Others will harm themselves or lash out at those who have prospered. Not him. He don't swim the river beggin others for a cup to drink out of. He and that Jane are just alike. It ain't up to the other fella to get you a cup; it ain't up to the other fella to buy you books; it is up to you if you want to drink or learn somethin. If the other fella wants to help, and many do, that's a good thing, but if he don't, it is up to you. Life is all about choices, takin responsibility, and doin what you know in your gut is right.

"The first thing you gotta learn is that life ain't fair. It just is. A fella's gotta take every day as it comes and make the best of it, the good and the bad. Fairness just ain't a part of it. Some folks will fail no matter how hard they try, and some folks will fall off a damn honey wagon into the clover. The difference is that those who prosper and succeed never give up. They just never quit!" he said. "They put one foot in front of the other, day after day. They don't stop. Sure some folks have sickness; others just ain't that smart and they need help. That is what the churches are for, family, or them that wanta help. But there will always be them that takes and them that gives, that is just the way it is—the nature of the critter. Them that gives are not always rewarded, and them that takes are not always punished, but life goes on.

"That Jane took matters in her own hands and figured out a way to get by in the world. It may not have been the best way, but it was the road she had to take. I'll bet if a fella were to look her up twenty years from now, he would find that she is doin just fine. Take them boys who lived in the barn years ago as an example: one prospered, one didn't. One made his own way and took responsibility and give up somethin to get somethin. The other, he didn't want to give up anythin. He wanted to drink liquor, chase them Janes, and lay out from work. They came from the same blood, but they chose different paths. There ain't no explainin it.

"Life is about choice. If you don't want to be smokin them cigarettes, don't be puttin them in your mouth. Buster's ole man chose to fail; his brother chose to succeed. Life is as simple as that. It really ain't complicated. Folks just try and make it complicated, mostly because they want an excuse. Them letters tell you who that Jane was and what she was made of. As you go about livin, you want to be like her. There ain't no shame in bein poor, and there ain't no shame in failin; the shame is in not pickin yourself up an keepin on movin no matter what life throws at you. Just put that one foot in front of the other.

"Now let's us go look at the barrels, so I can show you what you need to do to get ready to build us that bridge." He walked to the first barrel and picked up a five-pound sledge hammer and a cold chisel he had placed there that morning. "I want you to cut the bottoms out of every one of these bastards," he said. "You need to angle this chisel just right, and hit it hard enough to put a slice in the barrel. Don't be hittin your goddamn hand. Hold that chisel at the bottom and take aim. Move the damn thing like a can opener until the bottom is gone," he said with a smile and walked away. "You just remember that until them bottoms are cut out, we can't start on that bridge. It is up to you. Don't be a holdin up progress."

I stopped cutting long enough for dinner and was back at it again. It took about fifteen minutes to cut the bottom out of each barrel—three to four every hour. It seemed I would never finish. I counted and recounted the remaining barrels, thinking somehow counting them over and over would lessen my chore.

By mid-afternoon my right arm was stiff, and I could feel a subtle tingling sensation in my left hand and shoulder from the constant attack on the barrel with the metal chisel and sledge. The vibration continued long after the tops were removed and into the night. I had not thought to wear gloves, so it wasn't long before I had a blister the size of a quarter on the inside of my thumb and forefinger. It stung with perspiration.

Almost as if he could read my mind, I saw Frank approaching on his bicycle from the house with an extra pair of leather gloves in his hands. It was an easy lesson, and one he wanted me to learn. "I told you," he said, "wear them gloves when you are workin. I buy you books, send you to school, and you still don't know nothin. Think boy!"

I learned so many lessons that summer; one would have thought putting on a pair of gloves would have come easily. It didn't, and I had a burning sensation in my right hand to prove it. I had heard him repeat all summer, time after time, "Do it right the first time, and you won't have to do it over." *I always seemed to learn everything the hard way,* I thought.

I did not want the summer to end. I would have cut the bottoms out of a thousand barrels and blistered all of my fingers if I knew that I could just stay longer. Helping Frank build the bridge over Cedar Creek was the only way I knew how to repay him for his kindness.

I had several spectators as I hammered away. Three large black-and-white "camp robbers" watched me from their perch in the pine tree above me and from the roof of the garage. They would land on the canvas top of an ancient Hupmobile parked next to the garage and hop around on one foot and then the other. They kept up a constant chatter. They didn't seem to fear me and often would land on my shoulder if I had a piece of bread to feed them. They were big, beautiful birds often referred to as "magpies" because of the chatter. Two large red squirrels jumped from limb to limb along the roof of the garage transporting pine cones and nuts in their teeth. They would stop occasionally, sit back on their tails, and screech at me as if to say, "Stop that incessant racket!" It was just about dark when I finished. I just couldn't quit until the last barrel was cut. Frank brought me a sandwich at suppertime, and I barely stopped to eat it. Time was running out, and I wanted to get started on the bridge.

I was exhausted by day's end. I was sunburned from having taken off my shirt early in the day. My hand burned from the blister, and my shoulder still vibrated deep down in the muscle, but I was proud. I did it! We could start on the bridge.

Although it might not have seemed like much of an accomplishment for many, cutting the bottoms out of all those barrels caused me to feel like the man of the hour. Frank had ridden his bicycle down the lane a few times during the day but pretty much stayed out of sight until I finished. I think he knew how important this was to me—to be a part of something and make something happen. I would find out soon what my long day of labor was all about.

CHAPTER TWENTY-EIGHT

The barrels were all cut and ready to be made into the structure of the bridge. All of the ends were unobstructed, so water would flow through with ease.

Cedar Creek originated in Cedar Park at the high elevations. At its origin it was only a few feet in width and dry most of the year. It could not even be considered a creek but a drainage allowing water and melted snow to flow down the mountain and into the river below. By the time it reached the small dirt road crossing Cedar Cove and the concrete slab in the creek bed, it was no more than twenty-five feet across and then widened at its mouth into a small alluvial fan that emptied water into the river. Its banks were lined with boulders, time-worn river stone, and gravel that had been forced down the mountainside by the strength of the water over the millennium. High willows and wild flowers as well as water oak lined the creek banks.

The water rarely reached depths of more than six inches in the summer but following a heavy snow in the fall or spring, a torrent of water could course down the mountainside and often overflow its banks. Residents of the cove were often stranded for days, and occasionally, a week would pass before traffic would be permitted to flow again. This wasn't only an inconvenience but a safety concern that Frank wanted to eliminate.

He had met with the other residents, but they either did not want to spend the money, were not healthy enough to participate, or were weekend residents, and the problem didn't affect them.

He finally decided after the fourth or fifth unsuccessful community meeting that if anything was going to be accomplished, he was going to have to do it himself. After proposing several different plans and ideas for a bridge, Frank's nemesis across the creek found every reason to stall and thwart the construction. "It just damn well wasn't going to work," he would say or, "It is a stupid damn idea." He never proposed an alternative. "The first little bit of water to come down that creek next spring will wash the damn bridge away and destroy my property," he said in one meeting. He wouldn't admit that his house was thirty feet above Cedar Creek's hundred-year high water mark established by the Corp of Engineers, and Frank did not tell him that he had hired a hydrologist to give him a professional opinion. Ironically, his home was in the flood plain of the river and would easily be threatened if the river rose, but that was his problem, Frank thought. "The damn fool was right in the middle of a flood zone!" Frank said. "If the river ever rose even just a few feet, his house could be in jeopardy. He could lose everything."

Twenty years later that is exactly what happened. On the afternoon of July 31, 1976, a series of microbursts created so much rainwater in a few minutes that a dam was breached, and water rose forty feet in minutes. The result was the death of one hundred and eighty people downstream and the destruction of millions of dollars in property. One of the houses to be destroyed was Harrigan's. All that remained of his home in the aftermath of the devastating flood was some blue coping that surrounded the pool and a set of stairs leading to a good fishing spot in the river. The site where his home stood was river bottom, one of life's little ironies.

Once Frank, Fred and I began constructing the bridge, things went quickly. Frank and I raked and shoveled wheelbarrow loads of dirt, gravel, and river stone. We removed the trees and willows with a hand axe and two-man saw. We dynamited a large boulder blocking access to the bridge and flattened the creek bottom so the barrels would fit together horizontally and would not allow for any shifting or movement.

Before dynamiting the boulder, Fred instructed me to drill three six-inch-deep holes in the surface with a one-inch star drill. He then removed the explosive material, putty like substance, from a stick of dynamite, and he filled the holes I had drilled about halfway to the opening on the surface. After inserting a fuse that looked a little like a .22 caliber cartridge and a braided wire, he packed the three cavities with wet river sand and clay that he found along the bank of the creek. The dynamite had the same texture and substance of modeling clay or bubblegum after it had been chewed for a while. It looked innocent enough. I sure couldn't see how that little bit of clay could do any damage, no less split a boulder the size of a deep freezer. *He must know what he is doing*, I thought.

He laughed when I told him my reservations and how the Saturday afternoon westerns always depicted the driver of the wagon containing the dynamite driving so deliberately and being so careful. He didn't even seem to be cautious with the stuff. "That's a Hollywood myth," he said. "Them moviemakers never been on a horse, no less handled dynamite. Why a fella can damn near chew this stuff like tobacco without causing it to explode. I don't think I would chew it just because of the foul taste, but you could probably hit it with a hammer, and it wouldn't cause any damage. It explodes after a charge is installed and ignited. Hell, you can sit on a box of the stuff all day long and not worry a little bit. Now once you put a charge to her—Katie bar the door! It ain't going to take but a few well-packed inches of the stuff in order to blow that boulder to kingdom come. You'll see soon enough."

Frank covered the boulder with about a dozen old truck tires and a heavy canvas.

Fred said, "The only thing we have to worry about is if we get a dry hole. If the damn thing don't explode then we do have a problem." Looking directly at me, he said, "Actually, you may have a problem. I'll be alookin for a young lad to dig the blastin cap out and put in another. You figure I can recruit you?" He grinned.

Frank sent me fifty yards up the road and disappeared down the lane in the opposite direction. "Block that traffic," he said, "and I'll stop 'em on the other side. We wouldn't want someone to come whipping down the lane once we light the fuse; it would ruin their day."

About the time I got halfway up the hill, Fred touched the fuse with a railroad flare and hightailed it to the back of the truck. I didn't think a man his age could move that quickly. In about twenty seconds there was a *ker bam!!* The muffled explosion tossed the canvas and the tires twenty feet in the air. Gravel flew everywhere and rained down on the tin roofs of the closest cabin and the truck. The boulder had not appeared to move, but as I walked back down the hill and got closer I could see three very clear dark lines in its surface. It was split in three pieces as clean as if Fred had sliced a new loaf of bread. Frank had told me that Fred knew what he was doing, and if the boulder was any indication, he sure did! We hooked the remnants of the boulder to the jeep with a come along and moved them down the creek bed to the edge of the river. Access to our bridge was no longer a problem.

We placed all the barrels in the riverbed, chinked them with rock, river sand, and gravel and built a two-by-twelve form along the top of the barrels to contain the concrete that was expected to arrive first thing in the morning. We stopped briefly midday to gobble down a couple of bean sandwiches and consume a few cans of Vienna sausages, one of Frank's favorite meals.

The next morning the concrete trucks started to arrive soon after daylight. After each driver emptied his truck and washed down his chute and tools, Frank would thank him and stick a few dollars in his pocket before sending him on his way. He and I stood in the center of the bridge in our rubber boots as the concrete flowed out of the trucks and swirled around us like thick molasses. We directed its flow with our shovels and filled the many voids between the barrels.

Once the voids were filled, we started pouring the deck. We filled the forms Frank had built on the top of the barrels. Fred crossed from side to side pointing out low spots or cavities in the deck and directed our efforts to level the surface. While the concrete was still wet, we placed large round river stones along the edge and seated them so the concrete covered half of their surface. These stones became a barrier to prevent careless drivers from running over the edge of the bridge.

When the last concrete truck departed, we took a break for dinner and returned to our work just as the deck of the bridge had begun to harden. We swept the entire width and length of the surface with normal household corn brooms to make sure the deck surface had a rough texture and was not slippery.

Sometime during the second or third pour, Mr. Harrigan backed his long white Cadillac out of his drive without a glance and continued up the lane. I heard Frank mutter an obscenity under his breath, but he kept shoveling and chinking the barrels.

Several residents drove through the river and offered us encouragement while admiring our work. A neighbor's dog ran across the deck as we sat on the bank having our dinner. While none of the residents of the cove offered their help, they all seemed very pleased with the results. The two older women who lived in the cabin at the far end of the bridge sat on their porch all afternoon and kibitzed. They told us over and over how pleased they were to know they would be able to get out of the cove all winter and spring. They kept our water cups full and offered us hands full of cookies.

I was exhausted by the end of the day. Both Frank and Fred would laugh and tease me about how I "needed my rest."

We finished just before sunset. We erected a barrier at one end of the bridge and parked the truck at the other end in order to obstruct traffic. "As soon as she is dry, and we are able to drive over her, we are going to have a ribbon cuttin," Frank said. "Them big shots don't have nothin' on us. I'll get Lillie to take a few pictures, and you, boy, can be the first to cross her. You done the work, you earned it. You will remember these past few days fifty years from now, and I bet you dollars to donuts she'll still be here."

Fred even complimented me and said, "You worked hard boy." I knew that was a deep compliment coming from him. His face lightened a little, and he squeezed my shoulder with one hand and said, "I didn't think you had it in you, boy. You done good." I was not sure he had forgiven me for creating the dust all summer, but his compliment meant a lot to me. "You done good," he said again. "We all worked hard, and we done her. Ain't she a beaut?"

We stored our tools in the back of the truck and walked together toward the house in the twilight. As tired as I was, I was walking on proverbial air. I don't think my feet ever hit the ground all of the way home. I was so proud of what we had done and so happy to have pleased both Frank and Fred. We had built the bridge over Cedar Creek, and maybe, just maybe, I will be invited back next summer. There had been no word yet.

We had our ribbon cutting once the concrete dried and cured a few days. Frank, Fred, and I posed for pictures, and many of the residents of the cove gathered round. I was the first to drive the Dodge across the bridge. We all shook hands, and the same two women who watched us from their porch clapped for us and posed for pictures just as if they had poured the concrete themselves.

Now that it was finished, I thought about going home. There were just a few days remaining. I knew I would miss Frank threatening to "screw my plate upside down to the table," admonishing me not to "fly up on the corners and slam on the brakes." I would miss having him bang on the basement door in the morning and laugh about the bears getting me in my sleep. I would even miss Fred's severe looks when I passed his cabin on the Cushman. I knew I would miss trying to figure out what the next "hickey" was going to be or who some Jane was that he knew forty years ago. I would certainly miss watching him gambol with Smokey and Tuffy and see them snitch carrots and apples from his pockets. I would miss the trips to town, the visits with Wild Bill, and the daily "special" at the pool hall. I would miss the sound of the river and the cool mountain nights and riding the Cushman through the old canyon road. But what I thought I would miss the most was the genuine concern he seemed to have for me and the adult way he spoke to me. I was the "boy" but never the "kid."

I could not think of anything I had not enjoyed or learned that summer. I had pleasant memories of the tension breaking when the water from the broken sprinkler flattened my already short crew cut, of watching Melvin catch a creel full of trout while I snagged my line in the bushes and brambles along the riverbank, and riding Tuffy around the pasture with Smokey on our heels. I prayed he would invite me back.

That night at supper, Frank asked, "When does your bus leave?" I told him, "Friday morning, the day before Labor Day weekend." I had to be back in school on Tuesday. I was just beginning my freshman year in high school. He seemed to ponder what I had just told him and then asked me to pass the gravy. Peering over his fork, he asked, "How'd you like to join ole Rudy and me in Dodge City for Labor Day weekend? That is the weekend of them races I told you about."

I didn't know what to say. Of course, I wanted to go, but I already had a return ticket home. "Do you think they will let me cancel my ticket?" I asked.

"Sure," he said, "but you had better ask your mother. It is entirely up to her. If she agrees, I'll bet you that we can get you a seat on a bus leavin Dodge City."

I called my mother, and she consented and assured me that she could arrange with the school for a late start date. "A couple of days should not hurt a thing," she said.

I felt like a dying man must feel after getting a reprieve from the governor. I was going to the races. Summer wasn't over yet!

CHAPTER TWENTY-NINE

The day before we left for Dodge City, we drove to town as usual. We were going to stop by the shop, have dinner at the pool hall, and visit Wild Bill on the way back to the canyon.

Our first stop was the shop to say goodbye to Chili and Spot. Frank treated it just like any other day, but I felt as if I were going to the gallows. While waiting to go to dinner, I washed and swept out a customer's car. Frank exhorted, "Don't forget to air up them tires, boy. And get your ass out here soon so we can go to dinner."

Chili joined me out on the washrack for a few minutes for a quick smoke, while Frank helped Spot stab the transmission in a Chrysler he was working on. Chili took several hurried puffs on his Salem and extinguished it in the mop bucket while exhaling a thin cloud of smoke out of the corner of his mouth and nose. "Been good having you here this summer, boy," he said while furtively covering his nose and mouth with one hand. "I think Frank has mellowed. He surprised the hell out of me; it ain't like the old man, not to jump up and down once in a while; why he never hardly raised his voice. He was hell on wheels when I was a kid. I think you done him some good. I think this summer probably did you both some good. What do you think?" he asked. I agreed and told him it had been great.

I must have washed fifty cars that summer between Frank's personal cars and trucks and customer cars in the shop. By summer's end I could start and finish washing and vacuuming a car in about ten minutes. It would take a few more minutes to clean the windows and dump the ash trays and I would be done. I would time myself using the clock on the far end of the shop wall and try to break my previous record. I would finish the last few cars during the last days in less than ten minutes. I would even race the second hand to beat my previous best. It was fun, but what gave me the most pleasure was driving so many different cars to and from the washrack and the parking lot at the side of the building. One would have thought I had driven to Chicago.

Once, while I was waiting for Frank in the front seat of his Plymouth, a box truck backed into the alleyway. The car was running, because we had stopped briefly after dinner to pick up something that Chili had asked to be taken to the post office. I was distracted, and Frank was inside the building. I did not see the truck until it hit the fender. It happened so quickly. It crushed the driver's side fender and smashed the headlight in the blink of an eye.

I hadn't told Frank that I did not have a driver's license. I had a learner's permit, but it required a licensed driver to be in the car at all times. I was frightened.

When the police arrived, Frank said, "Let me handle this."

I was shaking and thought it was entirely my fault for not re-acting more quickly. I just knew I was in trouble, and he would never let me come back. I had to fight back the tears. "Why me?" I kept repeating to myself. Why hadn't I been more careful? *Damn, damn, damn!* When the cop asked Frank his version of events, he said, "The boy was sitting in the car waiting for me. No one saw the truck." The truck driver accepted complete responsibility, and no ticket was issued.

After I apologized several times for not being more careful or having seen or been aware of the truck, he said, "It was just one of them things, boy. It was a accident. Don't be so damn hard on yourself. If anyone is responsible, it was the truck driver. He should have been more careful when backin into a blind alleyway. Hell, it don't matter anyway, not a damn soul was hurt. It won't take long to fix the car. There just was damn well nothin to it. Forget it," he said. He never said another word about the incident.

"When you wash them customers' cars," he said, "it makes them run better. I'll bet you didn't know that did you? Sure enough, it does, but even if they don't run better, they seem to run better, and the customer is always happy. I never seen one turn down a free wash job. Why hell, that may be the only time some of these cars and trucks ever get washed. Most of these old boys are farmers and ranchers and live out on the dirt roads. You know, if a fella just does a little more in life than people expect, they will remember it for a long time. More important, you will remember it for a long time."

"If you see somethin in the road, pick it up; that'll save someone else from havin to do it, or it may even prevent an accident. The more a fella gives, the more a fella receives. Life is as simple as that. A fella don't have to be selfish about it, just do it and reward will come from it. It is the truth. But if you hear some fella braggin, like ole Harrigan, about all of what he's done, start dividin. That damn Harrigan will be sportin all over town braggin about all of what he is doin for the community, while he and his ole man are foreclosin down at the bank. He's a damn show horse, but what we need in this life is work horses. Hell, the bastard has walked around in Brussels carpet all his life and really never hit a lick at a snake. I don't believe in no flash. Flash is over in seconds, but substance lasts a lifetime. The fella or Jane that does the most for others usually says the least about it. Most people know. A man's circumstances reveal him, and he can't hide it."

We stopped in the pool hall for dinner. My "last supper" was a hot beef sandwich and iced tea. I said goodbye to Art and his wife and savored the sound of pool balls clicking and laughter coming from the backroom. We left the shop and drove slowly past the grain elevator, crossed the concrete culvert where the sheriff had died so many years ago, and crossed the railroad tracks on First Street heading westerly. Frank seemed to always be in a time warp. He spoke to me of people he knew and events that had occurred sixty years ago as if we had been together then. Occasionally, he would ask if I remembered old Joe, only to learn later that he had died years before I was born. "Remember ole 'Gold Mug,'" he would say or, "Otto that farmed the Ferguson place." I just listened. "Hell that damn 'Gold Mug' was the fastest man on an Excelsior I ever seen. He'd burn up them board tracks! It was the damndest thing a fella ever seen. He had no fear."

We passed the high school athletic field, crossed over the river bridge, and cruised down First Street until we reached the feed lot. I always enjoyed driving down the small hill in front of the shack, because it was so steep. It seemed like the drop of a roller coaster when we left the pavement.

This would be my last time to feed the "jackasses." That's how Frank referred to the four burros rooting around in the sage brush and dust inside the fence. "You try and ride one of them little sons a bitches," he said, "and you'll get the surprise of your life. They think they are rodeo bulls and buck just about as bad. Ole Pedro," the name he had given the largest of the four, "sure surprised Chili one afternoon. It was funny him being a rodeo rider and all when he was younger. He didn't last ten seconds before he was on his backside in the dirt. Them are tough little critters."

I climbed the ladder into the hay loft and stumbled over an old motorcycle sidecar before my eyes became accustomed to the dark. Pinholes of light streamed through the nail holes in the tin roof and dust motes danced in the light once I opened the door to the hay trough. I broke open a tightly bound bale of fresh alfalfa, and more dust exploded in the bright light of the framed opening.

The dust particles sparkled like effervescence in the wake of a slow-moving ship at sea. I fed the burros a few flakes of hay each for the last time and watched them push and shove playfully with their green-stained teeth bared and their long ears pinned back on their necks. I filled the old footed tub that served as a water trough and unloaded four of the remaining bridge barrels from the back of the truck. I placed them next to the sidecar in the loft.

"I'll find a use for them barrels," Frank said. "Maybe I can use them as part of the septic drain field at the back of the house in case you come back next summer and take all them showers again. I never have seen a person with a taste for cleanliness like you. Hell, there was a time when a fella'd be lucky to get a real shower once a year and have to use the horse trough for his baths all the summer." He laughed. "Showers are for rich folks in town, don't you know. If I didn't know better, your mama will be accusin me of shrinkin you when you get home after all that damn water. Damn good thing we was on a well." He laughed again.

I patted the largest of the burros on the rump, being careful to avoid his hind feet, and climbed back into the front seat of the truck.

"Let's go on by and see old Wild Bill," he said. "I think he has taken a likin to you, boy. I bought him one of them pints of Jack Daniel's sippin whiskey that I know he has taken a liken to. He will take a drink in the winter to keep out the cold. It gets damn cold on that dump in the winter, but I never seen him miss a day. He is as regular as clockwork. He always has him a big fire going, a bottle of whiskey close by, and a warm smile on his face."

When the dump man saw us enter the gate he, flashed us a grin and waved. He looked the same as the first day we met. One suspender was dangling, one boot was untied, and he had a cigarette in the corner of his mouth. Both front teeth were missing. When we stopped next to him, he threw the cigarette to the ground, wiped his right hand briskly on his pants, glanced at it, and extended it to me. "Heard you be a leavin soon, boy. I hope ole Kunce ain't killed you so you will be a wantin to come back. I know you been a lot of company. Chili has been keepin me up with all your doins. Heard, too, that you, Frank, and Rudy will be headin over to Dodge City for them races. You had better be ready; that place is hotter than the hubs of hell. I growed up in Oklahoma, and it is just like that damn Kansas. A fella never seen it so hot. I couldn't wait to hightail it out of there."

Frank said, "The boy is goin to end his summer with a bang, hot as a firecracker. We ain't worked him yet. He smiled.

"Think old Kunce will let you come back next summer?" he asked.

I didn't say anything, only looked at Frank who winked at him. I couldn't respond, not only because I didn't know, but I was too choked up. I really liked this hard-looking, toothless old man. I couldn't tell him that I hadn't had the courage to ask. Sensing I was upset, Bill reached into his pocket and pulled out a can of Copenhagen, screwed open the top, peered at it, and then offered me "a pinch." "This here is good for a lot of things," he said. "It'll calm you down; it'll pick you up or just give you a pleasant little buzz. You ought to try some. Sure you won't have a pinch?" he said as he pulled back his lower lip and stuffed a marble-sized lump between his lip and his gum. "Nothin like dippin," he said. "It helps a fella to relax. Are you sure you don't want to try some?" he said as he thrust the container in front of me with a smile. "It is good for what ails ya." I declined, and he laughed again. "Better off, I guess, you'll get to liken the damn stuff before too long." He reached out his hand again and said, "Sure hope to be seein you again son. You be careful heading home on that Greyhound, and be a thinkin about us back here in Colorado."

As we drove off the property, I looked briefly over my shoulder and saw him waving frantically at another patron. I could almost hear him say, "Stop her over here. I won't be letting you fall in." He looked away just long enough to give me a huge grin and wave and turned back to his work. I had no idea at the time what a prominent role he and his family would play in my life over the next few years. I looked in the rearview mirror as we headed west and saw a black four-door Ford round the corner and enter the dump in a cloud of dust. It came to a sliding stop next to Wild Bill.

CHAPTER THIRTY

My last day in Cedar Cove that year was spent working around the place. I cut the lawn one last time, being careful not to hit the sprinkler heads. I checked the oil and water on Lillie's car before she went to town and helped Frank repair a fence on the hillside that he used to contain Smokey and Tuffy when he wanted to graze the mountainside.

Frank helped me grease and change the oil on the '50 Plymouth. We rotated the tires, washed the outside, and swept out the inside.

The car was ready for our trip to Dodge City. While we rarely drove the Plymouth, Frank said I would be doing all the driving. He said he and Rudy planned to sleep most of the way.

I packed my suitcase late in the day and then walked down the highway toward the narrows and the small café. I thought I might see the girls and say goodbye but was surprised to see a sign in the window on which was printed: "Closed for the Season, See You All Next Summer."

I left the highway at the Canyon Inn and walked down the dirt lane as the sun set and sent long grey shadows down the road. I could see Cliff, Frank's older brother, and his wife Emma moving around in their cabin on the river. I stopped briefly to say goodbye. The barbed wire gate enclosing the pasture was opened by slipping the wire noose over the fence post and closed by leveraging the gate with a short piece of wood secured to the post. It allowed the person opening the gate to pull it tight and replace the noose over the post.

I didn't want to be bothered, so I crawled under the lowest wire and caught my shirt on a barb. As I pulled myself through the fence, I heard and felt the shirt rip. I was in a hurry. I wanted one last look at Smokey and Tuffy before I left, and I wanted to take one last deep breath of the smells in the barn: the pungency of the alfalfa hay, the horse smells, the cedar and pine scent I knew would be commingled with dust, and dry, late afternoon, cool mountain air.

I felt a cold pocket of air envelop me and saw the horses coming my way. I wasn't looking forward to the heaviness of the south Florida nights or the dull and sweltering days. I didn't miss the harsh smell of peat moss and humus or the diesel fumes from the busses that passed the house all night. I never enjoyed the noises of the city night, the honking of a thousand cars, or the many sirens that pierced the darkness. I had become accustomed to the roar of the aircraft engines and the rattle of the aircraft as they passed low overhead, but I was sure going to miss the quiet repeat of the water as it tumbled over rocks and boulders in the river on its way down the canyon.

The horses nudged me as if they knew I was leaving and followed me to the little house that served as a barn. I fed them for the last time and sat a moment in the open window above the feed trough while they munched on their hay and sweet feed. As soon as they finished eating, we walked together to the gate leading to the footbridge that crossed the river. Smokey nudged the middle of my back, and Tuffy made a soft sound. It seemed as if they were saying good-bye, and my eyes welled with tears. I heard the click of their hooves as they stepped on rocks and struck one another. I scratched the big iron grey's forehead and pulled gently on his forelock, while I patted Tuffy's flat chest. They shook their huge bodies at the withers and slapped at flies with their tails while I said goodbye.

As I turned to walk across the bridge, my eyes were so full of tears, I could hardly see where to place my feet. I felt the edge of the bridge with my shoe and kept walking. *I hate to be such a crybaby,* I thought. I sat briefly on a boulder at the river's edge in order to gather my composure. The horses lingered by the gate as if they knew I was not happy to be leaving and watched me until I got up from the rock and rounded the corner toward the garage.

I started the Cushman and took one last ride down the road. I passed Fred's small white house and crossed the new bridge, up the hill where I had first met Melvin, and continued into the old canyon. I killed the engine, extended the kickstand in the electric plant park, and briefly listened to the tick of the hot motor in the cool evening air. I sat on the grass next to the river and listened to the river sounds. It was almost dark. The sun had set and the only thing left on the horizon was the red-and-pink remnants of the day. Hundreds of small bugs were walking on the water in the eddies and gentle pools or hovering above the river in the twilight. A small speckled trout broke the surface of the water and snatched the first serving of his nightly meal out of the air. The white water burbled over the rocks in the river, and the sound swept across the park and enveloped the trees and buildings in a soft caress. I could see the remnants of Willie Papa's small cabin at the river's edge, and I could visualize him and Frank tending to their cattle on the mountainside when I closed my eyes. *What had it been like,* I wondered, *living in a small cabin miles from town fifty or a hundred years ago.* It was time to head to the house.

It was still dark when I loaded my mother's old suitcase in the trunk of the Plymouth. I could see the peacocks asleep in the trees with their heads under their wings. The river continued to rush by, and the light on the middle garage cast long shadows across the gravel drive. The old pine tree in the center of the lane painted an eerie shape down the road. The moths circling the light punctuated the night in little commas and colons.

There was a faint glow coming from Fred's cabin, and I could see the trace of light created by automobiles descending the mountain. Lillie had cooked a big sendoff breakfast consisting of country-style eggs, elk sausage, thick slices of bacon, and waffles that I loaded with butter, syrup, and chokecherry jam. It was too early to feed the chickens, so we just piled the remaining waffles in a pan and placed it on the wall above the walk where they would be sure to find it.

I felt the gravel crunch under the tires as I pulled the gearshift lever down into first gear, and the car started moving forward. Lillie stood on the sidewalk smiling with her arms crossed. She offered a small wave but said nothing. She had already said her goodbyes.

I could see the ghostly outline of Smokey across the river and a flash of Tuffy's white forelock in the light fog hovering above the water as we exited the gate. We stopped briefly on the bridge, and I found our names etched in the concrete. "That damn bridge will be there long after you and I are gone," Frank said. "Old Harrigan won't be around either. Only person that fella is lookin after is himself. He is one of the orneriest and most disagreeable people I know. I am athinkin it comes from years of bein served from the left."

I swung the Plymouth wide onto the highway, and the luminous strips on the guardrails started to flash by me. I passed the Canyon Inn and could just make out the Coors sign lighted behind the bar. I entered the canyon just beyond the water diversion and the secret place I had shared with Mary Ann. The Pillar of Hercules loomed ahead just as Frank reminded me to slow down for Dead Man's Curve.

CHAPTER THIRTY-ONE

When we arrived at Rudy's farm just outside of town, he was sitting in the yard on an old tractor seat mounted on a tree stump. A yard light threw his shadow against the building, and the headlights revealed a white line across his forehead where his tan line began and ended. His hat was pushed back on his head, and he gave us a quick salute. He picked up his bag and a box of cookies, opened the rear door of the old Plymouth, and slid both he and his luggage across the cloth seat. He greeted Frank and me and waved goodbye to Mary, who was standing in the kitchen door in her white apron. It was almost dawn.

Light grey streaked the sky, and the high clouds were luminescent and fringed in pink. I pulled the car into first gear, and we slowly entered the dirt road in the direction of the state highway. The oil well was pumping as if two children were on a teeter-totter in a school yard.

The farther east we went, the smaller the mountains became in the rearview mirror. It was not long before I could no longer see them. The road opened up onto a flat expanse bordered by sandy shoulders, a line of fence extending beyond the horizon, and brittle brown grasses and sage brush. An occasional tumbleweed would scurry across the highway ahead of me and once caught under the front bumper, dragged along with an irritating scraping sound.

Long after sunrise Frank and Rudy were still sleeping. The little Plymouth purred along alone, mile after mile. Occasionally, a pickup or a long haul truck would pass in the other direction, but that was rare. We had the highway to ourselves.

Huge cylindrical silos would suddenly appear as if rising from the earth long before I saw any further evidence of a town. Frank's left eye popped open once, and he cautioned me, "Them troopers are goin to pinch you, boy, if you keep up with that lead foot. I don't know that you got the money to pay the bill, so slow this baby down just a little." As quickly as he spoke, his heavy breathing returned, and his chest rose and fell as if he were sound asleep. With the exception of an occasional snort, Rudy did not make a sound; he just seemed to slump lower and lower in the seat as the miles clicked off.

Many of the small towns had water towers that rose hundreds of feet above the ground with the name of the town emblazoned on the tank or evidence of some long-lost acclamation of love... Larry loves Sally.

I slowed for a couple of blinking amber caution lights in the middle of the larger towns but rarely had to reduce my speed. A large sign posted on the right of way just after leaving a small town read: "You Are Leaving Colorful Colorado." *It certainly had been colorful*, I thought as the sign flew by.

Western Kansas was not different—small towns, miles and miles of fence with an occasional cow grazing along the highway and huge barns off in the distance dwarfing small unpainted farmhouses surrounded by corrals and cattle pens. I passed several diners with parking lots full of pickups and a truck stop where tractor trailer rigs were idling three deep. The many small stores and storefronts glistened from the bright morning sun, and their reflected light could be seen for miles.

It had been a desolate morning. The beautiful white-snow-capped and green-fringed mountains had been replaced with miles of brown grasses, tumbleweed, small farmhouses, and trails of dust that followed the farm vehicles on the roads crisscrossing the prairie. Although Colorado was behind me, the summer was not quite over. Dodge City was only a few hundred miles ahead.

As we passed the cemeteries on the outskirts of many a dusty town, I wondered if there were more dead people than those alive in the community. *What would cause people to remain here after they were grown*, I asked myself. *Where did they all go when they left? Everyone couldn't farm or operate a gas station*, I thought. *What about the girls? Where did they go*, I wondered as we passed the small diners and restaurants with waitresses bustling around inside. *Every girl can't be a waitress or stay and live on a farm.* I had never given it much thought in the past. *What would hold people to these dusty wide spots in the road?* The world had become much smaller for me that summer. It had just started to dawn on me when I met the young Army private: the world was a mighty big and diverse place.

We came to the top of a rise, and there Dodge City lay before us. In an instant we went from mile after mile of tumbleweed and wheat field to a dusty, sprawling community. Most of the streets were brick and traversed the small hills behind the low-rise downtown area. The only evidence that this was once the thriving center of the cattle industry was a large brick railroad station at the foot of town. There were no wooden sidewalks, and Boot Hill was only a tourist attraction.

We stopped in a diner just inside of the city limits and had a late lunch. Earlier in the day, Frank had dispensed Vienna-sausage-and-bean sandwiches while we drove. We washed it down with a thermos of coffee and followed with some fresh-cut tomatoes Rudy had plucked from Mary's garden. We had already eaten all the cookies.

We stopped only once to quickly refill the gas tank and empty our bladders. When we arrived in Dodge City, Frank said, "Ought to eat a little before it's too late. We will be a needin to stop by the track and then get on to the motel to rest up for tomorrow. It is sure enough goin to be a long hot day. I been thinkin that we ought to be workin before daylight in the mornin to take advantage of the cooler mornin air. We got a lot of daylight to burn in order to get the track ready."

We left the diner and followed a dirt road north for a few miles until we saw a hangar and an old rickety control tower on the flattened top of a hill off in the distance. When we arrived the old yellow-painted hangar's massive doors yawned open, and I could see two north-south/east-west runways intersecting somewhere in the middle of the field. The control tower leaned a little to the east as if the harsh prairie winds had tried to push it over in their journey across the continent.

Someone had already set up a row of bleachers for the VIPs, and bales of hay were stacked around the airfield. Grass was growing out of the cracks and breaks in the concrete, and there was gravel in places that had come from crumbling concrete that needed to be swept up. Our job was to lay out the course, remove the grass and gravel, place the hay bales strategically on the corners of the track, and help with admission and in the concession stand. In the next day or so, the city's population would grow by thousands.

There were a couple of cars and trucks parked haphazardly around the field. Several of the trucks had the names of racing teams stenciled on the side, and the occupants were raising tent shelters and placing hay barriers in front of the pits and seating areas. Enclosed trailers containing motorcycles and parts were parked behind the tents. The American Motorcycle Association conducted the event, while the many vendors and suppliers to the motorcycle world sponsored it.

A tall man wearing Levi's and a short-sleeved western shirt came from the direction of the hangar. He had a broad grin on his face and a plump but very attractive teenage girl at his side.

"Howdy Kunce," he said. "Good seeing you and Rudy again!" They shook hands, and he extended his hand to me.

"This here must be the boy you told me was a comin. Howdy," he said. "Frank told me about you; glad you could come help. This is Jamie, my daughter. She is goin to be helpin out this year."

I said hello to both he and his daughter and learned she was going back to school on Monday. She was my age. She blushed deeply when he introduced her and looked at me as if to say she hated it when he embarrassed her.

"I'm going to work in the concession stand," she said.

The adults talked a few minutes about their plans for the next day. I spoke with Jamie, and we walked together toward the hangar. She was entering the ninth grade on Monday but had the physical attributes of an adult. She had large breasts and wore a flowered skirt and blouse that accentuated her womanly figure. *She still had a little of her baby fat, but it had settled in all the right places*, I thought. Frank saw me looking her over out of the corner of his eye and winked. *These motorcycle races might not be all that bad*, I thought. We were standing near the hangar when her dad approached carrying a single-barreled, sawed-off shotgun.

"I use this piece here to blast them damn pigeons," he said. "We had pigeons crappin on payin cutomers last year. This here hangar is where we set up many of the booths and a viewin area for VIPs to get out of the sun. We cook in here, and last year damn near got pigeon droppins in the chili. Weren't too appetizing."

About that time two pigeons rounded the corner of the hangar, flew through the open doors, and settled in the steel rafters above our heads. He leveled the shotgun and fired a load of buck shot that struck close by. When they scattered he said, "Don't really like killin the damn critters, just want to get their attention. This ain't the place to be nesting durin the races."

The next day, Frank, Rudy, and I worked on the track all day. Unlike the dry heat of Colorado, the humidity was oppressive. The sun struck the acres of concrete at an angle causing me to squint until it was fully overhead. We all stopped at noon and rested inside the hangar where it was cooler. A thermometer on the concession stand read 105 degrees. The big bay doors were open, and several rollup doors on the back of the building allowed a warm wind to suck through the building. When I heard the pigeons flutter, I knew the explosion of the sawed-off shotgun was soon to follow.

Jamie and I ate several hamburgers and guzzled about a gallon of cold water and a handful of greasy French fries while we sat on the bleachers talking about our lives. Someone had mounted a ten-gallon wooden barrel on the side of one of the trucks and filled it with crushed ice and water.

Before I finished eating, I heard the shotgun explode two more times and could only guess the pesky pigeons were beginning to get the message. I saw a few heading in the direction of the hangar and then abruptly turn and land on several telephone wires about fifty yards away.

Vendors were setting up booths and display areas inside the hangar. The Norton Motorcycle Company had several of its latest models on display, and there was a beautiful dark blue and chrome Jawa mounted on a dais with a sign reading: "Dealers Solicited, Inquire."

People were starting to congregate in the hangar, around the concession booth and in the pit area. Riders could be seen in the crowd wearing high-laced boots, leather pants, and unbuttoned shirts with sleeves rolled up. There were several attractive young women milling around the pits in abbreviated dungaree shorts with the fronts of their blouses tied in a knot beneath their ample breasts. Frank said, "Seems a fella will find women anytime there is a scent of testosterone, gasoline, and money. Camp followers. Don't know where the hell they come from; they just show up at every event. Don't find too many riders complainin," he said as he shook his head.

I heard the subdued sound of the shotgun, the whine of a motorcycle in a distant corner, and the buzz of the people working around their machines as I walked through the pits with Jamie. She received more than a few furtive glances as we strolled by the roped off areas.

Waves of heat rose off the unprotected concrete, and I could see my arms and neck were growing redder as the afternoon progressed. I left Jamie and started helping Rudy chip away the remaining grass growing out of the seams in the runway. Frank followed us and burned what remained with a burner that emitted a steady flame. We were about done with the track surface. As we scraped away at the grass with shovels that were no longer pointed but concave on the tip, my arms and shoulders began to ache, and my feet felt as if they had been dipped in lead. The time trials were to begin late that afternoon, and we had to have every inch of the track surface ready.

I watched as more and more trucks and travel trailers began to assemble in the pit area. Large tents were being erected, and there were spaces roped off designating the work area. Engines began to start, and rear tires burned as the riders began warming up and exercising their motorcycles on the long taxiway.

Some of the riders were older and hardened, but there were several that did not look to be much older than me. Frank had said on several occasions, "This is a young man's sport, and like pilots, there may be some old ones, and there may be some bold ones, but there were no old, bold ones."

The smell of rubber burning, gasoline, and hamburgers broiling in the concession stand permeated the late afternoon air. The wind was still hot, and the old abandoned airport had come alive. The airfield had been a World War II bomber training base. The excitement of the races must have resembled the excitement generated by fifty B24s lined up readying to take off for Europe during the middle of the war. Young whiskerless men surrounded the motorcycles much like the crews of the B24s must have in 1943, both wishing the operators good luck and Godspeed.

"Them machines," Frank said, "Will exceed one hundred miles per hour just before enterin the corners. Riders often will be scrapin their leather chaps on the concrete as they round them. They will stick to their machines like a flea on a dog in a drivin rain," he said. "It's in their blood; the more the adrenaline pumps, the faster they go. Hell, I seen em fall, slide twenty, thirty, fifty yards and tear their leathers all to pieces, hop back on, the machine still runnin, and win the event. All these boys are tough owlhoots."

It was obvious he loved the thrill of racing and the rush of adrenaline. Although I knew he hadn't raced in forty years, I could see a faraway look in his eyes as he watched the young riders careen down the straightaway and slide through the corners with sparks flying from the nails in their boots. I know he longed for the old days.

We had placed bales of straw strategically at each curve in the course several layers deep and had lined the straight a ways with a continuous line of straw bales. Jamie had helped by pushing the bales off the back of her dad's flatbed truck while Rudy and I lined them up in a long single line. By the time the trials began, I just wanted to find somewhere to lie down, since my arms were bleeding from having to manhandle the bales in my short sleeves, and my neck was singed to an iridescent red. I didn't think the day would ever end.

Once we finally placed the last bale of straw at the finish line, Frank laughed and said, "Looks like we damn near killed the boy.

He is goin to need to get his rest tonight, so probably won't be strong enough to go to the dance they hold after them races." He and Rudy were in their late sixties and still going strong. All I could think about at the moment was finding Jamie, a cold drink, and a shady spot to sit. *A dance,* I thought, *I just might be able to get my strength back.*

The races were thrilling. The riders were daring and skilled beyond my wildest dreams. They defined the man I had spent the summer with. As Frank predicted several riders slid through the hay barriers we had erected on their backs at speeds in excess of one hundred miles an hour. They seemed to challenge their machine, recapture them, and hurl on down the track. They looked like dying cockroaches with arms and legs extended in the air sliding on their backsides with bales of hay exploding around them. It seemed a battlefield of sorts. Surprisingly, all but one rider picked themselves up, dusted themselves off, remounted the machine on the fly, and continued on. There were a few bruises and bent metal, and although an occasional ego was pummeled, no one was seriously injured. The ambulance never left its spot on the tarmac during the entire two-day event. The noise was deafening as the motorcycles passed the bleachers, and the crowd roared as its favorite rider or team crossed the finish line. I had never seen anything quite like it.

Jamie, her father, and I sold cold drinks, grilled hamburgers, and hot dogs by the hundreds. There was not a cloud in the sky the entire weekend as if the gods had willed it so. By the time the last motorcycle crossed the finish line on Sunday afternoon, I wished to never see another hamburger or breathe the smell of hotdogs and hamburgers roasting.

The odors of the track, the grease and charcoal, and the burning rubber permeated my clothing and seemed to ooze from my every pore. We had sold thousands of hamburgers and hot dogs and dispensed iced Coca-Cola by the case. The cash and silver in the till at the end of the day could have inspired another great Brink's robbery. The shotgun leaning against the concession stand wall may not have only been a means to thwart pigeons.

Frank and Rudy mingled with the riders in the pits and introduced me to the people they knew on each team. The Harley Davidson team and Floyd Clymer of Clymer Publications treated Frank with reverence. Several were sons and grandsons of great competitors on the Harley team forty years earlier. Mr. Clymer regaled Rudy and me with events of the past and laughed out loud when Frank kidded him about almost losing his leather chaps when riding an Excelsior. He had stayed on the fringes of the industry and become a successful publisher of magazines and books on the subject of racing and motorcycles. He talked about coursing around board tracks in a sidecar with Frank, his face inches from the boards. He laughed about the time they faced their fears while ascending Pike's Peak on a gravel road with throttles full open and little or nothing for brakes.

"These kids today are better than we were, and that is hard to admit. Those were glorious times, and this is a glorious sport," he yelled as the Harley team crossed the finish line.

It has been quite a day for me, I thought. *What an incredible way to end my summer.* It certainly had not been anticlimactic.

Jamie told me school started for her on Monday morning. She attended a one-room schoolhouse not far from the track. She asked if I would like to join her on the first day. This would be her last year before entering the new consolidated school in town, and she thought I might find the experience interesting. Since my bus did not depart for home until late Monday afternoon, I happily agreed to join her.

Jamie and her father picked me up at the motor court around 7:00 a.m. Frank, Rudy, Floyd Clymer, and I had already had an early breakfast. Classes began at eight, but Jamie had to arrive early, because she was the teacher's assistant. She said upperclassmen always were called upon to help. She was the only person entering high school at year end.

I was entering high school when I got home, but I would be riding a city bus for miles and entering a large, long-existing school with very few people I knew. Most of my former classmates had chosen to attend a high school in Hialeah, but many had family means of transportation. I did not, and there were no school buses.

It was Jamie's responsibility to open the school, turn on the lights, be certain the blackboards were clean, the floors swept, and arrange all of the desks and chairs according to grade level. She had attended the school since the first grade.

We drove west away from the airport and out onto the plains. In a few minutes, after passing several farm houses, grain silos, large barns full of hay, lines of barbed-wire fence, and a small cemetery, we came upon a white building with a cupola sitting prominently on a small rise. It looked exactly how I had imagined a one-room schoolhouse should look. The cupola contained a bell, and the yard around the school was dirt swept clean. There was no grass, and the path in the dirt to the outhouse was edged by whitewashed rocks. An old swing set and a basketball hoop attached to a single pipe were at the back of the yard.

Jamie introduced me to the teacher, who wore a full skirt, blouse, and comfortable shoes. She could have been the subject of a Norman Rockwell painting. As the classroom started to fill, Jamie explained to the teacher why she had invited me.

The room was large, surrounded by high windows opened at the top. A large blackboard covered the back wall with a clock mounted above it. Several desks and benches were arranged in small clusters, and each had a blackboard and small bulletin board facing them. There were about twenty chairs aligned in rows facing the front of the room. Each was to accommodate a child of varying age.

There were no first graders this year, but the room was made up of children from every other grade level. A boy both taller and heavier than me, perhaps my same age or older, was the only person entering the eighth grade that year. Each child was talking animatedly, but once the clock struck eight, the chatter stopped. There was not a sound.

The teacher smiled and said, "Good morning," to the class. "Please welcome Michael. He is from Florida and will be spending the day with us. This is his first visit to a one-room schoolhouse. Please make him welcome. I would like him to leave our classroom with a good impression of our community and our school."

She asked if anyone knew where Florida was located or had ever been there. None of the children responded. The teacher laughed and said while she knew where it was located on a map, she had never been east of Kansas City. She then asked the class to stand and recite the Pledge of Allegiance, and Jamie then led the class in "The Lord's Prayer." Next, the teacher asked Jamie to open a group discussion about everyone's individual summers. Each child was called upon to stand and tell what she/he and her/his family had engaged in that summer.

Only one child had left the community on vacation. He and his parents had rodeo'd in Wyoming. The majority had worked with their families on the surrounding farms and ranches. Some had shown livestock and produce at the county fair, and one had earned a blue ribbon for her heifer. She modestly pulled a wrinkled blue ribbon from her pocket and held it up for everyone to see. The entire class applauded.

The class was divided into small groups. Each grade level seated themselves at the desks and benches arranged around the room. The second grade was assigned to Jamie. The teacher assigned each group a chapter to read or math problems to work out on the blackboards. Jamie was assigned to read Rudyard Kipling's poem, "If" to the entire class after the recess.

We spent about an hour in quiet. At nine thirty each group member was asked to explain to the class what he or she had read. Those assigned math problems were required to work the problem in their small group with an upperclassman's assistance. The teacher moved from group to group talking to each pupil individually after giving each a hug.

The class was dismissed for a fifteen-minute recess at ten thirty. The day was closed at noon with homework assignments for everyone. Jamie and I sat on a bench at the back of the classroom and ate the lunch her mother had prepared for us both. I had not thought to bring a lunch. We helped the teacher clean the blackboards and then waited outside on the swing set in the yard for Jamie's father to pick us up at two o'clock.

It was a morning I would never forget. The children were well behaved and respectful. The teacher was warm and welcoming. The room smelled of chalk and scrubbed bodies.

The experience has remained with me my entire life. I still recall a stanza in Kipling's poem: "If you can dream—and do not make dreams your master, if you can think—and not make thoughts your aim; if you can meet with triumph and disaster and treat those two imposters just the same…"

CHAPTER THIRTY-TWO

My bus was waiting at the depot when I arrived. Frank, Rudy, and I visited the local armory earlier to watch displays disassembled and to meet and talk with the riders who remained. I admired the Jawa motorcycle that had been moved from the hangar to the armory. It was dusk, and my bus was to depart sometime shortly after 8:00 p.m. It would take me to Oklahoma City, across Arkansas, Mississippi, and Alabama and then to Atlanta, Georgia where I would change busses. After a brief layover, I would be on an express to Miami by way of Jacksonville. I should be home late Wednesday, Frank said.

A magenta sky filled with haze created by the dust in the air, and the hot afternoon sun obscured what I could see of the horizon. I could smell a hint of rain. I felt dull. I did not want to leave, and I could feel my words sticking in my throat. I didn't want to cry in front of Frank and Rudy, but there was a subtle pressure in my chest, and the muscles in the small of my back and neck were tight.

I finished a hot roast beef sandwich that I thought was not near as tasty as the one from the pool hall, slurped down some bitter iced tea, and shifted around in the booth nervously. The few cars that passed seemed stuck in glue. I could hear the noises of the street and the rattle of pots and pans in the kitchen. All these sounds seemed amplified. The streetlights had just come on, and the scenic cruiser was now idling at the curb with its two baggage doors yawning open.

Our supper together had been quiet. I said little as usual while the two older men only engaged in idle chatter. *Did they know I was about to cry?* It seemed as if the other passengers knew and stared at me. *Did they think I was just a child?* I tried to focus on anything that would hold back my emotions. The several ceiling fans overhead were making a high-pitched noise, and the hot air moved slowly. "Air Cooled" it had said over the door. *Ha, what a joke,* I thought. Someone dropped a dish in the kitchen, and the two waitresses scurried from table to booth.

"Well, it has been a good summer, boy. I am proud of what you done," Frank said. "Rudy and I were talkin about how hard you worked at the track. Cuttin them barrels to make that bridge was quite a job too." He handed me a handful of bills and said it was a little pay for the times I cut the grass and washed the cars.

"Never you mind that sprinkler head," he said. "You did a good job, boy. I am glad you didn't head out when we got in the defugalty over the sprinkler." The bills totaled sixty dollars. I had never thought about being paid, and I still had a few dollars left from selling the bicycles at the sale. I would have paid Frank if I would have had the money, but it sure would be nice to have a little money on the trip home.

"I guess I didn't tell you," he said, "I bought that Jawa they had in the armory. It is a 125cc job and seems like a dandy. If you want to come back next summer, you will have it to ride."

I turned away from Frank so he wouldn't notice my tears while he was paying the waitress. Rudy smiled sheepishly as I picked up my suitcase and started walking toward the door and onto the bus. The driver shoved my bag into the baggage compartment and pointed to the stairs while Frank and Rudy stuck out their hands to shake my hand. Frank didn't say anything, only smiled as I turned, mounted the stairs, and found my seat.

I was seated directly across from the toilet on the lower level. There was a young woman in the seat in front of the restroom who had a pillow covering her head and was sobbing. I was choking back tears but trying to look strong as I waved my good-byes to the two men standing on the curb. The door closed with a whooshing sound as if a chamber had been sealed, and the big bus pulled away from the curb. I waved one last time as Rudy and Frank turned and walked toward the Plymouth and then turned my head to the wall. The tears flowed.

The bus contained only a few passengers. Several had moved to the rear, and I could see someone sprawled out on the bench seat which spanned the entire width at the very back of the bus. I didn't know why I hadn't thought of that. I could hear an occasional sob coming from the seat adjacent to me. I had yet to see the occupant.

The bus swayed from side to side as it picked up momentum, and the windows began to condense around their edges. It was sweltering outside, but the air conditioning was turned up high. I found a small pillow and blanket located in the baggage rack above my head and quickly fell asleep. Occasionally, I would awaken to the sound of the door opening to the restroom, the light shining into the aisle, and the muffled pulsing as the toilet flushed, but soon I would be back to sleep.

I was startled awake at the first rest stop. It was close to midnight, and I was thirsty. I hadn't felt the bus stop or the passengers disembark, but I felt the thud of the baggage door opening beneath my seat. One of the passengers was getting off at this stop.

The depot was merely a small gas station with a lunch counter. A young woman was sitting at the counter talking to a fellow passenger. I sat down and overheard her say she had come home for her father's funeral. Her mother and father had been married for thirty-five years, but she didn't think of them as old.

The last time she had seen her father, he had been in perfect health, and she never dreamed he would not live forever. Her father's death was sudden. There had been no warning. He had never even been sick. What a shock to the entire family. They had been close, but she had moved to Oklahoma City to attend court reporter school. She had spent the summer with her parents and had just returned to Oklahoma City a week earlier to finish her last year. She started to cry and told the woman she had so much to say. "Why didn't I say it?" she asked.

The other passenger reached over and gave her a motherly hug but said nothing. I knew then she was the person who had been sitting in the seat adjacent to me.

The young woman's relationship with her father had ended, and their life together was over. There would now and forever only be memories. Whatever they had known together over the years would have to live in her heart. While she had not spoken to me, she had known I had been crying earlier. She looked at me as if to ask if she could help, but she didn't say anything.

I did not think it was the time to tell her my tears were of joy and of the knowledge I was valued and that I could come back to Colorado the following summer. I had measured up. I was sad to have to leave, but I knew it was the beginning and not the end. I removed a cold Coke from the cold water-filled cooler, poured a small package of peanuts into the bottle, offered her a crooked smile, and reentered the darkened bus.

When we arrived in Oklahoma City, I watched her remove her belongings from the overhead rack, gather up her purse and a book, and exit the bus. The driver removed her bag from beneath; she accepted it, clutched her purse and the book in one hand, and picked up the suitcase with the other. She crossed the island separating our bus from the others waiting to depart, entered the depot, and disappeared.

The rest of the ride home was uneventful. I watched all sorts of people of all ages, all sizes, and all colors enter and depart the bus at a succession of stops at wide spots in the road, small towns, and an occasional large city. As we left the western states, I watched the colored people move farther toward the back of the bus. A Negro would occasionally sit upfront, but it was rare, and for the most part, they congregated in the back. I thought it strange they would sit anywhere they wanted while in the west but moved rearward as we progressed toward the south.

When we arrived in Atlanta, the waiting room was divided as it always had been in Miami. I had never noticed before. The section reserved for colored people was small, crowded, and dimly lit with pulsating florescent light bulbs emitting a buzzing sound or not working at all. There were two fountains in the corridor leading to the platform. One was an old porcelain bowl with a green, tarnished drinking source and the other a new refrigerated fountain that was sparkling clean. It was clearly marked Whites Only. It gave the impression coloreds were unclean.

While I had lived with the separation of the races all of my life, it now seemed strange. I had never given much thought to it before. The colored waiting room was separated from the white-only waiting room by a glass wall and a large faded sign reading:Colored Only. There was a separate lunch counter and separate toilets for whites and colored. I had never thought about it before going to Colorado. It just was.

Frank never spoke of the races. He spoke of "sorry" people and always made it clear he had only distain for people who wanted something for nothing and tried to live off the labor and perspiration of others. Denver was home for a few coloreds, but Mexicans were more prominent. Chili was a Mexican, and Frank never gave it any thought. He made no distinction between white or black, red or yellow, Catholic, Jew or Protestant, tall or short. He spoke fondly of Willie Papa and had taken Chili to raise. One's character is all that mattered to him. He despised a thief and saw a liar as a contradiction of terms.

I met my mother in Jacksonville. She met me at the bus depot and said she had decided to drive up and "carry" me the rest of the way home. She told me my dog Rowser had died, and we both cried. She said she thought he had died of a broken heart, because I went off and left him. She said every morning when she opened the backdoor his head would come up as if looking for me and then settle back on his front paws with the saddest look in his brown eyes. He rarely left the backdoor all summer.

After spending the night at my aunt and uncle's house, we departed for Miami around 4:00 a.m. to avoid the oppressive heat of the drive. By the time we got to Ocala, my mother was intoxicated, but she wouldn't let me drive. She kept a bottle of gin under the seat and refilled her paper cup every few miles.

I hadn't recognized her drinking until I was about ten. I didn't notice the mood changes and the change in the timbre of her voice. It wasn't until others called it to my attention that I recognized the problem.

She and a respected neighbor, a former Marine fighter pilot who had befriended me, got into a shouting match one afternoon. She told him he wasn't even smart enough to read, and he said that all she ever read was the writing on the bottom of a beer bottle. He had been a friend, and it hurt to see her behave in such a way. She broke up a birthday party when I was twelve and forced everyone to leave while roaring drunk. I was humiliated. There were many painful experiences.

Rides in the car would have been humorous if they had not been so dangerous. One of her friends fell down in the center of the road after backing into the street and having her car struck by another. When the police arrived, my mother was almost jailed for her display. Fortunately for her she lived in the house where the accident occurred, and the police could not cite her for drunken driving. Nothing had changed over the summer. I had begged her to stop drinking.

I realized I had not thought about my friend Rowser all summer. That hurt even more. I felt terrible

Rowser was dead. I couldn't imagine living in Miami with Rowser gone. My mother filled her cup again, and I cried for another hundred miles. When we pulled into the front yard at last, the reality of Rowser being gone hit me. I cried again. *Life can be tough*, I thought but then again Frank had told me that this summer.

CHAPTER THIRTY-THREE

The school year dragged until Frank returned to south Florida for his winter hiatus. Occasionally, he, Buster, and I went to the Royal Castle for hamburgers and birch beer in a frosted mug on hot afternoons. He brought me up to date on Rudy, Chili, Spot, Wild Bill, and the Longmont sale. He had gone hunting on the western slope with Chili, Rudy, and Melvin and shot an eight-point buck. Tuffy and Smokey pulled their load as usual. Mr. Becker from the farm in Wiggins had asked about me and sent his regards. He had seen Clay Wells in the street, and he had asked about me.

On the first Saturday following the end of the school year, I was back on the bus heading for Colorado. I met a young military couple early in the trip who had been transferred from Ft. Stewart in Georgia to the mechanized division in Colorado Springs. They accompanied me all the way to Colorado and were very solicitous and helpful.

I was reminded of the young Texas rancher's son who sat with me the previous summer and wondered how he was doing. We travelled across the aisle from one another most of the way and played hundreds of hands of cards, five-card poker and gin rummy.

The landscape flew by, and I found myself in Colorado almost before I knew it. It was great to have people to latch onto, and I was comforted by their presence. They were childless, but in some ways, acted as surrogate parents for the trip. We ate together at almost every meal and shared our waiting time when in a new strange city waiting to make a connection. I enjoyed their company and still think of them many years later.

The summer was very much like the previous summer. I met a new friend who worked at one of the local motels and was allowed to drive his employer's car. We went to Estes Park together and grew to be confidantes and friends.

I cut the yard soon after I arrived and was careful to avoid the sprinkler heads. I had grown accustomed to not stepping on the threshold when I entered the house, and there was a fresh piece of elk jerky hanging up in the basement. I greased and washed the cars and trucks, went to the sale, and rode the Cushman and the new Jawa through the old canyon. I drove the old Dodge pickup all over the state, back and forth to Frank's farms in the eastern part of the state and to Kremmling to visit Freddie and Frances.

One night a nephew of Frank's and I rode back from eastern Colorado in the cab of a model T pickup that was being hauled on the back of a stake-bed truck. We just about froze. It turned cold, and my new friend and I huddled together like lovers to keep warm.

The summer passed quickly, and Frank asked me to stay on for the winter if my mother would permit, and I promised I would attend school and not be trouble to anyone. My mother and I both agreed so we renovated Chili's old shack in the feed lot over the summer and made it ready for my occupancy. That is another story for another time.

I never learned who killed the sheriff. Old Clay Wells and I shared separate rooms and became neighbors during my stay in the Arcadia Hotel that winter. I lost track of him soon after. The Dodge City motorcycle races survived a few more years, but I never attended them again. I was never able to learn anything about Jamie's experience at the big consolidated school in town; the one-room school-house on the hill was closed for good a few years later, and our friendship for those few days is but a pleasant memory. Mary Ann just disappeared. I never learned how her life turned out.

The Longmont livestock market and sale barn is a shopping center, and the diner across the street is a dress shop. The small town became a suburb of Denver, and America evolved into the jet age.

Wars were fought, and presidents and presidential candidates were assassinated as was Martin Luther King Jr., the leader of the nonviolent group who initiated integration of the schools and the country. Eddie Fisher and Elizabeth Taylor were divorced and went on to marry a succession of people. Transcontinental buses all but disappeared off the nation's highways.

All that remains of Fred's house is a concrete slab. Most of the people and personalities of that first summer are long gone. Wild Bill's fiefdom is now a city park and walking trail. The lake is covered over. The feed lot is the site of an ice-skating rink. Rudy and Mary share a common tombstone in the local cemetery, and the shop is an antique mall. The pool hall is gone, replaced by an upscale gift shop.

Frank found Tuffy dead in the river one morning, and Smokey grieved for a year before he was gone too. Chili died of cancer, much too young, and Melvin just disappeared never to be seen or heard from again. Perhaps he is fighting some fire in the west somewhere or pearl diving in a restaurant in Oregon dreaming of his escape.

Buster went on to become a successful theatrical producer and lives with his second wife in a fifteenth-century carriage house in a beautiful part of England. We have remained lifelong friends, and he was the best man in my wedding many years ago.

The last time I saw Jimmy, he was in his mid forties and living with his mother. She told my children that she had worked in "entertainment" as Princess Delago. We laughed together after we left.

Soon after we reached an amicable truce, my mother died after a lifetime of too many cigarettes and too much alcohol. In spite of the pain that passed between us, I love her and miss her dearly. Even with her demons, she was a remarkable woman in so many ways.

My father decided one day in his mid eighties, he had lived long enough, and within a week, he was dead. I was able to say my good-byes. My stepmother passed a short time later. He seemed at last like the nice neighbor next door.

The long sad story of segregation is ancient history, and the technological age has replaced the Industrial Revolution.

Lillie died shortly after falling and breaking her hip. Frank lived into his nineties and was able to enjoy his last successful elk hunt. He is buried next to Lillie, his brother Fred and his wife Ann, his sister Fonte, her husband Lester Foote, and their son George who died in an automobile accident. I visit their grave every year and cry like a baby.

That summer was a seminal time in my life. I crossed the country seven times over the next few years. I finished high school while living in Chili's old shack and the Arcadia Hotel.

Frank never believed in organized religion, but he maintained an abiding faith. He was deeply spiritual and believed strongly in the Golden Rule. His life exemplified the many teachings of the world's religions. While he was disdainful of most "preachers," he acknowledged a divine principle and first cause. He believed in the notion of personal responsibility, honesty, truthfulness, right action, fairness, integrity, and goodwill. His emotions were not for public view, and he never asked for thanks or praise. He always maintained a strong and stoic personality and yet he felt deeply for others. He was a no-nonsense, no-excuses kind of guy. He expected action, not words. He replaced tears with doing and reached out to others in need yet never spoke of it. I saw tears well in his eyes when we learned that my new young friend had died that summer afternoon. I saw them well up when he spoke of his favorite two Chesapeake Bay retrievers long since gone and of the death of both Tuffy and Smokey. He grieved for Lillie for the rest of his life, but I never knew him to cry.

He taught me more about love, respect for myself and others, hard work, strength of character, and personal responsibility than anyone else in my life, and although I am sure I have not always lived up to his expectations, I know he would be proud.

I have been influenced and loved by many and thankful to have lived an interesting and varied life. The many people who have come and gone have all brought something sacred.

My beautiful wife has been my soul mate and one of the most forgiving and thoughtful people I have ever known. She has been a helpmate, and although she did not know Frank the way I did, he was proud of me for taking her as my wife.

Every person and every animal that have arrived in my life did so when either I needed them, or they needed me. There are no coincidences. It is said that "when the student is ready, the teacher will appear." I have been blessed by many teachers. Frank is one of the most prominent. I have heard God can only be known through faith. I know God through all of the clues he has left along the way.

The bridge over Cedar Creek still stands today.

Made in the USA
Charleston, SC
14 March 2014